# VITAL SIGNS

Bel Air General

# VITAL SIGNS

Jessica Sutton

**HEADLINE**

British Library Cataloguing in Publication Data

Sutton, Jessica
Vital signs
I. Title
813'.54 [F]

ISBN 0-7472-0146-3

Printed and bound in Great Britain by
Richard Clay Ltd, Bungay, Suffolk

HEADLINE BOOK PUBLISHING PLC
Headline House
79 Great Titchfield Street
London W1P 7FN

# Acknowledgments

This is a work of fiction, but every effort has gone into making the medical information as accurate and up to date as possible.

This book would not have been possible without the expert knowledge and advice of surgeon Richard L. Clark, M.D. He has a rare talent for translating technical terminology into layman's terms. Thanks also go to Professor Robert M. Doyle of the University of Windsor, Windsor, Canada, and Mrs. Susan Crosby Taliferro of Baltimore for their contributions. And special thanks to Jean Liston, who helped with the manuscript.

J.S.

# Chapter 1

If he had ever doubted it, the ringing phone convinced Brian Hecht, administrator of Bel Air General Hospital, just how much he needed an assistant. Here he was, trying to interview someone to fill that vacancy, and he had already been interrupted three times. Couldn't be helped. It was a rule that all admissions to this "hospital for the rich and famous" had to be approved by either the administrator or his assistant. And since Jenny Corban had left, Brian was constantly in the hot seat.

He glanced at Judd Forbes, seated across his desk, made a gesture of futility, said he had to take the call, and picked up the phone. Addie Weickel, Brian's secretary, said Dr. Hamilton Dodd's office was on the phone.

"Very well, Addie, but only admissions calls, do you hear?"

"That's what this one is."

1

He sighed, flicked a switch, and said, "Brian Hecht here."

"Oh, Mr. Hecht, it's you. Will you hold just a moment for Dr. Dodd?"

He had no chance to reply and probably couldn't have, for the woman's voice startled him. How very much she sounded like Jenny Corban! A pain very much like grief stabbed at him. Jenny, his one true love, had only been gone a week, but it seemed forever. She was in Buffalo, endeavoring to start a new life, and he had promised to stay away from her for three months. He'd never make it.

As he waited for Dr. Dodd, Brian glanced at Judd Forbes, an applicant for Jenny's job. For two years she'd been his assistant administrator and a damned fine one. The two of them worked so well together. Falling in love had been inevitable. Then had come the terrible assault and rape. Jenny was lucky to be alive. Terribly scarred, both physically and mentally, she had rejected his entreaties to remain here with him and moved to Buffalo to live with her parents. Going back to school. Starting over. He understood. But, God, it was hard. He missed her so. . . .

"Brian? Ham Dodd here. I've a patient I'd like to admit, if that's possible."

Brian formed a mental image of Dr. Hamilton Dodd, the so-called obstetrician to the stars. He'd delivered so many show-biz babies, the kids almost didn't count unless he brought them into the world. Aside from that, he was a first-class gynecologist. If a woman in Hollywood, Beverly Hills, or Bel Air, California, had female or pregnancy problems, she first thought of Hamilton Dodd. The man was good, no doubt about it. "Are you about to deliver another thespian?"

"I hope so. I'd like to admit Adriana Barre. Today, if that's possible."

2

Brian Hecht arched his dark brows. "Did you say Adriana Barre?"

"I did. As you probably know, she's been trying to have a child for some time. Several miscarriages, a couple of stillbirths."

"Is she pregnant now?"

Dodd laughed. "You must not read the papers. It's the most widely reported pregnancy since Princess Di."

"Problems?"

"Not sure. She's in her eighth month and I just want to take every precaution. I'd like to bring her in. Bel Air General will afford her the privacy and medical supervision she needs."

Brian Hecht didn't hesitate. Bel Air General had been established just for patients like Adriana Barre. Italian by birth, she had become a truly international star, winner of Academy Awards, Golden Globes, and just about every other accolade the film world had to offer. Her exquisite face, with its honey-blond hair, almond-shaped green eyes, and full, sultry mouth, not to mention her tall, statuesque figure, made her instantly recognized and admired the world over. "You know we have a place for her. Do you prefer OB-GYN?"

"If that's possible."

"Let me check." Brian glanced at his chart. The OB-GYN unit at Bel Air General was small, only four beds since the hospital hardly advertised for patients. "Yes, we have a vacancy—two, in fact. I'll reserve two-twenty-seven for Miss Barre." He listened to the thanks, then hung up.

Judd Forbes looked at him with interest. "Adriana Barre is being admitted?"

Brian studied him. Young. Didn't look thirty. Probably too handsome—blond, blue-eyed, firm mouth, small cleft in the chin. Beach tan. But there was a rugged masculinity to him that kept him from being "pretty." Women probably fell all over him. "Yes. This hospital was designed for

3

people like her. She will receive the finest medical care in the world here. That is the responsibility of our medical and surgical staffs. She will also receive the ultimate in privacy, confidentiality, and personal security. That is primarily the task of the assistant administrator, the position you're applying for." Brian had raised his voice a trifle, adding authority to it.

"Yes, sir, I understand."

"This hospital abounds with celebrities, Mr. Forbes, as well as the wealthy and powerful who do not wish to be celebrities. If you are overly impressed by the rich and famous, if you have any tendency to gawk at them, ask for autographs, or treat them as anything other than the ill persons they are, then I don't think assistant administrator of Bel Air General is the proper job for you."

"I understand."

"Do you also understand that any tendency to regale your friends with anecdotes about the patients in this hospital—indeed, any discussion whatsoever of any patient, including the fact he or she *is* a patient—is grounds for immediate dismissal? That rule applies to all personnel. It also applies to talk both inside and outside the hospital. There is to be no discussion of patients other than that necessary for medical care."

Judd Forbes felt the hazel eyes boring into him. In his forties with dark hair, graying at the temples, Brian Hecht both looked and acted the part of head of this prestigious hospital. Forbes knew that Hecht had the total confidence of Laura Carlyle, the matriarch who owned Bel Air General. Hell, wasn't he married to the old woman's granddaughter? Brian Hecht was the Boss with a Capital B.

"I understand, Mr. Hecht," Forbes said again. "As assistant administrator I would be in charge of enforcing the rules you just described. I could

4

hardly do so if I were not entirely circumspect myself."

Brian eyed him a moment. Very good. Forbes had stood up to him. If he had any hope of doing this job, he had to be tough-minded. For a moment the image of Jenny Corban flitted across his mind. How tough she had been! She'd disagreed with him, stood up to him, even argued with him during the day. Then at night they'd been lovers, all softness and sweetness. . . . *Oh, hell!*

"I know you told me in our first interview, but tell me again why you want this job."

Judd Forbes looked him straight in the eye. "I don't know how to be anything but totally honest with you. I came out here from back East to be an actor. It's the same old story. I quickly found out it takes . . . well, more than I had. I froze up in front of the camera. The only part I was any good at was playing a wooden Indian. I did a little modeling, then tried local TV here in Los Angeles. I didn't have the journalism background to break into news, so I was the weatherman. I wasn't very good at that, either, and I knew I'd last only until a prettier face came along. I quit before that happened." He hesitated. "I don't know anything about hospital administration. But I can learn. To answer your question, I'm thirty, and I want to get started on a career with some substance to it. I have a brother and uncle who are doctors. I worked as a hospital orderly during college. I just feel this is the right job for me."

Brian nodded. Hospital experience was not a prerequisite for the job, nor even desirable. Jenny had had none. Indeed, because Bel Air General was so different from most hospitals, it was better that his assistant start from scratch and learn. And Brian liked the straightforward honesty of Judd Forbes. At least a half dozen others he'd interviewed in the past week had tried to impress him

5

with their administrative and medical knowledge. He'd been unimpressed.

"Mr. Forbes, have you had a chance to study the hospital rules that I gave you?"

"I have, yes."

"That means you have a rough idea of how we do things around here."

"Yes, sir."

"Okay. Just now you heard that Adriana Barre is being admitted as a patient. She's about as big an international star as there is. Her efforts to have a child are well known. She is now in her eighth month. The fact she is entering this hospital suggests there may be some medical reason other than delivery of the child, perhaps some complication. The press is going to be intensely interested in every aspect of her stay here. At the same time, Miss Barre is going to require the utmost in privacy and confidentiality. How would you go about protecting her and keeping the press at bay, which is one of the main duties of the assistant administrator?"

Forbes hesitated, looked away, then back at Brian. "The press *does* know she's here?"

"We have to assume they'll find out if they don't know already."

"Then we can't stonewall it. The press has to be told *something*. I'd suggest issuing regular medical bulletins saying as little as possible. I'd consult with Miss Barre, her doctor, manager, family, whomever, then prepare statements to the effect that Miss Barre entered for tests and a rest from her strenuous schedule. All quite routine. She is resting comfortably, spent a good night, is looking forward to the birth of her child—that sort of thing."

"And if she were seriously ill and about to lose the child?"

Forbes sighed. "Again, I'd work out some sort of statement with her doctors and other people re-

6

porting the least that can be said. Meanwhile, I'd keep all reporters and photographers outside the gate."

"And if that didn't satisfy them?"

"You mean a press conference? With yourself and maybe a doctor answering questions?"

"Could you handle that?"

"I could. I may not have made it as a TV newsman, but I know them, understand how they think and operate. I know what they want and need."

"Which is often at cross purposes with the needs of this hospital and patients like Adriana Barre."

Forbes smiled. "Then we'll just have to tough it out, won't we?"

Brian did not return the smile, only nodded. "Very well, Mr. Forbes. One of your qualifications for this job is that you can come to work immediately. Is that true?"

"Yes, sir, at once."

Brian rose. The interview was at an end. "Let me think about this a bit. I'll get back to you. I have your phone number. I suggest you stay by it today." He extended a hand, felt Forbes's firm, masculine grip.

"Thank you. I'll hope to hear from you."

"If you do, please be aware that it will be only probationary. You'll be on trial for some time. A lot depends on how well you and I can work together."

"I realize that. All I want is a chance."

"Do you really think it's necessary for me to be hospitalized, Doctor? After all, it is a very slight pain and a couple of extremely small spots of blood."

Ham Dodd looked at his celebrated patient. In more than twenty years of medical practice he'd had intimate knowledge—just about the most intimate knowledge—of some of the most beautiful and desirable women in the world. But none of

7

them had such allure as Adriana Barre. He'd tried to figure it out. It wasn't just that splendid face with *those* eyes, *that* mouth, or the tall, voluptuous figure that seemed to evoke all that was womanly and earthy. Nor was it her remarkable range as an actress, which had allowed her to go from playing chorus girls and harem slaves, to sensuous women, to shattering portrayals of human suffering and courage that won universal critical acclaim.

What drew him to her, he decided, was what she was as a *person*. Now forty-three, she had gone from an impoverished childhood in an Italian slum to become a beautiful woman and a consummate actress—and more, an intelligent, caring, considerate, sophisticated, and entirely civilized woman of the world. She was, Dodd concluded, a genuinely good person, one worthy of admiration and respect.

The examination was over. She was dressed now—how elegant she looked even eight months pregnant—and her husband was with her in the consulting room. "I think it's wise, Adriana. Just as a precaution. You know your own history better than I do."

She did indeed. She'd lost count of the miscarriages, but not of the two babies she'd carried to term, only to see them stillborn. Oh, the pain, the suffering, the anguished disappointment! She smiled, that brilliant array of fine teeth, all natural, filling the wide mouth, positively brightening the room. "But I've been so *well* with this baby, Doctor! I've never felt better in my life. Isn't that true, Charles?" She looked up at her husband for agreement.

Charles Bridges stood behind and a little to the side of her chair. In his mid-fifties, he was tall and slender with thick salt-and-pepper hair, dark brown eyes, and even features set off by a neatly trimmed beard and moustache. Although thoroughly American, he affected Continental manners and dress, including boutonniere, derby, and cane. He had inherited money, made a good bit more in the construction business, and thereafter devoted his life to Adriana Barre as lover, husband, manager, companion, and friend. In twelve years of marriage he had come only to love her the more. He remained hopelessly smitten, loving even her unpredictable moods, sometimes demanding petulance, and occasional titanic rages that the public knew nothing about. And in his love he suffered with her in her determination to have his child. It had become *everything* to her. No other accomplishment in her life meant a thing if she wasn't a mother. Secretly, he wished she'd give it up. So much suffering and pain, both mental and physical. At her age the risks of childbirth were . . . He tried not to think of it.

"Yes, my dear, you have been well. I've never seen you more glowing, in fact." It was true. Adriana Barre, always the epitome of beauty and sexual appeal for him, had never been more lovely than during these past months.

"There you are, Doctor. I'm sure my little discomfort is entirely normal." She rendered her generous, earthy laugh. "I refuse to allow you to make me into an invalid!"

But Ham Dodd shook his head. "Hardly that, Adriana. I just want to run some tests. I want to have a look at our little infant via ultrasound. And a few days of rest will do you good."

Charles Bridges cleared his throat. "Why do I feel you're not being entirely honest with us, Hamilton? Is something wrong that we should know about?"

Dr. Dodd sighed. " 'Wrong' is hardly the word, Charles. I'm a little concerned, perhaps, and even that may be too strong a term." He looked at her. "Adriana, you are a bit hypertensive. Your blood

9

pressure is one-sixty over a hundred. That's too high."

"In my eighth month?"

"It's still a little high. You were in Italy when this pregnancy started, so I don't know what your blood pressure was before. I wish I did. Did you have your BP taken?"

"No, I felt fine. There was no need to. I finished the film and came straight here to you."

"Is her blood pressure a cause for alarm?" Bridges asked, frowning.

Dodd looked at him. "Hardly alarm. I'd just like to put her in the hospital for a few days and stabilize it."

"Oh, Doctor, I hardly think—" Adriana began, but her husband cut her off.

"No, my dear. I think we should both do what the doctor wants. The hospital it is." Bridges hesitated. "I guess you know Adriana can hardly make a move without the paparazzi and press—"

"Which is why I'm putting her in Bel Air General. She'll have all the privacy and protection she needs there. The place is practically a fortress," Dodd assured him.

As she listened to the fussy little lawyer, Bobbi Hecht wondered what was wrong with her. She felt numb. Nothing seemed to matter anymore. Her life was in tatters, ruined.

The absolutely ghastly week had begun with her mother's suicide. Connie Payne had somehow gotten into Bel Air General late at night, threatened to shoot Jenny Corban, held a security guard at bay, then turned the weapon on herself, blowing her brains out. Dear God! What a nightmare!

Bobbi had tried to grieve but really couldn't. The estrangement between them was too bitter and had gone on too long. There were things to admire about Connie Payne, however, Bobbi had to admit. She had parlayed a big bosom and a

10

modicum of talent into a small career as a minor
movie star, then into a larger career as a celebrity
and eccentric. She had managed a brief marriage
to Willard Carlyle, Laura's only son and Bobbi's
father. After his death, Connie Payne had adopted
a flamboyant life-style as an "ageless sex symbol,"
looking the part even in her sixties, thanks to repeated visits to the "plastic man" at Bel Air General.

If Bobbi had learned grudgingly to admire her
mother for her singlemindedness in making so
much out of so little—at least she knew who she
was and how she wanted to live—Connie's death
and her own lack of grief proved how little there
was to love about the woman who had given birth
to her. Connie Payne was utterly flamboyant,
lewd, vulgar, narcissistic, and totally unprinci-
pled. Her sending a two-bit porno king to rape
and nearly kill Jenny Corban had proved that. The
police were about to arrest her for it, and Connie
Payne took her own life in a moment of manic
rage and despair.

The funeral was a ghastly, garish travesty, all
prearranged by the deceased. Thousands of
"mourners" had come, but really only to see Connie Payne's last performance. She had not disappointed them. She'd arranged in her will for choirs
of angels, vestal virgins in diaphanous gowns, and
little "cherubs" strewing laurel leaves and rose
petals. Topping it off was the gravestone. Connie
had sometime previously commissioned a larger-
than-life staute of herself, nude, so that her awesome dimensions would be immortalized. Bobbi
Hecht had nearly died of mortification, grateful
her grandmother hadn't come to the interment.
She did think, however, that her husband might
have at least gone through the motions and stood
beside her. She couldn't blame him, though. Brian
Hecht had detested his mother-in-law in life. Why
should her death make any difference?

Bobbi sighed. Face it. Her marriage to Brian was over, finished, kaput. He blamed her for sending the rapist to Jenny. He would not believe otherwise. Even Connie Payne's suicide hadn't convinced him.

The lawyer's voice droned on. "The wording of your mother's will is very simple, direct, and, I think, touching. It says, 'I hereby bequeath all my worldly possessions to my beloved daughter, Roberta Carlyle Hecht.' "

Bobbi had been standing in the living room of her mother's home in Bel Air, looking out toward the pool where Connie Payne had so often tanned herself—topless, of course. It was a smallish pool and a small house, at least by Bel Air standards, but commodious for a woman living alone. She turned now to look at the lawyer. Cary Knowlton was bald, with a small, pinched face and nervous, obsequious manners. A most unappealing individual. Why had her mother ever chosen him as her attorney? She liked her men young, sexy, and right off the beach. Paid enough to get them, too.

"Did you say everything?" Bobbi asked.

"Yes."

"This house?"

"Indeed. Mrs. Hecht, you are—"

"Sell it. I'll need the money to pay for that ridiculous funeral."

The lawyer looked affronted.

"Sell it? I hardly think you want to do that."

"Look, Mr. Knowlton, I've seen the bills for the funeral. They're astronomical, and I have no money to pay them."

"Oh, but you do, Mrs. Hecht. Miss Payne's affairs are quite in order. She was most careful about things like that. I'm sure the will can be probated within a few days. Then you'll—"

"Then I'll what, Mr. Knowlton? My marriage is breaking up. Let me amend that. My marriage is *already* broken up. I have no career, no idea of

12

what to do with my life, no one to turn to. I have all these bills from my mother. I want to get them paid, clean up my mother's affairs—I'm sure they're a first-class mess—get her things out of here, dispose of what's disposable, and get on with my life."

Cary Knowlton looked at her through his steel-rimmed glasses. He thought she was a very strange woman. Beautiful, even stunning. Irish coloring. Dark hair, worn short, the most vivid blue eyes he'd ever seen, luscious red mouth, flawless skin the color of milk. Fantastic figure. What was she so unhappy about? Obviously, it wasn't mourning her mother. Her white sweater and pants indicated that. Maybe she was a little nutty?

"Mrs. Hecht, you are going to be able to get on with your life in any way you want. You are a very wealthy young woman."

Bobbi stared at him. "What did you say?"

"I think you heard me. Your inheritance is quite significant. Weren't you aware of how much your mother was worth?"

She was still gaping at him. "No, I've no idea. She never seemed to have very much or spend much. She always seemed to be mooching off friends."

Knowlton rendered a lipless smile. His orthodontia was good and helped his appearance. "That was Miss Payne for you. She always said why spend a nickel when you can beg or borrow it."

Bobbie was stunned. "Mother had money?"

"Oh, indeed. In fact, Mrs. Hecht, it might be said that your mother, God rest her soul, had one outstanding virtue. I believe it's called thrift. I'd hoped to have a complete tally for you by this time, but there are a couple of safety deposit boxes which I need a court order to open. I believe they contain jewelry and cash, along with some securities. But I would estimate that with this house, her other real-estate holdings—there are at least

13

two apartment houses, Mrs. Hecht—her various stocks and bonds—she owns ten percent of Bel Air General Hospital stock, as you know—I would conservatively estimate your inheritance at between seven and eight million dollars."

Roberta Carlyle Hecht didn't actually faint, but she did feel weak and a little dizzy. Her knees gave way and she slowly crumpled to a nearby sofa. (A sudden shock will sometimes do that to people, especially when they haven't had breakfast.)

When her mother showed up, Susan Raimond had a sense of inevitability. She'd hoped it wouldn't happen, but knew it probably would. She tried to accept it, rather like an element of nature. She couldn't stop the rain and wind any more than she could stop her mother.

The tirade had been going on now since early morning. Rita Farrell was in full voice, layering on the guilt like a master plasterer, or maybe a Japanese craftsman applying coat after coat of lacquer to a piece of pottery. Her mother could have been a tour guide specializing in guilt trips. "How *could* you, after all I've done for you?" "How ungrateful can one person *be?*" "Don't you care about *anyone* but yourself?" "Do you realize how I've *sacrificed* for you?" These were some of the commoner themes, but Rita Farrell knew endless variations on them.

Rita Farrell had had an extremely minor career as an actress twenty-five years ago. Mostly, she had been an extra. What bit parts she landed usually ended up on the cutting-room floor. She had spoken lines in two films, a total of fourteen words: "Have you got a light, mister?" and "Tea is served in the drawing room, madam."

But in another sense she had been a great success. She had married Dusty Raimond. When they met, he was a stunt man and a bit player in Westerns, mostly as a bad guy. His prospects were no

14

better than her own. But he had the good sense to recognize his limitations and turn animal trainer. Ultimately, he made a great deal of money in theme parks. Rita stuck it out with him, so that when he died she was left with a home in Beverly Hills and a tidy sum in the bank.

But that wasn't the best thing that happened to Rita Farrell. Her greatest good fortune was to give birth to a daughter who had big, soulful brown eyes, a little pouty mouth, and the ability to shed tears on command. Rita Farrell became a stage mother, and unabashedly so. Susan Raimond became her whole life, and Rita pushed and shoved, fought and clawed, to make Susan a child star. Whether Susan actually became a star was open to dispute. Shirley Temple or Margaret O'Brien she was not. But she had considerable success, beginning as a model of diapers and baby powder, and progressing through a series of film roles, some notable, as well as a long-running TV series.

By age thirteen Susan Raimond was a has-been. She hadn't turned out to be a great beauty. The eyes were still appealing, but the mouth was just too small, and the lower lip pouted too much. Her face became a little too square. She didn't photograph well. Even a nose job and thousands of dollars worth of orthodontia couldn't do much to improve her.

But Rita Farrell refused to believe any of this. Susan was just going through an "awkward stage." As soon as the hormones stopped raging through her, her growth subsided, and her features "settled," she'd be able to resume her career. And the sooner the better, because that "tidy sum" in the bank was running low.

Susan hadn't minded being a child actress, sort of enjoyed it, in fact, but the death of her father when she was fifteen really shook her. He had been the anchor of her life, the antidote to her mother, the one who kept her feet on the ground and made

15

her feel like a real person with some semblance of normalcy. She had always been able to depend on him to curb at least some of her mother's excesses.

With the death of her father, Susan now hated the incessant acting, singing, and dancing lessons, the continual harping on diet, the grueling efforts at fitness, the endless auditions, rounds of casting directors and trumped-up appearances to keep her name before the public. She didn't really hate her mother, but she was sick to death of her and had to find a way to escape.

In desperation, Susan decided that becoming pregnant was her way out. She also knew that if she told Rita and submitted to an abortion she would be forever chained to her mother. So she concealed the pregnancy for three months, then stole some money—it was hers, after all—and fled, hiding in a small town in the Sierras. She was eight months pregnant and not quite eighteen. She figured the baby and her majority would come about the same time. When her mother finally had found her and showed up this morning, Susan knew Rita Farrell could do nothing to stop either from happening.

"If I'd known you wanted an affair, I would have arranged something. I'm not a prude, you know," Rita wailed.

Susan sighed. "It was hardly an affair, Mother."

"All right, a one night stand. I could have found someone *suitable*, seen that proper precautions were taken!"

"It *wasn't* a one night stand, Mother. How about a half-hour stand? No, make it a five-minute stand."

"God, Susan, how *could* you?" Rita shook her head and flung her arms out in a gesture of despair. "Do you know who the father is?"

"Of course."

"Well, who *is* he?"

16

"Tex."

"Tex who?"

"That's all I know. I met him on the beach. He wanted to. I let him."

"But you do *know* him?"

"Only in the Biblical sense, Mother," Susan said dryly.

Rita tried to get control of herself, saying, "You have been most foolish, Susan, and *most* cruel to me. But there is nothing to be done about it now." Sigh. "You shouldn't have had an abortion, but it's too late for that now. We'll just have this baby and put it out for adoption."

"*It*, Mother?"

"Well, do you know whether it's a boy or girl?"

"No."

"Have you been to a doctor?"

"No."

Rita Farrell was shocked. Her blue eyes widened and she shook her head in despair so hard her dyed red hair quivered in spite of all the hair spray she'd applied. "Heavens, Susan! Are you all right?"

Susan Raimond wanted to say she was fine. She wanted to prove she could run her own life. But the plain truth was she was scared, a lot scared, and that won out. "I'm not sure," she whispered.

She might be the most manipulative stage mother in Hollywood, but Rita Farrell did love her daughter. "What's wrong, honey?" She saw Susan hesitate, the lower lip protrude just as it always had. Rita came to her, put her arm around her, said, "You'd better talk to your mother, Susan. Let's not fool around about this."

The arm did it. Susan's resistance melted. "I'm passing some blood. It's—it's getting . . . worse."

"God, Susan! We're returning to Los Angeles at once. You're going to get the finest medical care available!"

\* \* \*

17

Most weekdays Brian Hecht breakfasted with Laura Carlyle at eight A.M., discussing hospital affairs, but he had canceled today because of his interview with Judd Forbes and other matters. So it was after ten when he entered Laura's private elevator and pushed the button that carried him five flights up to the Carlyle Tower atop Bel Air General.

Laura Carlyle, second wife of Dr. Oliver Carlyle, founder of the hospital, was now the principal owner, indeed the heart and soul of Bel Air General. Far more than her late husband, Brian knew, Laura Carlyle had turned the hospital into a leading medical facility. It might be exclusive, luxurious, and posh, but the clientele received (admittedly, for a high price) the finest nursing and medical care in the world.

Brian considered Laura Carlyle to be, even at age seventy-two, the most beautiful woman he'd ever known, in the fullest sense of the word. She was physically beautiful, so petite, seemingly frail, with great character in her delicate, oval face, those immense and astonishing blue eyes, that wreath of silver hair that gave her an ethereal appearance. Always, but always, she was elegant and so steeped in genteel courtesies that she seemed to command respect and consideration simply by entering a room. She had often disarmed the angry and vituperative with little more than her presence.

But beneath all that frailty and gentility lay a very tough woman, as Brian well knew. The hospital was her whole life. She set the highest standards and demanded total performance. Furthermore, she had an uncanny knack of knowing, sometimes before anyone else did, virtually everything that transpired in Bel Air General. The person who crossed her or tried to thwart her should beware. Laura Carlyle always got her own

18

way, using the most patient, devious, and manipulative means.

At the elevator Brian was met by Rosella Parkins, Laura's longtime secretary, companion, and, Brian was sure, protector. Rosella was a black woman of Southern extraction, friendly, polite, dignified, and soft-spoken. But she would not tolerate any affront or threat to Laura, as Brian himself had found out more than once. They exchanged pleasantries as she escorted him to "Oliver's Study," where coffee was laid out and Laura received him.

"I'm sorry to have missed breakfast, Laura. I promise not to make a habit of it," Brian said as he entered.

Laura smiled. It was merely exquisite. "I will try to forgive you. How did your interview go?"

Brian bent, brushed her cheek with his lips in greeting—one of the little courtesies she expected, regardless of how often they saw each other—and sat in a leather chair opposite her. "Well, I think I'd like to hire him."

"You know you needn't ask permission. The staff is entirely up to you. Your choice of your assistant most certainly is."

He smiled. "So you always say, Laura, but over the years I've learned how wise it is to receive your—shall we say—advice and consent?"

She looked at him out of the corners of her eyes, a gesture of mild disapproval. Brian might be right, but no one else she knew would say such a thing to her. That alone was proof of how much she loved and needed him.

Brian laughed, disarming her disapproval. "These things are always a bit of a . . ."—he wanted to say "crap shoot" but thought better of it; Laura had very definite ideas about what was proper language—". . . risk. But I need someone desperately, and he's available immediately. I'll

19

keep him on probation awhile, see how it works out."

She nodded approval, then said, "Are you sure you want a male assistant?"

"Most definitely." He grimaced. "I've enough females on the staff as it is."

She didn't believe him for a second. She virtually never referred to it, but she had been totally aware of his affair with Jenny Corban—decrying it, hoping for the success of his marriage to her granddaughter. But some time ago she had decided to let him have his affair with Jenny, if that was what it took to keep him here as administrator. She couldn't run the place without him. Still, she had been surprised by how much he loved Jenny. He had been almost destroyed when she was attacked and nearly murdered.

"Have you heard from Jenny?" she asked now.

The question told him what she had been thinking. "I phoned her, just to see if she arrived safely. Apparently she has settled in, plans to check on courses at the University of Buffalo."

"I know you must miss her dreadfully, Brian."

He blinked. Her concern was genuine, no doubt of that. But how strange, considering how much she wanted him to patch up his marriage to Bobbi. "Yes." He sighed. "Life goes on. I've agreed to make no further contact with her for three months, give her a chance to—"

"I think that's wise, Brian. The poor girl has been through a dreadful ordeal. First, that terrible attack, then . . ."—she made a gesture indicating just how hard it was for her even to speak of it—" . . . then that ghastly scene in her hospital room." Laura Carlyle had so detested her daughter-in-law, Connie Payne, that she had rarely referred to her, at least by name, in life. She wasn't going to speak of her at all in death, if she could help it. "Jennifer needs time to adjust, to come to

20

grips with herself and with all that has happened."

"I know. But that doesn't make it any easier."

She sought to change the subject. "Why didn't you go to the funeral, Brian?"

"The same reason you didn't. I detested her when she was alive. Her death hardly changed that."

"But you're her husband. You should have stood beside Roberta. I now wish very much that I had done so." She saw him shrug. "Is there no hope for your marriage?" she asked softly.

"I don't see any, Laura. Let's talk about something else."

"You know how much I love you both and want your happiness," Laura persisted, then smiled. "And heirs."

There was bitterness in Brian's voice as he replied, "As I've said before, we don't always get what we want in this life, Laura."

Laura's smile faded. "Can't you believe Roberta had nothing to do with that . . . that *person* who attacked Jenny?"

He knew better. Bobbi had admitted sleeping with the man. But that was old news now. He said nothing.

"Can't you see that her mother's suicide confirms that it was she who arranged for the attack?" Laura pleaded.

"We've a new patient coming. Adriana Barre, no less," Brian said, trying to change the subject.

But Laura would not be distracted. "I intend to offer Roberta a seat on the board of directors. This very afternoon, in fact. I'm sure she has inherited Willard's ten percent. That awful woman had the good sense not to dispose of it, amazingly enough. Don't you think it only right that Roberta take her seat?"

Brian sighed. "That is entirely your decision,

21

Laura. I have nothing to do with the directors. I am not a stockholder."

She made a face at him. "My, aren't we testy today? I just think Roberta will make everything much easier for us both. Her ten percent and my forty-one will give us total control. It will be as I intended when I gave Willard those shares in the first place."

"No doubt—if Bobbi does what you want her to, something I've never managed to accomplish."

Laura shook her head at him, slowly, sadly. "How did you two ever get to such a state?" At once she dismissed the question with a wave of her bejeweled hand. "Since you don't want to talk about anything having to do with your personal life, let me ask another question. Do you have any idea of what is bothering Hillary George?"

"Bothering her?"

"Yes, she seems—I don't know, *distracted*. It's as though she's terribly worried about something. Do you know anything that's happened?"

Brian well knew his employer's sensitivity to people, particularly someone she cared about as much as she did Hillary George. Laura had brought Hillary, an abused child, into the hospital at age sixteen, made her an aide, sent her to nursing school, and brought her along, eventually making her Director of Nursing.

"I'm sorry. I really don't. I have to admit I haven't seen enough of Hillary lately to notice any change in her."

"Well, you *should* notice. It's part of your job," Laura snapped.

He sighed. "Now that I'm about to have an assistant, maybe I'll have the time."

# Chapter 2

Hillary *was* terribly worried, virtually beside herself with worry, in fact. The last word from Arthur had been that she was to do nothing until she heard from him. He had made her promise that she would take no action independent of him. That was a week ago. She had not heard from him since, not a note, not a phone call. Where was he? What was happening?

Sleep became virtually impossible, and when it came it was filled with horrid dreams of what was a real-life, fully awakened nightmare. The memory was burned into her brain, tormenting her— the motel room door bursting open, a flash going off, bathing Arthur and her in light as they lay naked in bed, in the act of love.

Almost as bad had been the confrontation with Dana Shaughnessy, Hillary's first-shift supervisor at Bel Air General. She had produced the photograph, but Hillary had refused to look, knowing

23

only too well what it showed. Shaughnessy and the other two supervisors, Kathryn Quigley and Barbara Brookes, had joined together to force her out as Director of Nursing. She either resigned, or Arthur's identity would be revealed. Hillary had said she would resign, but she had not yet done so in obedience to Arthur.

The situation at the hospital was hopeless. Dana Shaughnessy had again confronted her, and Hillary had begged for more time, again saying she would resign. Shaughnessy had seemed to agree, but for how much longer? Meanwhile, the nursing staff was in disarray. Hillary avoided her supervisors and they her. They were ships passing in the night. Everyone knew something was wrong. Nursing care at Bel Air General, one of the hospital's claims to fame, was facing total collapse if something didn't happen soon.

Hillary kept showing up for work, but could do little more than remain in her office, staring out the window, the immaculate lawns and gardens of the hospital quite unseen. It was as though she was paralyzed. Only the most dire emergencies were attended to.

*Arthur, oh, Arthur!* It was all her fault. Wasn't it always the woman's fault? *Arthur.* She sighed. Better stop calling him that. Long ago, almost from the beginning, she'd made up the name, referring to him always, even in her thoughts, as Arthur to avoid even the remotest possibility that she might inadvertently say his real name, even in her sleep. She never wrote, spoke, or thought his real name. She had almost forgotten it. Now, looking out the window, when she said it aloud, "Quentin Cardinal Stillwell," she knew just how great her folly had been.

He had been a patient at Bel Air General for some forgotten malady, she his nurse. The attraction between them had been powerful, but both had fought it hard and for a long time before they

24

succumbed—a white man, a Bishop of the Roman Catholic Church, she his nurse, a black woman. Their affair had continued over the years while he became an Archbishop and finally earned the red hat of the Cardinal. Their secret, sporadic lovemaking didn't even stop then, although it became far more difficult for them to find time to be together secretly.

When she thought of it now—Quentin Cardinal Stillwell, not Arthur—it was so wrong—terrible, ghastly, blasphemous ugliness, people would think, and weren't they right? But it had never seemed wrong to her while it was happening. They loved each other deeply and truly. He was the one man in her life who understood her, the one man she could be totally honest with, the one man who awakened her long-suppressed sexuality and helped her accept it.

In all honesty, she could now admit, she was unsure what she meant to him. She knew only that he loved her and seemed to need her desperately.

With hindsight, it had been so easy for her, too easy. She had hardly ever seen him in his clerical garb, so she could pretend to herself not to know who and what he was. But she was not totally dishonest. She knew. And she knew what a terrible price he paid as well. Frequently she saw the suffering, the agony in his eyes, particularly when their titanic, insatiable lovemaking had ended. She'd reach out to him, say they must stop. He'd say no. It was his problem, not hers. Yes, *he* had made it easy for her. Too easy. . . .

They hadn't been together very often, especially in the past few years. He was on the East Coast, she on the West. He traveled abroad a great deal on church affairs. He was said to be a favorite of the Pope. Twice, maybe three times a year, they managed to meet—that was all. Stolen hours, an occasional night. A few secret phone calls to stay in touch. So very little. *Why* was it so ugly? *Was* it such an evil?

Hillary had told herself she was content with the arrangement. She loved him and knew she was loved in return. And she had Tommy. Her son was her whole life, her darling, his twelve-year-old body wracked with cystic fibrosis. Between caring for Tommy, providing a home, and her career at Bel Air General, she needed nothing more. Or so she told herself.

Then two changes had entered her life. One was Maximilian Hill, the celebrated black film star. He was like a magnet to her, though she had been convinced that no man could ever interest her again except Arthur. And Max wanted her. They saw each other, quite chastely. Tommy adored him—Tommy, who knew nothing of Arthur. She fought the attraction between herself and Max, tried to get rid of him. It hadn't worked. Then she had succumbed, discovering that another man could arouse her deep sexuality, and love her as well. Max sensed there was another man—"Mystery Lover," he called him. She'd admitted it without identifying him, promised to break it off, to give Max a chance. She had talked about it with Arthur, and he agreed she should find happiness with Max. Their relationship was at an end. She *did* feel free. Had to admit it.

The second change had been Hillary's appointment as Director of Nursing at Bel Air General. She had been promoted from floor nurse, passing various head nurses and supervisors. Laura Carlyle had insisted on it. Most of the nurses had accepted her, but not the three supervisors. They were determined to force her resignation on the grounds of moral turpitude, and hired a detective to follow her, which of course she did not know.

She had met Arthur again to discuss how he might legitimately have a place in her life as her friend. But the attraction between them, always

26

there, was too powerful, and the flesh was weak. He was insistent. She gave in. One last time. Door, flash, shame, disaster. . . .

The phone rang. She leaped to answer it. *Arthur!* At last. She listened, said, "Yes, I know the place. I'll be there, waiting." Hesitation. "Arthur, are you all right?"

"We'll talk about it over lunch."

Click.

She was ridiculously early, and waited for him, fingering her glass of white wine. The place, The Wine Cellar, had apparently once been just that. It was dark, like a cave. Probably didn't even need air conditioning. It occurred to her that this would be the first time she had ever been out in public with Arthur. *Stop it! Not Arthur. Cardinal Stillwell.*

She saw him coming, tall, so very slender, somehow imposing even in dark glasses, a straw hat, and casual clothes. He needed the disguise. His nearly white hair and violet eyes made him one of the more easily recognized public figures in America. How could she have been so stupid as ever to believe she could carry on a secret love affair with this man?

He saw her sitting in a booth to the rear of the restaurant. She was to him unutterably lovely, so much so that just seeing her caused him physical pain: the dark hair falling in waves to her shoulders; the expressive eyes, dark brown flecked with gold; the soft, sensual lips he knew so well; and her skin, *café au lait* in color, almost glowing with an inner light. A man's hands ached to touch it. He knew his did. And he had. The memory of it would be forever burned in his brain.

But it was not Hillary's beauty alone that made her irresistible. Nor was it her statuesque figure— she was almost six feet tall. Nor was it her innate dignity, the hard-won elegance and sophistication with which she carried herself. What made Hillary George special was her aura of sexuality, which she tried very hard to suppress and negate. The effect she had on men had always caused her personal torment. As a child, growing up in Watts, she had been grossly abused by men, boys, menboys, not understanding why it was so, hating herself and her body, until Laura Carlyle had rescued her.

Her marriage to Lester George, a young black doctor, had offered no refuge, for he had beaten her repeatedly, beyond all reason. She had retreated into a shell, which only Stillwell had broken. He'd released her true sexuality, loved her for it, helped her understand and accept her own nature.

At first Quentin Stillwell had tried to convince himself that he had performed an act of charity, helping a suffering woman learn to live with herself. But he'd always known that was a rationalization. Hillary George had become his own private torment, a craving that demanded to be satisfied no matter what the cost.

He slid into the booth opposite her, his back to the door, and removed his hat, then his glasses. When Hillary saw the pain in his eyes, her own filled with tears. "Oh, Arthur. . . ." She smiled, or tried to, wanly, lips quivering. "I keep telling myself I have to . . . stop calling you . . . Arthur."

He had eyes only for her. Voice choked with emotion, he said, "I—I . . . don't want you . . . to stop." He longed to touch her. His hand started forward, across the table, to clasp hers, but he restrained it. Not here.

She understood, tried to brighten her smile. "Do you realize this is the first time we've ever been out in public together?"

"Yes." Still he struggled with his physical desire. "And I think we'd better try to behave."

"Yes."

He ordered wine from the waiter, a welcome distraction.

"Where have you been? I've been so worried," Hillary said.

He nodded. "I know. I'm sorry. But I did what I had to do." The wine came. He sipped it. "I went off by myself. It doesn't matter where. I needed to think, and I needed to pray. I did a lot of that." He smiled slightly. "My knees are sore. It's the first good feeling I've had in a long time."

"Oh, Arthur." She shook her head. "I should have been stronger. I should have spared you all this pain."

"No. It takes two, Hillie. Always has, always will. The fault was mine. This is no time for blame, recriminations, or guilt. It *is* time for confession and amends. That is precisely what I'm going to do."

She stared at him, waiting for him to go on, and finally said, "I don't understand."

"I'm going to do what I must, Hillie. I'm going to confess my sin, then resign. After that . . ." He shrugged. "I know a little monastery in the Italian alps—Trappist, very severe in its discipline. I'm going there, if the Holy Father will permit me, and dedicate the rest of my life to . . ."—he smiled again—". . . to what I should have been doing all along."

"Oh, God, Arthur, no! I won't let you!"

"I must, Hillie. It is the only way for both of us."

"No, it isn't, not at all!" She shook her head violently. "Oh, God—what do I call you? Quent, Quentin, Your Eminence—what?"

"Arthur. I want to be Arthur—always."

She saw the emotion in his eyes. "Oh, Arthur, I'm sorry. I can't help it. I love you—I always will. I—I—I'm sorry, but I have . . . no regrets." She saw the pain she was inflicting on him. He clearly had regrets, and he was prepared to pay an enormous price for them, a hugely unnecessary price. "I won't let you do it, Arthur. All Dana Shaughnessy wants is my resignation. She can have it. I'll go." She saw him shaking his head. "I'm a good nurse, Arthur. I can get a job anywhere. I won't even lose a paycheck. I'll probably be better off."

Still he shook his head. "It won't work, Hillie."

"Yes, it will!"

"They want money, Hillie," he said quietly. "A great deal of money."

She stared at him, she couldn't believe him and now she shook her head in denial. "You're wrong. I asked Dana Shaughnessy if she wanted money for the photo and negative, and she accused me of being a tramp for even suggesting it. She wouldn't touch any of my *filthy* money. That's exactly what she said."

"It's not her, Hillie. A man named Wallace Dykes came to me. He wants a half-million dollars or he'll sell that photograph to the highest bidder."

"Oh, my God!" Her hand came to her mouth in shock. She stared at him, trying to come to grips with this new information. Finally, she asked, "Who's Wallace Dykes?"

"A most unattractive, venal little man. He's the one who took the photo. I had him checked." He sighed. "It seems he's an insurance investigator. He's also the son-in-law of Dana Shaughnessy."

Hillary gasped. "Yes—Dana Shaughnessy has a daughter, Maureen. Maureen Dykes. Lord save us!"

"Which both of us should have been asking Him to do for quite some time," he said wryly. "I haven't got a half-million dollars, Hillie. I cannot compound my sin by stealing—misappropriation is hardly the word—from the Church. My only choice is to go to the Holy Father, confess, and let him decide what must be done."

30

Hillary kept shaking her head in numb disbelief.

"I've thought about simply not paying the blackmail or going to the police," he continued.

"You can't, Arthur! The scandal will—"

"Exactly. With so many other religious and sex scandals so much in the news lately, I cannot permit this to tarnish the image of my Church. I am, after all, expected to set a moral example to the faithful."

She saw his bitterness, heard his self-flagellating sarcasm, and her own suffering was compounded by the knowledge that it was her love that had brought him to this state.

"That is why I must go to the Vatican. I have no choice."

Somehow, slowly, Hillary tried to come to grips with herself so she could begin to think clearly. "No, Arthur—at least not yet."

"I said I have no choice. I've made up my mind."

She saw the dynamism and command in him. He was indeed a Prince of the Church. But she did not waver. "You asked me to give you time, Arthur. Now I ask *you* for time, a few hours at least, a couple of days."

"To do what?" he asked wearily.

"Dana Shaughnessy was most emphatic that she didn't want any money. Apparently her son-in-law does. She ought to be told that. Maybe she can stop him."

"No good, Hillie. I must confess and resign. I am no longer worthy of the exalted position I hold."

Perhaps for the first time since she'd known him, Hillary was annoyed with him. "Will you please stop thinking only of yourself?" She saw him stare at her as though she'd slapped him. "You say this scandal—*our* scandal—must not tarnish the

31

Church. I'm trying to prevent that. Let me try, Arthur. Please at least let me *try*."

In a moment he nodded reluctantly. "Yes. Very well. Forgive me, Hillie, if you can."

"Roberta, I deeply regret not going to the funeral. It was too thoughtless of me."

Bobbi Hecht was more than a little surprised at Laura Carlyle's words. If her grandmother had ever apologized to her before, she couldn't remember it. "It's just as well, Grandmother. Mother had arranged for what qualified as a three-ring circus." She sighed. "At least a *one*-ring circus."

Laura had a fairly good idea of what the flamboyant Connie Payne might have concocted for her last scene on earth, but she hardly wanted to know the particulars. "I suppose I assumed Brian would be there. If I'd known he wouldn't, I most assuredly would have attended."

Bobbi shrugged. "It's just as well he wasn't, either."

Laura looked at her disapprovingly. Bobbi wore an attractive lightweight suit, off-white in color, and matching heels. She was artfully arranged—a term Laura was fond of using in reference to women—quite stunning, really. Being old-fashioned, Laura tried to honor the amenities, and felt that her granddaughter should wear black for at least a month. But she decided not to mention it, saying instead, "I was not fond of your mother, as you know. There is no sense in pretending otherwise. But she *was* your mother, Roberta. I want you to know you have my deepest sympathy."

Bobbi looked away. This was too much. Or was it? When she had first learned of her inheritance, at least when she had recovered enough to realize the extent of Connie's wealth, she had been deeply affected. There had been a stricture in her throat and her eyes had smarted, although she had not

32

actually cried. What had gotten to her was the memory of the many times Connie Payne had said she'd take care of her. Bobbi had thought it meaningless, just her mother being maudlin. The woman could be exceedingly histrionic at times. If the situation called for an expression of sympathy, Connie Payne would render a bucket of tears. Color her excessive. When Bobbi understood that her mother had accumulated all this money for her sake, she was deeply touched.

Then she realized it was only money, after all. If she hadn't grieved for Connie before, why should she dissolve just because her mother had left her a fortune? It was as if she was being paid to grieve.

It had taken a while for Bobbi to think it through, but she had decided that she must try to feel less antagonistic to Connie Payne. As that funny little lawyer had said, thrift was a virtue. It was nice to know her mother had *some* virtue. She had promised herself to think of her that way—as a woman of virtue.

"I'm not grieving for her, Grandmother." She turned back to look at the silver-haired woman, now her only living blood relative. "She was all the things you always thought she was. She was not a very good mother, but. . ."—suddenly emotion stabbed at Bobbi—". . . but she did . . . love me."

Laura was moved. "I'm sure she did, Roberta." They were sitting in the morning room, that bright, airy room where Laura and Brian usually had breakfast. More shaded now, it was cool in the afternoon. She reached out and patted her granddaughter's hand. "Is there anything I can do for you?"

Bobbi was not given to displays of emotion. Tears were not her thing. Quickly she collected herself. "I guess I'd like a drink, a little dry sherry or something."

33

Glad for something to do, Laura motioned to Rosella, who poured a drink and handed the glass to Bobbi. "I invited you here this afternoon, Roberta, to ask you to assume your mother's place on the board of directors of Bel Air General Hospital."

Bobbi sipped her sherry and made no comment.

"As you know, I gave ten percent of the shares to your father. He in turn bequeathed them to your mother." She spoke matter-of-factly, not revealing her inner anguish at her only son's folly in marrying Connie Payne, then dying in a plane crash. "Your mother did not sell them. I would have known if she had. I assume she bequeathed them to you."

"Yes, I just learned that this morning."

Laura smiled radiantly. "I can't tell you how that pleases me. To think, what I intended so long ago with your father has finally come to pass—a person of my own flesh and blood joining me in the administration of this hospital."

Bobbi looked sharply at her. She hadn't thought of it that way. "I suppose that's true."

"My, my!" Laura squeezed her hand with surprising strength. "I am so delighted. I think we will make a great team, Roberta. I look forward to having you at my side."

Bobbi was somewhat taken aback. All her life, she had been torn between two women who hated each other, her mother and her grandmother. Much of the time her grandmother had lost out. Connie had called her an old fuddy-duddy. Laura was steeped in gentility, always calling her "Roberta." Her mother, calling her "Bobbi," had been more fun—Hollywood, movies, celebrities, parties—however shallow and licentious. With her mother's approval, Bobbi had sowed a lot of wild oats, a whole granary full, enough to feed the entire country breakfast for a week. Yet during it all her grandmother had been there, beckoning to her

34

better nature, appealing to her sense of honor. Now Connie Payne was dead by her own hand and Laura Carlyle remained. Virtue—true virtue—had triumphed. Funny how things worked out. . . .

Laura was speaking again. "I must ask you, my dear—do you need any funds to tide you over? Dividends are paid quarterly. I think you will be surprised what a substantial amount that is. But the next payment is not due for a couple of months. I can let you have an advance if you wish. I'll be happy to do so."

Bobbi smiled, almost laughed. For the second time today, money was being thrust at her. It never rained but it poured. She hesitated. The idea that she was now a rich woman had not completely sunk in. She wasn't sure how to handle it, hadn't told a soul. What the hell—this was her grandmother, and she just *had* to tell *somebody*. "I met this morning with a fussy little man named Cary Knowlton," she said. "Do you know him?"

Laura repeated the name as though tasting it. "I don't believe I do."

"He's been Mother's lawyer for a number of years, and her business manager. Apparently he's good at it, although you wouldn't guess it to look at him. Anyway, he read Mother's will. It was a short one. She left everything to me." The words *beloved daughter* flitted across her mind.

"Of course she did," Laura said calmly. "You are her only child—only relative, as I remember."

Bobbi opened her purse and pulled out two sheets of paper stapled together. "Mr. Knowlton prepared this as a statement of my inheritance. It's not complete—there are still a couple of safety deposit boxes to be opened."

She handed it to her grandmother, watching her unfold the sheets, begin to read. Laura had acres of aplomb. She made a point of never being surprised or shocked—too unladylike. Now Bobbi watched her eyes, those immense blue pools, sometimes so immeasurably deep. They darkened first, then widened as they read. The eyes left the page, fastened on her, then returned to the page. Her grandmother wasn't about to faint, but she was clearly in a state approaching shock.

Finally Bobbi said, "As the lawyer put it, if thrift is a virtue, my mother was *extremely* virtuous."

"My dear!" Laura's mouth stood open a moment. "I simply would not have dreamed . . . all *this?*"

"Nor I." She laughed now. "I still can't quite believe it."

Laura looked at the second page again, specifically the bottom line. A little in awe, she said, "You're a very wealthy young woman, Roberta."

Another laugh, almost a gleeful giggle. "Aren't I!"

But surprise would only last so long with Laura Carlyle. Her poise slid back into place like a familiar garment and made a perfect fit. She handed back the papers. "I hope you're not going to do anything foolish. You must preserve this estate for your future."

"I have no intention of being foolish, Grandmother. Since Mr. Knowlton has done so well for Mother, I've retained him. I'll live off the income and hopefully invest a good deal of it." She smiled. "Like mother like daughter. Maybe I take after you a bit, too. You had little before Grandfather died, or so I've heard."

"That's true," Laura said. "Oliver left me a substantial amount, mostly the majority shares in this hospital. I've strived both to preserve and enhance my inheritance, as Oliver would have wanted me to do." She hesitated. "What are you going to do, Roberta? I mean—differently?"

"I hardly know. I just found out this morning.

I think, however, I'll keep Mother's house and move into it."

Laura was shocked, but she didn't show it. "Do you think that's wise?"

Bobbi pretended not to know what Laura was driving at.

"It's small by Bel Air standards, but I think I'll be quite comfortable there."

"I'm talking about Brian. What does he think of your moving?"

"I haven't discussed it with him. He knows nothing about any of this. I'm not at all sure I'm going to tell him."

"You must, Roberta. He is your husband." The old woman's expression was stern, her voice sharp.

Bobbi shrugged, demonstrating a lack of concern she did not feel.

"So it says on a piece of paper somewhere. Let's not kid ourselves, Grandmother. Brian and I not only aren't living together, we hardly speak."

"Much to my personal grief. The fact remains, Roberta, he is still your husband."

Now Bobbi stared at her, her eyes narrowing. "You mean community property?"

"I was hardly thinking of anything so crass as money, my dear. I had in mind love, affection, mutual respect, and trust between husband and wife."

Bobbi hardly heard her. "I can tell you right now he won't get a nickel of my inheritance. Just let him try!"

"My dear, my dear!" Laura shook her head, seemingly in total despair. "Can't you see that this inheritance may be a means for you to patch up your marriage? I know how much you love Brian. Don't deny it."

Yes, it was true, dammit! She *did* love Brian. "You want me to *buy* his love?"

Laura's back straightened in a characteristic

muted display of anger. "That's insulting, Roberta. I will not entertain such talk."

"But isn't it what you meant? Now that I have money, do you really think Brian will come running back to me, declaring his undying affection?"

The back remained straight. "That is absurd and you know it. I will not be spoken to as though I were a fool. You know perfectly well what I mean. Your inheritance may be viewed as a door opening on a new life for you both. It will take time, patience, mutual give and take. But the effort must be made."

Bobbi sighed. There was no sense in arguing with her. "I suppose so."

"And has it occurred to you that your mother might well have intended to save your marriage when she arranged your inheritance?"

"Now *that* I refuse to believe." Bobbi stood up, slinging her purse over her shoulder. "I have to run."

Laura stood, too. "All I ask is that you think about what I've just said."

"Very well. I will think about it." She bent and kissed her grandmother's cheek in farewell. "I think I'm going to enjoy being a director."

"It's a great pleasure for me as well, Roberta. I want you with me."

Bobbi hesitated, looking at her intently. "Yes, that's a good way to put it. It's what I want, too. In fact, I'd like to ask you to find something for me to do here at Bel Air General. I'd like to participate in the affairs of the hospital. I have no intention of being nothing but a coupon clipper."

"Do you mean that?"

"I've never meant anything more in my life."

Laura nodded, then smiled. "Very well. I'll work something out."

# Chapter 3

"Oh, isn't he beautiful!"

Adriana Barre heard the exclamation of Jane
Tawari, her nurse in obstetrics. Of Japanese extraction, Nurse Tawari was middle-aged, tiny as
a button, and so good-natured and enthusiastic
Adriana could not help but like her. "Where? I
don't see."

"There!" She pointed with her finger to the
monitor for the ultrasound. "See? A tiny leg . . .
another. There's an arm."

Adriana raised her head, peering intently at the
small screen. A sort of television, but distorted,
wavy. Then she figured it out. "Ohhh."

The image moved. "There! See the head?"

"Oh, yes, yes!" Adriana began to emit a series
of cooing sounds, as she saw images of the baby—
*her* baby—she carried within her body. It was to
her a miracle of miracles. "Oh, he's so beautiful!
Look at him. I love him. Oh, I *love* him!" Actu-

ally, no view had yet showed the sex of the fetus, but that didn't matter to Adriana.

It was just such natural spontaneity that had already endeared Adriana Barre to every member of the staff who came in contact with her. Her admission had caused a stir. Even the most blasé doctors and nurses were impressed and eager to meet her. Adriana Barre. Imagine! Rules were rigidly enforced to spare her a parade of admiring visitors among the staff. Room 227 had been declared off limits to all but the OB-GYN staff and senior medical personnel.

"Isn't he just darling!" Nurse Tawari enthused.

Adriana agreed. "Oh, yes, yes!" Right now, despite her persistent pain, she loved the whole world. "I'll keep him, thank you, and take him home with me."

Hamilton Dodd only half-heard the exclamations as he applied the transducer to Adriana's distended abdomen. Nor was he looking at the fetus in much more than a cursory way, noting that it was in a normal position and apparently quite healthy. His attention focused on something not even Nurse Tawari was trained to see. He was looking at the placenta, that nutrient-rich sac that supported the life of the fetus through the umbilical cord. Specifically, he studied a couple of spots, showing dark on the ultrasound monitor, behind the placenta where it linked with the uterus. Couldn't be sure what they were. He could only hope they were not what he feared.

He moved the transducer again, giving him fresh views of the infant. When he returned to the backside of the placenta, the spots were still there. He hadn't been imagining them. Damn! Quickly he took still photographs for later study.

"See, Hamilton? Didn't I tell you everything was okay? I've a perfectly healthy boy growing inside me," Adriana said, beaming.

Dodd didn't want to tell her about the spots.

No sense worrying her about something as uncertain as this, something hopefully manageable. Instead, he said, "He certainly is an active little bugger."

"You will *not* call my son a bugger, Doctor." Her laugh, so famous, was musical. "I can feel him. I'm sure that's what is causing my little pains."

"I'm afraid not, Adriana. Babies have been moving and kicking throughout the ages, and not one of them has caused a persistent pain on the mother's right side."

"Oh, posh, Hamilton! It's so slight I hardly notice it. There's no reason I can't go home. Everyone is nice here, but I must insist on my own bed."

"You may insist all you want, Adriana, but it is simply not going to happen. I'm keeping you here until that pain goes away or until I find out the cause of it." He saw her start to protest. "No buts, Adriana. You either do as I say—which is complete bed rest—or I'll sic Charles Bridges on you!" He gave her a mock scowl.

She laughed. "Now, *that* would be terrible."

A few minutes later Dodd had sought out Dr. Leon Kazinsky for a conference. Although twenty years his junior, Kazinsky, Chief of Surgery at Bel Air General, had earned Dodd's respect. He was not only a crackerjack surgeon and getting better daily—his emergency heart transplant on pianist Gregory Claiborne had proved that—but a first-class administrator running a tight ship and attracting good people. The surgical department at Bel Air General, which had sunk to journeyman status during the long tenure of Dr. Ernest Wilkerson, who still hung on with the meaningless title of Director of Surgery, had gained a new lease on life under Kazinsky. Bel Air General was now one of the "in" places to perform surgery, as long as the patient could pay the freight.

41

"On the right side, you say? Could it be appendicitis?"

Ham Dodd looked at Kazinsky. The man was far from handsome. Flat Slavic face, mouse-colored hair, unruly, probably seldom combed it. The man was too interested in medicine ever to give a damn how he looked. Good. "Maybe, " Dodd said. "I looked at it with ultrasound. Seemed okay. I've ordered a blood count to be sure, but I don't think we're dealing with a bum appendix."

"Then what?"

The door to the surgical office opened and Pete Guarneiri, the senior resident and Kazinsky's right-hand man, entered, along with Dr. Garson Shedd, the junior resident for OB-GYN. Dodd waited while Kazinsky brought them up to date on the consultation. When Kazinsky turned back to him for an answer to his question, Dodd said, "I sure do hope I'm wrong—Lord, how Adriana Barre has suffered trying to have a child!—but I think we may be looking at an *abruptio placentae*. Can't be sure. The spot is small, if that's what it is. But we have to assume it is and take every precaution." He saw them nod agreement. "I'm ordering complete bed rest. I don't want her to get up even to go to the john. She's an energetic woman and more than a little willful. I'm counting on the staff to do whatever is required to see that she stays in bed. Blame everything on me. Doctor's orders."

Guarneiri nodded; Shedd, too.

Kazinsky asked, "Have you told her?"

"No, not yet. She's a little hypertensive as it is. She wants this child so damned bad, Leon, I'm afraid that if she thinks anything might happen to it, she'd—"

"I understand. Why not try to bring her blood pressure down? Diuretics, at least."

"I intend to. And an ACE inhibitor, too. Use Basotec."

Kazinsky nodded concurrence, then watched Shedd write the order.

Guarneiri said, "If it is an *abruptio*, that doesn't necessarily mean it has to be serious, does it?"

Dodd replied, "No, not if it stays the way it is. Let's just hope that if we manage her properly it will do just that. Maybe we'll blunder through."

"I hope so, too." Guarneiri shook his head. "When I met her today I felt I was in the presence of a queen. I felt like kowtowing—bowing, at least. A remarkable woman. You just gotta love her."

Dodd smiled. "You noticed that, did you?"

Then Guarneiri looked at Leon Kazinsky and laughed. The chief of surgery was famous for knowing virtually nothing about Hollywood celebrities. Apparently he'd hardly ever gone to a movie. "Leon, I'll bet you have no idea who Adriana Barre is."

Kazinsky glanced at him, unperturbed. "Of course I do. She's a patient at Bel Air General Hospital."

The confrontation was bittersweet for Hillary. Part of her hated it. It was something she thought she'd never do in her life. Another part of her welcomed it as a relief. At least she was doing *something*, fighting back. She was not completely helpless.

When she asked Dana Shaughnessy to come to her office and close the door, she felt she was seeing the older woman for the first time. Shaughnessy truly was "the battle axe," as the nursing staff privately referred to her, built square, steel-gray hair tied back in a severe bun, hard, passionless mouth, cold eyes— very cold eyes. She was a prune of a woman. All the juices of life had been squeezed from her. A speck of Hillary thought she ought to feel sorry for her, but she couldn't, not under the circumstances. Later, perhaps, some

43

other time. She promised herself to try to work on that. Later.

"Ms. Shaughnessy, I believe you and I made a deal," Hillary began. "I was to resign as Director of Nursing, leaving the way open for your appointment, in return for a certain photograph and negative showing . . ."—she hesitated, mostly out of long practice of secrecy, but it was pointless now; she forced herself to say the name—". . . showing Cardinal Stillwell and myself together."

What passed for a smile touched the thin lips. "And a most revolting photograph it is. One of the most disgusting I've ever—"

Hillary cut her off. "You said all that before, Ms. Shaughnessy. You needn't repeat it. And I really don't care how much pleasure it brings you to do so. The point is that I agreed to resign in return for the photograph and all negatives. I am prepared to do that." She gave a small shrug of her shoulders. "Unfortunately, Ms. Shaughnessy, you have not lived up to your side of the bargain."

Shaughnessy drew herself up, the picture of outrage. "I have so!"

"You have not. One of your faults, Ms. Shaughnessy—I strongly suspect it is one of your minor faults—is that you lie," Hillary said evenly.

The first-shift supervisor bristled. "I will not be talked to that way by a . . . a *harlot* like you. You're nothing but a *whore!* I will not be—"

"By definition a whore does it for money. I did it for love, which I'm sure you couldn't possibly understand. Be that as it may, you have lied, canceling our deal."

"I have not lied! I won't listen to such talk!"

"Ms. Shaughnessy, an individual named Wallace Dykes—quite a loathsome person, I understand—has demanded payment of a half-million dollars from Cardinal Stillwell in return for a certain photograph." She watched Shaughnessy's eyes widen. The woman was clearly shocked. "I believe this Wallace Dykes is your son-in-law, the husband of your daughter, Maureen. He was also your cohort in your nasty little scheme. It was he who burst in the motel door and took the photograph."

"I—I—"

"You need neither admit it—I know it's the truth—nor try to explain. The simple fact is that you are an accessory to attempted blackmail, Ms. Shaughnessy. I suspect Kathryn Quigley and Barbara Brookes might also be viewed as accessories."

"You wouldn't!"

Hillary smiled faintly. "You're right. I probably wouldn't. But if all this is going to come out anyway, I might as well drag you down with me. As your superior here at Bel Air General, I respectfully suggest that you stop lying, rethink the deal you want to make, and get back to me. The rules of this game have just changed."

Hillary watched as the woman stared at her a long moment, eyes filled with virulence, then stood and stalked out of the room. At once Hillary slumped in her chair, overwhelmed by fatigue and despair. She was only bluffing, and she knew it. Would this ghastly mess ever end?

Dr. Sheryl James, staff psychologist at Bel Air General, hung up the phone after her conversation with Jenny Corban in Buffalo. Jenny had been her patient, and Sheryl had given Jenny her home phone number, inviting her to call if she needed help, or just someone to talk to. This had been the first such call. Not much news—Jenny had settled in, signed up for courses. She was okay. Brian Hecht had phoned, asked how she was. She'd told him not to phone again for three months, to give her a chance. Sheryl had supported her in that decision.

Now Sheryl stood in the kitchen of her Westwood apartment, hand still holding the receiver of the wall phone. Jenny might just make it. She was tough and resourceful. She had pride and a sense of herself—or she had once had before she'd been raped. But it was going to be a long, painful road back—no, not a road *back*. Rather, a road to a new and different Jenny Corban, a road that Brian Hecht, her lover, might never traverse. Jenny was right in keeping him away. All this, Sheryl James knew for certain. She was a specialist in rape counseling. Having been a victim herself at the hands of her stepfather when she was a teenager, she knew just how hard it was for a woman to win back her self-esteem after such a traumatic experience.

Sheryl relinquished the phone and went to the refrigerator, pouring herself a little chablis. Brian Hecht. Now, there was a basket case. Estranged from his wife—and we are talking gorgeous woman here—and abandoned by Jenny Corban because of the rape, which Brian insisted, however pigheadedly, that his wife had engineered. The woman who got involved with Brian Hecht would be infecting herself with psychological leprosy.

She shook her head. The prime candidate was no less than Sheryl James. She knew it, knew that Brian knew it. The physical attraction between them was . . . Better not think about that. A week ago he had grabbed her in her office and impulsively kissed her. She'd been astonished at her intense response. Purely physical, of course, but still . . . She raised her glass of wine, swallowed, as though cooling her lips. No way, buster. Then he had come to her apartment late at night, wanting her. It would have been so easy—the man was a hunk, face it. She'd sent him away. *Good girl, Sheryl. Real good girl. Keep it up. Forget Brian Hecht. You're a tough lady. You've got your act together. Keep it. Don't play with dynamite.*

46

*Don't play Russian roulette. Don't play games
with Brian Hecht.*

The phone rang. She answered.

"Like Chinese?" a male voice asked.

She laughed. "No, but I like the person bringing
it. Come on over."

A half-hour later, following a quick shower and
the famous change into "something comfortable,"
Sheryl sat opposite Leon Kazinsky at her kitchen
table, licking her fingers. She simply wasn't handy
with chopsticks.

"Do you ever wear a dress?" Kazinsky asked,
eyeing her loosely tied cotton robe.

"Not around you. What's the point?" She
laughed. Teasing Leon, so uptight about his sexuality, so easily shocked, was so much fun.

He shook his head in pretended disapproval, or
what he thought of as disapproval. Growing up in
Gary, Indiana, struggling to get through college
and medical school, then internship and resi-
dency, Leon Kazinsky had given little thought to
women. He'd zeroed in on surgical medicine. Anything else was a waste of time and a distraction.
Oh, he figured to marry someday, a nice, plain,
mousy woman, probably long suffering and un-
demanding, a suitable companion to someone like
him. The last thing he'd ever consider was someone like Sheryl James. She was a really beautiful
woman, like a movie star, someone a man looked
at but never thought about touching. Rich, luxu-
riant auburn hair fell softly to her shoulders. A
lovely face, delicious skin, delectable mouth . . .
and those eyes. They were dark blue, but from the
pupil radiated streaks of silver, giving them a crys-
talline, gemlike quality. Just plain startling. And
her figure. She'd admitted to having breast-reduc-
tion surgery, but Kazinsky figured they hadn't removed much. Men like him didn't get women like
her. No way. Yet there she was across the table,

47

licking her fingers seductively, wearing nothing under that robe, virtually inviting him to make love to her.

Again he shook his head. "There's something wrong with us, you know."

Through a mouthful of sweet-and-sour pork, she said, "You noticed that, did you?"

He blinked. "Noticed what?"

She chewed a moment, swallowed, wiped her lips with a paper napkin. "For one thing, here we are at my place again. Do you realize I've never been to your place? You *do* live somewhere, don't you? You don't bed down in the backseat of a car or a cot in your office?"

"I have an apartment. Not far from here."

"That's nice. Your wife like it?"

"I don't have a wife. You know that."

"A roomie, then."

He was shocked. Where was this heading? "I live alone."

"Then why haven't I ever been there? I get turned on by men's beds." She saw his consternation and smiled at it. "I know it's too much to expect us to go out all the time—dinner, a concert, a walk in the park, maybe even a movie. But I thought I could at least sneak into your apartment some night—after dark, when nobody can see me."

"Aw, c'mon, Sheryl." Kazinsky was distinctly uncomfortable.

"C'mon, yourself. Are you ashamed of me? Am I some piece you have stashed on the side?" At once she saw she'd gone too far, hurt him. She reached out and clasped his hand. "Leon, you're such a dope! I like you, respect you, admire you. I may even love you. I've been going to bed with you for all those reasons—and because you are something else in the sack."

Now he was actually blushing. "I am not."

"I'll be the judge of that. You're a fantastic

48

lover, precisely because you don't know it, because the last thing you are is a preening peacock putting on a performance. Why can't you just accept the fact that—" She smiled. "You're a hunk, Leon. A nice, shy, sexually retarded, grossly inhibited, and uptight hunk who brings out the predator in me." She laughed, couldn't help it.

He joined her, but only for a moment. "I don't know. We just don't *belong* together. You're too . . . too gorgeous, that's all."

"And you'd feel you were on display if you went out with me. You'd be uncomfortable."

He stared at her. "How'd you know that?"

Another laugh. "Leon, my love, you are so easy to read. You're a comic book—and I do mean funny." Her laugh deepened, as she stood up. "C'mon. Let's finish this later." When he hesitated she took his hand, brought it inside her robe, and pressed it to her breast, feeling the thrill of being so bold. "Now that's not too hard to take, is it?" she said, her voice husky, just before she bent and kissed him.

She had taught him to be a good kisser, and his fingers caressing her breasts were something else. Still, she was again surprised by her reaction to him. Oh, she'd understood it the first time. The man was a virgin. That was a first for her, too— a man in his thirties who'd never done it and who wasn't gay! But why her continued interest? She positively lusted for him. Amazing! For Sheryl, the proof that she had at last recovered from her teenage trauma was that she had learned to enjoy sex, thanks to her dear, good friend, Dr. Ben Singleton. She considered herself a nice, healthy, normal woman with the usual appetites. Good. Wonderful. But she was frankly surprised by her near-insatiableness when it came to Leon Kazinsky.

As they lay entwined in bed a short while later, her urgency at its peak, seemingly driving the air

49

from her lungs, she realized again why making love with this man was almost addictive. He was a surgeon and he brought to bed all the gentle skills, the careful thoroughness, and the total concentration that made him one of the finest young surgeons in Los Angeles. She felt completely dominated by him, totally in his hands—as though she were being operated on by the most precise, clinically approved methods. No anesthetic needed, thank you, although she sometimes swore she passed out. He gave her orgasm after orgasm, which was nice. No doubt about it, Leon Kazinsky's technique was *thorough*. He left nothing undone that needed to be done. The patient was quite satisfied with his treatment.

She was still contemplating the wondrous healing process when he said, "There's a new patient I think you ought to talk to."

She lay inside his arm, one leg draped over his, and smiled. From one patient to another. She had no complaints.

"Yes, Doctor. Who?"

"Adriana Barre."

"*The* Adriana Barre?" Then she laughed. "I suppose you don't know who she is."

"I guess I must have heard of her, but . . ." —he sighed—". . . frankly, no."

"Leon, she's just about the most famous film actress in the world."

"I figured as much, the way my whole staff is practically slavering to meet her. Anyway, she's pregnant."

"Which the whole world also knows. The papers and magazines have been full of how this time, finally, it looks like she's going to have a healthy baby. They're practically selling tickets."

"Not yet. Dr. Dodd fears she might have an *abruptio placentae*,"

"Explain." Sheryl was a psychologist, not a medical doctor. As she listened she slowly sat up

50

in bed, looking down at him. "That's terrible, Leon. Ghastly."

"Maybe not. It's small, barely visible on ultrasound. We're trying complete bed rest, some drug therapy. Maybe it'll be all right."

"God, I hope so."

"But maybe you ought to put in an appearance. She might need some counseling down the road."

She nodded. "Of course I will. But Lord, Leon, it just *can't* happen to that poor woman again!"

Every dog has its day, and Wally Dykes figured his had come. Ever since he developed that negative and saw what his camera had wrought, Wally had become a new man, his own man. He wasn't about to take any shit from anybody. A half-million bucks, maybe more, could do that to a fellow.

So when Dana Shaughnessy stood in his living room ranting and threatening, declaring what she would not have, he was amused. To think only a week ago he would have been scared of this old bag! Not anymore.

"Are you quite finished, mother-in-law dear?"

"You will not be sarcastic with me, Wallace, you—"

"I'll be whatever I wanna be, Mom, baby. I practically have a half-million big ones in the bank, maybe more, maybe a whole lot more. There is nothing you can say or do to stop it. Believe that or not, Mrs. Ripley."

"You stupid little man! You only have a print. I have the negative."

"Not anymore." He grinned. "You should've hid it better."

She gaped at him. "You broke into my *house?*"

"Yep, and into the bureau drawer. Yes, indeed." Wally laughed. "I assure you I've got it in a safer place than that."

Dana Shaughnessy was fuming so much that she could hardly speak. Then she saw her daughter

51

standing in the doorway to the kitchen. "Maureen, speak to him. You can't let him do this!" she wailed.

Maureen Dykes, short, dark, hugely unfavored, sighed. "I'm sorry, Mother, but Wally's right. It's our big chance. We have to take it."

"But it's blackmail!"

Dykes laughed. "Black, white, purple with yellow polka dots—what's it matter? We got a Catholic Cardinal with his pants down." Another laugh. "I mean *down* down, *real* down, way, *way* down—and dirty!"

"All I wanted was that . . . that *woman's* resignation. I never dreamed of anything like this. You should've heard the way she talked to me today. She threatened to make me an accessory to blackmail!"

Wally Dykes was really enjoying himself. "Is that all that's bothering you? Forget it. She's not gonna call the cops. No chance, no way. We got a photograph of a high mucky-muck in the Catholic Church changing his luck with a black broad. The only thing that's gonna happen is those guys in the funny collars are gonna scrape up a lot o' bucks to buy it from us. Think of it as a simple business transaction. They got gobs of dough. We got somethin' they want. Happens every day."

"Yes, Mother," Maureen added. "It was an awful thing that Stillwell did. It's only right he be punished for it."

Shaughnessy looked at her daughter uncertainly, then sighed. "I suppose you're right. But all I wanted was that black bitch's resignation."

"And you'll get it, mother-in-law, dear. And Maury and I will have big, big bucks. Just leave it to me. I know just how to handle everything."

Her name was Lorraine, and Brian had met her in the bar of the Beverly Hills Hotel. She was beautiful enough, an aspiring actress, real blond,

built, clean, interested, and accommodating.
Brian figured it was over two months since he'd
been to bed with a woman, and he needed her
bad. He also figured it had been years since he'd
had a one-night stand. Almost forgotten how it
was done. Since he was still staying at Jenny's
apartment, he couldn't take another woman to
that bed. They went to a motel.

It had felt so damned good to kiss Lorraine,
hold her, feel the smooth softness and savor her
response, not to mention being touched, fondled,
then guided. Yes, damned good. He'd had a return. Even better. She hadn't faked it. He was
sure of that. She'd really been turned on. Good to
be able to do that to a woman again. She'd given
him her phone number.

Then why did he feel so rotten?

# Chapter 4

Raf (for Raphaella) Spina was surprised and disappointed. Of all the applicants Mr. Hecht had interviewed, Judd Forbes was the last one she expected him to hire. Couldn't he see what Forbes was and that he was never going to fit in?

Raf had little to go on other than a gut feeling. But her intuition told her Judd Forbes was an *operator*—handsome, friendly, *too* friendly, adroit at manipulating people. He was a chameleon, changing his personality to match that of whoever he was with. He could be whatever a person expected him to be. Judd Forbes was an actor, all right, starring in his own very long-running play.

Too bad. He was her boss and she was his secretary. Nothing to do but make the best of it. Why did Jenny Corban have to leave? Jenny had been the genuine article, so very good, a real pro at a most difficult job. Raf respected her, loved working with her, and thought of her as a friend. No wonder Mr. Hecht had fallen in love with her.

Now Raf stood across the desk waiting while Forbes read the bulletin to be released concerning Adriana Barre. Just routine tests. Comfortable night. Excellent spirits.

He looked at her, smiling. "Excellent. Just what I had in mind. Do you know how to distribute it?"

Of course she knew. She did it every day. "Yes— the wire services, afternoon papers. The switchboard operator will be prepared to read it to anyone inquiring."

"Very good." He looked down at his desk, an act of dismissal, then changed his mind. "Do I call you Raf or Raphaella?"

*How about Ms. Spina?* "Whatever you prefer, Mr. Forbes."

"Very well. I'll ring when I need you."

Raf returned to her desk feeling vindicated in her reservations about him. The bulletin he had dictated earlier had been in the wrong form and quite unsuitable. She had changed it to the form generally used by both Mr. Hecht and Miss Corban. Frankly, Raf had expected him to ask why she'd changed his dictation. But he'd said nothing, either not noticing, or—more likely—planning to claim credit for what she herself had done. He didn't even say thank you for saving him from a mistake that Mr. Hecht most assuredly would have noticed.

Another thing. Judd Forbes didn't know how to treat subordinates, especially female subordinates. Raf knew her place. She ranked second on the clerical staff—no, third. Rosella Parkins was definitely first, but one didn't usually think of her as a secretary. Then came Addie Weickel, Mr. Hecht's secretary. Forbes treated Raf like she'd just been promoted from the steno pool, and she knew why. Judd Forbes was obviously one of those infuriating men who treated all women as sexual ob-

55

jects. If she was beautiful, the charm was ladled on. Addie Weickel had gotten that treatment for being both pretty and his boss's secretary. Raf knew she herself was not beautiful, although she thought her dark brown eyes and black hair were nice enough. She did not appeal sexually to Judd Forbes. She was his inferior; therefore, she was of no importance to him. *Better stop it, Raf*, she told herself. *You're going to have to work with him, you know, whether you like it or not.*

Courtesy was ingrained in him and Brian Hecht stood up when his wife entered Laura Carlyle's morning room at breakfast the following day. He also squelched any visible manifestation of his surprise, and no small annoyance, at seeing her. Another of Laura Carlyle's little manipulative ploys, no doubt. He returned Bobbi's cheerful "good morning" and watched her kiss her grandmother's cheek in greeting, then shake hands with Rosella Parkins.

At one time Brian had reveled in having a beautiful wife. Now that they were estranged, he simply acknowledged it as a fact. In a cool, lightweight dress, white in color, simply and stylishly cut, Bobbi looked perfectly stunning. The woman knew clothes and wore them well. She also spent a lot on them, as he damned well knew. But in terms of elegant chic, he got his money's worth. Would he ever get her completely out of his system? Bobbi Carlyle had once been a total turn-on for him, drove him wild, and made thoughts of all other women vanish from his mind. Their lovemaking had been tempestuous and intensely satisfying, until her bitchy temper and scathing tongue ended even that. She'd tried to patch things up between them and had almost won him back. He still desired her. She was a chronic disease, he figured, like something they treated in the isolation ward. He'd been in bed with Bobbi when he

56

had promised to be with Jenny. If he had kept that promise, he could have prevented the assault and rape that had ruined both their lives. . . .

"How have you been, Brian?"

Her smile was brilliant. Again he felt her considerable allure. Thank God for Lorraine! He was more physically relaxed than he'd been in weeks. Otherwise, this might be more difficult.

"Just fine, Bobbi. Yourself?"

"Oh, you two!" Laura reacted with obvious annoyance. "You sound like a couple of old chums or casual acquaintances, rather than husband and wife."

A response formed in Brian's mind, but Bobbi, always so quick, beat him to the utterance. "Maybe that's what we are, Grandmother. At least we're being civil."

Laura let the remark pass and turned to him. He sat on her right, a subtle courtesy not practiced much anymore. "Roberta has had some remarkable news. Has she told you yet?"

He glanced at Bobbi. So that explained her special radiance so early in the morning—or it would if he knew what had happened.

"No."

"I tried to call you last night, but you weren't at home," Bobbi said.

"No, I was out—quite late."

*Very* late. Bobbi tamped down the temptation to say it.

Laura looked at her, smiling. "Is it all right if I tell him?"

Bobbi shrugged. "Why not? He'll be pleased, I'm sure."

"Tell me what?" Brian was becoming increasingly exasperated.

"Roberta is coming into a great deal of money— several million dollars. Isn't that something?"

It certainly was. His raised eyebrows conveyed his surprise.

"How did you manage that?" he asked Bobbi.

"Mother's will."

"Connie Payne?" Now he was astounded.

"Actually, I was as flabbergasted as you are, Brian. I had no idea she was worth so much. I'm told it's between seven and eight million."

Brian was indeed stunned, and a whole lot more, although he hardly had time to sort out his reactions. He wasn't exactly penniless, but he did live on his salary, which was substantial. He'd made several small investments, but he really didn't have much in the way of assets. Even the house he and Bobbi had lived in actually belonged to Laura. Oliver Carlyle had built it for his first wife, silent screen actress Hetti Morgan, and had bequeathed it to Laura as part of his estate. She had insisted that they live in the dank, cavernous monster because it gave them a good Bel Air address at no additional expense.

He smiled. "Congratulations. I think you'll wear seven or eight million extremely well."

*Did he mean it?* Bobbi wondered. He seemed to. She smiled, too, in relief. "It will be sort of fun getting used to it."

"You'll manage," he said dryly.

*He didn't mean it!* "Does it bother you, Brian?"

*Damned right it does!* Another smile. "Not at all. I'm genuinely quite happy for you."

"I'm sure he is, Roberta," Laura added. "We both couldn't be happier." She reached out and clasped the hands of the two people she loved most. "And I do think financial independence will make things easier for both of you."

"Both of us?" Brian repeated. "I thought it was Bobbi's money."

Bobbi glanced at him. Yes, he *was* upset—jealous, most likely. *Do him good.* "I think I know what Grandmother means, Brian. The inheritance is mine and I intend to hold on to it, but you will have a share in it, at least indirectly. I

58

won't require any more . . ."—she had been about to say alimony, but that wasn't correct, since they were still married; not even legally separated, for that matter; she'd never had to go to court to get money from him; Brian Hecht had always been generous—". . . *funds* from you."

Inwardly he bristled. So this was how it was to be! "I intend to continue our current financial arrangement," he said stiffly.

"That's silly. I don't need it. And I'm sure you can put it to good use. Furthermore, Brian, since I have also inherited Mother's house, I'm going to move into it. I'm almost packed. I'll be gone this afternoon. You can move back into our place. You must be cramped where you are now."

"Stop it, you two, this instant!" Laura commanded. "If you can't live as husband and wife, you can at least share a common roof."

Brian looked at his employer. "Hardly, Laura."

"But how are you ever going to get back together if you don't?"

Brian glanced at Bobbi. At least they agreed on something. He tried to put it tactfully. "I believe that is something you're going to have to let us settle ourselves, Laura."

"Yes, Grandmother. Brian's right."

Laura let out a long, deep sigh. "The two of you will be the death of me. Very well, finish your breakfast." She might have been addressing two naughty children. They ate in silence a few moments. Then Laura said, "As of noon today, Roberta, you are officially a director of Bel Air General Hospital."

Bobbi smiled, genuinely. "Director of Bel Air General. I like the sound of it." She looked across the table. "Do you mind, Brian?"

He did, but he was in no position to say so. "Laura told me the situation yesterday. I concurred at that time." He forced a smile. "Welcome aboard. Meetings are held irregularly, so it shouldn't be too taxing for you."

"Roberta is going to do more than simply attend meetings, Brian," Laura told him. "She has asked for an active role in hospital administration, and I intend to give her the opportunity."

Brian squelched a groan of outrage and disbelief, saying only, "Is that so?" She couldn't mean as his assistant. Thank God he'd filled that slot. "I think we're quite well staffed at the moment." He longed to say he could no doubt find her something in maintenance or gardening, but thought better of it. Why pick a fight?

"I have something in mind, Roberta, which I think would be appropriate for you as a director and which might interest you," Laura was saying. "I do hope you'll consider it."

"What might that be?" The question came from Brian. His anger was rising rapidly, as he sensed another of Laura's devious manipulations.

"Let me explain, please. For some time I've been concerned about the role of Bel Air General in community affairs. After all, we are part of Bel Air, Beverly Hills—even Hollywood—society. We should do more for the communities, help improve them. Therefore, I'm proposing, Roberta, to create a Community Outreach Program and put you in charge of it."

"What *are* you talking about, Laura?" Brian growled.

"Don't be dense, Brian. I'm talking about charity. I've never liked Bel Air General being called the hospital for the rich and famous. I've always wanted to do more *pro forma* work, as the legal profession calls it—share with the needy some of our great good fortune."

He burst out laughing, couldn't help it, even though he saw Laura stiffen in annoyance. "You can't be serious! Are you proposing to admit bag ladies and drunks? I have an idea our present clientele, who create the 'good fortune' you speak of, would dislike hobnobbing with them."

"Stop it this instant, Brian! I will *not* be ridiculed by you or anyone else. You know I'm not talking about any such thing." She dismissed him with a wave of her hand and turned to Bobbi. "Let me talk to *you*, Roberta. I'm sure you'll be *far* more receptive. Of course, we can't admit the general public, except perhaps on an emergency basis as we do now, but we can make donations to suitable charities which provide health care to the needy. Some of our staff can be made available at clinics from time to time. We can provide medicines where needed. Something can be done in the way of educating the public about health problems. Some brochures, perhaps. What do you think, Roberta?"

In truth, she didn't think much of it. Grubbing around among the dirty and diseased was hardly what she had in mind. Still, she realized how very much Brian objected to her involvement in hospital affairs, and that alone enhanced Laura's scheme in her mind. But she said, "I'm not sure, Grandmother."

"I think you'd be splendid at it, Roberta, the very best possible person I can think of. You're most presentable and make a splendid impression. You'd meet with—oh, I don't know exactly—the Salvation Army, United Way, the various religious charities, explain that we want to help, work out a program which fits the nature of the hospital. . . . Do you understand what I'm talking about, Roberta?"

Bobbi's eyes brightened as she looked at her grandmother. Not bad. Not bad at all. "I like it, Grandmother. As a matter of fact, I think it's splendid. I'd meet with the leaders of charities, work out ways Bel Air General can assist the needy and take a more positive role in community-health programs. I think I might be good at that."

61

"I do, too, Roberta. I can think of no one better. We'll find you an office somewhere, a secretary, perhaps." Laura Carlyle positively glowed with enthusiasm, even as she turned to her hospital administrator. "I expect you to implement my plan, Brian, however much you might personally disagree with it."

He shrugged, conceding defeat for the moment. "As you wish, Laura."

Bobbi laughed. "Try not to put my office *too* far down in the sub-basement!"

The quality Charles Bridges most admired in his wife was her courage. She had had a difficult life, first as a child of the slums, then as a bosomy starlet struggling to prove she was also an actress, finally as a woman desperate to have a child. She never complained, never felt sorry for herself, though she occasionally flew into a rage when others let her down or proved incompetent. But in his love, Charles Bridges had learned to know and read her quite well. It wasn't her pallor or the beads of perspiration on her face, but the expression in her eyes that told him she was in great pain.

He went at once to the nursing station, which produced a flurry of activity from Nurse Jane Tawari. The junior resident, Garson Shedd, was summoned, then Pete Guarneiri, and finally Leon Kazinsky, as soon as he could free himself from the OR.

Adriana Barre was no help. She would admit to nothing, insisting she was fine even when she grimaced and spoke through clenched teeth. Both Guarneiri and Kazinsky admired her fortitude, but they were not fooled. Adriana Barre's pregnancy was in deep trouble. Her pulse was up, and so was her blood pressure. The fetal monitor showed the baby's heart rate speeding well above the normal one hundred forty, then slowing sharply. Bright red clots of blood escaped her vagina. When the port-

62

able ultrasound was brought in and used, the cause of it all showed clearly on the monitor. The hematoma behind the placenta was no longer a barely visible spot, but an area the size of a fist. Adriana Barre had serious, perhaps even massive, bleeding behind the placenta. Nothing could be worse.

"Are you in much pain, Miss Barre?" Kazinsky saw her grit her teeth, firm her lips. She did not speak, probably couldn't. "Miss Barre, this is no time for heroics. The degree of the patient's pain is important to the diagnosis. I ask you again. Are you in much pain?"

She held her expression, a sort of grimace, for a moment longer. Then tears rolled out of the corners of those famous eyes and down her cheeks. Finally, she let out her breath in a sharp groan. "It's agony!"

"I thought as much. And there's no need for it." He turned to Jane Tawari. "I want her to have Demerol at once. And start an IV drip, glucose and saline." This much was standard maintenance, to relieve pain and prevent shock from the bleeding. To Shedd he said, "I want a complete blood workup. Type her and see that whole blood is at hand. Also plasma. And I want to know her fibrin levels at regular intervals." He saw him nod, go to work.

"What's wrong, Doctor?"

Bedside manners were not Kazinsky's long suit, but he could not help appreciating this woman's stoicism. Most patients complained at the first twinge, but this one had been in severe pain for some time and had said nothing. If only she had.

"You have some internal bleeding, Miss Barre," he said.

"I'm aware of that, Doctor. Is the baby all right?"

He was impressed by the fact that her first concern was not herself but the fetus she carried. He hesitated. No sense in alarming her and raising her

**63**

blood pressure higher. "The baby's fine, Miss Barre."

"Are you sure?"

"Good strong heartbeat." No sense in telling her how irregular it was. "What we want you to do is try to rest and relax. That should be easier with the Demerol." He smiled. "You are in the right place to get the best possible care."

A very concerned Charles Bridges spoke. "What's wrong, Doctor? You said internal bleeding. What does it mean?"

Kazinsky hated the question. He should have sent the husband out of the room. Had to keep from alarming the patient. "Hopefully nothing serious. I'm summoning Dr. Dodd. He'll answer all your questions."

Abruptly he wheeled around and left the room for the nursing station, picked up the phone, and asked the operator to find Dr. Hamilton Dodd at once.

Dodd was with a patient in his examining room, had her in stirrups, in fact. But when his nurse said it was Dr. Kazinsky and an emergency with Miss Barre, he left the patient and went to the phone in his office.

"Dodd here." He listened to the short, clipped phrases from Kazinsky. The man was good, providing just the essential information about the patient and what was being done. No extraneous comments, nothing important omitted. "*Abruptio placentae*. I've feared it," he said grimly.

"I know you have."

"I'm with a patient but I'll be there as soon as I can. Meanwhile, hurry up the lab with the blood workup. I'll want several pints when I get there."

He hung up the phone. No good-byes were said. When he returned to his patient, he apologized for the interruption, adding that he had an emergency at Bel Air General and had to leave as soon as possible. He donned fresh gloves and bent over the patient, hurriedly completing his examination. He didn't like what he discovered, not at all.

"Miss Raimond, you have been most foolish." He stood up, stripped off his gloves, slipped out of his surgical gown. "I have a most seriously ill patient at the hospital, so forgive my abruptness. To go eight months without proper prenatal care is unconscionable. If you are suicidal and don't care about yourself, you might at least give some thought to that helpless infant." His blunt words surprised him. He usually didn't talk that way.

"What's wrong, Doctor?"

He looked at Rita Farrell, the girl's mother, his annoyance at flood level now. Why did these Hollywood women always have two last names? Why couldn't they just be Mrs. So-and-so like everyone else? "Rita Farrell" was hardly a household word that had to be preserved for posterity. "I'm sorry, but I'm needed elsewhere. It's a genuine emergency. I can tell you that we are dealing here with a *placenta previa*, but I truly don't have time to explain the problem right now."

Rita Farrell's eyes widened. "Is it serious?"

"Potentially, yes, but usually easily managed." He reached for his jacket. "I really must run. Here's what I want you to do. Take Miss Raimond home, put her to bed. Meanwhile, pack a bag with whatever she might need. As soon as I can get her admitted to a hospital, my nurse will call you. Take her there at once."

"*Hospital!*"

He glanced at Susan Raimond. "That's where babies are usually delivered these days."

"But, Doctor—"

"Please, I haven't time to explain. Just do as I say." He was already striding toward the door.

"Very well, Doctor. I want her in Bel Air General."

Didn't they all? "I'll do the best I can. No promises."

At the hospital, Hamilton Dodd was convinced by the ultrasound, and the blood workup left absolutely no doubt. Hemaglobin count way down. an Adriana Barre had an *abruptio placentae* and serious bleeding. There was no question about what he had to do.

Dodd dismissed all others from her room and sat with his famous patient and her husband. "I'm sorry, Charles and Adriana, but I have very bad news to report. There is no way to gloss it over, make it more palatable. I'm sorry, more sorry than I can say." And he was. He felt rotten. Such terrible luck.

"What is it, Hamilton?" Adriana asked. "I want the truth."

He looked at the beautiful face. The evidence of pain was still there, though reduced by the Demerol—and fear. Yet she had the courage to face the fear. He took her hand in both of his, hoping to comfort her. "You have a condition known as *abruptio placentae*, or sometimes *abruptio placentarum*. Whichever way it is said, it is"—he shook his head—"one of the worst things to happen in a pregnancy."

"Explain."

"A hematoma, an area of bleeding, has developed between the placenta and the wall of the uterus. It is a most serious condition, Adriana. I'm being completely honest with you."

"For the baby?"

Her eyes were huge, green, almond-shaped pools of concern. "Yes." He wanted to say for the mother, too, but didn't. Why be more alarmist than he had to be? "I want to take the baby by cesarean at once, Adriana."

"Will he live?"

He signed and ran his hand through his sparse

66

hair, a gesture of frustration. "There is always hope, Adriana. But I must tell you the risk to the child is considerable."

"Then I won't permit it," she said quietly.

"Adriana, listen to me. I know how much you want this child, but you don't understand."

"Nor do I." Charles Bridges spoke with firmness. "I don't understand any of this, Hamilton. Please explain."

Dodd welcomed the chance to describe the situation in technical rather than personal terms. "The placenta is a large sac, shaped something like an elongated football." He made a motion with his hands, then had a better idea. "Let me draw you a picture." He went to the desk, extracted a sheet of hospital stationery, and quickly sketched the pear-shaped uterus leading to the os and vaginal area. To the left of his picture, the mother's right, he drew in the placenta and the umbilical cord leading to the fetus, which he roughly outlined. When he showed it to Bridges, he explained, "The placenta is here, filled with blood to nurture the baby through the umbilical cord. All the mother's oxygen and nutrients for life and growth pass from her body into the placenta and through the cord to the fetus. The baby's wastes pass in the other direction."

Quickly he added to his sketch, drawing in an oval area in back of the placenta, quickly darkening it with his pen. "What has happened is that, here, a pocket or sac of blood has formed, interrupting the flow of oxygen and nutrients from Adriana to the placenta and hence the fetus. It is most regrettable—and serious."

"Let me see." Adriana took the sketch and looked at it, seeming to understand what she was seeing. "What causes this?"

"No one knows, Adriana. It is just something that occasionally happens. Frequently the hematoma is small, manageable with bed rest, some drugs. I had hoped that would be the case with you." He sighed.

"I asked what causes it, Doctor?"

Her tone was imperious, which surprised him. He had expected her to be upset, weeping. Instead, she was angry, fighting back. "Your hypertension—elevated blood pressure—may have been a contributing factor."

"What can be done about it?"

"As I said, we take the baby by cesarean and hope for the best."

"And *I* said I won't have that. What else can be done?"

Dodd looked at Bridges but got no help there. "We can take a huge risk, Adriana. I can give you whole blood, a drug such as Heparin to encourage clotting, and hope your bleeding stops. It's possible that the hematoma will reduce in size and that the baby will receive enough oxygen and nutrients from the area of the placenta that remains uninterrupted." He arose, walked across the luxurious room. "I cannot in good conscience recommend such a course of treatment, Adriana. It is too big a risk."

"And so is taking my baby."

"True."

"Then I choose the risk of maintaining the pregnancy." She actually smiled. "Proceed, Hamilton. I will be the best patient you ever had."

"Adriana, listen to me—" Again he ran his hands, both of them, through his hair.

"No, *you* listen to *me*. This is *my* child, a healthy, normal child, almost ready to be born. I am going to have my baby. Nothing you or anyone can say or do will change my mind." She patted her swollen belly. "He and I will work our way through this together. I know it. I'm sure of it."

Dodd pursed his lips, shook his head. When he looked at Bridges for support, he saw he was smiling ruefully.

"Now you know what I have to live with, Hamilton. She is one tough lady."

Dodd sighed. "All right. I guess we can wait a few hours, monitor the situation, see what happens."

"Thank you, Doctor." Adriana's throaty, musical laugh was pure triumph. "I do so like a reasonable man!"

"I'd better get things started, then." He headed for the door, opened it, then hesitated and looked back, managing to signal with a movement of his head for Bridges to join him. Outside in the corridor, he huddled with Adriana's husband. "I didn't want to say it in there, Charles, upsetting her any more than she is already, but I have to tell you that if this condition goes on much longer or gets much worse, there is a grave risk not only to the baby but to Adriana, too."

"I thought as much. I knew that's what was bothering you."

"I'll give it a short while, Charles, try to do what she wants. But I warn you to be ready to bite the bullet and make the decision she won't, if you want to save her life."

"I'll do what I must. You know that. Nothing must happen to Adriana. That is paramount."

"I know. Just don't let her tie my hands too much longer, Charles."

Quentin Stillwell recognized the voice at once. He had been expecting it, dreading it. "Yes, I remember you, Mr. Dykes."

"Good thing. I'd almost decided to visit some of my friends in the press."

Stillwell registered the threat but made no reply. He'd made up his mind what he had to do. He wasn't going to beg.

"You were outta town for almos' a week. I began to figger you'd bugged out. Won't work, Yer Eminence." He laughed. "I looked that up. That's what yer called, ain't it? Well, Yer Eminence, there ain't no place to hide."

Stillwell hesitated. This person revolted him, very nearly made him physically ill, but he must regard Dykes as the agent of retribution for his sin. "I was trying to raise the . . ."—he was using a private office in diocesan headquarters; it was always possible someone might be listening on the phone, but what did that matter now?—". . . the money." It was a lie, but a small sin compared to his others. He had to have time to carry out his plan. "It is not easy."

"Oh, you can manage, Reverend—excuse *me*—Yer Eminence."

"I took a took a vow of poverty, Mr. Dykes."

Loud laugh. "I'll bet that wasn't the only vow ya took!"

Stillwell winced. "I do not come from a wealthy family. It is very difficult. I need more time."

"You got no more time. And don't give me that baloney. There ain't no outfit richer than yer church. I been readin' up on it."

A grimace of pain, but Stillwell's voice remained controlled. "It still takes time, Mr. Dykes."

Hesitation. "Okay, ya got till Friday. Four days. That's the absolute limit."

Four days. Was it enough time? It would have to be. "Very well, Friday. Late Friday. Where can I reach you?"

"No way, buster. I'll call *you*."

"But I may have it sooner."

The appeal to greed didn't work. "I said I'd call you."

"Don't call me here again, please. You'll ruin everything."

Hesitation. "Okay, you can reach me at this number."

He gave it. Stillwell jotted it down, but had no idea of what use he might make of it.

70

* * *

Judd Forbes spent most of his first day on the job in intense study of the files, determined to discover all he could about Bel Air General's history, procedures, finances, clientele, and key personnel. The place ran well, damned well, and made a ton of money. Ought to, at those prices. Forbes was shocked by them. And the patient list read like *Who's Who*, not just in Hollywood, but around the country, even abroad. Downright amazing who'd been treated in that place. Couldn't blame them. Lap of luxury, service better than the poshest hotel. Apparently the medical care was first-rate, too.

Because it was to be his prime responsibility, Forbes paid detailed attention to the security system. Now, *that* was something else. One couldn't get in the gate without a pass or specific approval. Everyone in the place, including patients, visitors, and staff, wore a color-coded badge indicating where they could go in the hospital. If people were found wearing the wrong color badge for the floor or section, they were politely escorted to where they belonged. Any arguments and they were escorted out of the gate and barred for life. Closed-circuit TV monitored everything in the corridors. Forbes was impressed. The security system worked effortlessly and unobtrusively, and was just about flawless. A lot of attempts had been made to sneak into Bel Air General to photograph its famous patients, but none had ever succeeded.

Forbes interrupted his studies to meet with Ben Riggins, the ex-LAPD captain who headed the Bel Air security force. Forbes was nominally his superior, but he knew better than to interfere with the grizzled veteran. Riggins seemed okay. Apparently one just spoke to him about a security problem or the possibility of one and Riggins took care of it. Forbes felt they'd be able to work together when they got used to each other.

Shortly before noon, Forbes was asked to ap-

71

prove his first admission. He was on thin ice, he knew, not quite certain of all the criteria. Susan Raimond, the former child star, qualified as a celebrity, but she'd never been a patient before. Obstetrics. Must be having a kid. Forbes hadn't realized she was married. Maybe she wasn't. Dr. Dodd's office wanted the admission. Forbes hesitated. There was an empty room in OB-GYN. Might as well fill it. He said okay.

Over lunch—a sandwich and milk at his desk, sent over from the employee cafeteria—and for some time thereafter, he dug into the files to learn what was most important to him: the key personnel and the relationships between them. He had a talent for ferreting out human relationships, and seemingly innocuous facts and figures, a few dull minutes of a meeting could reveal a lot to him. Laura Carlyle owned only forty-one percent of the stock, but she ran this place, all of it. No mistake about that. Her stepson, Oliver Carlyle, Jr., owned thirty-nine percent, but he was out of it—totally. He had nothing to do with the place and he and Laura hardly spoke. Couldn't blame her. Forbes knew "Junie" Carlyle to be a fat, corrupt fag. Ten percent of the stock had been owned by Connie Payne, Laura's daughter-in-law, someone else Laura didn't speak to. Connie Payne had killed herself. Her shares probably passed to the granddaughter, Roberta, Brian Hecht's wife.

Five percent was not owned, but voted by Dr. Sean "Mac" McClintock, the director of medicine, and five percent by Dr. Ernest Wilkerson, the director of surgery. It took Forbes a while to figure it out, but he did. The two docs controlled the stock, sat as directors, clipped the coupons as part of their recompense, but they did not actually own the stock. It was held in trust for whoever held those positions. Neat arrangement. So that was how Laura Carlyle kept control, though owning only forty-one percent. A little further reading deepened the story. Wilkerson was still director of surgery and controlled the five percent, but he had been reduced to a figurehead. Leon Kazinsky had been declared Chief of Surgery and given full authority over the surgical department. Interesting. Wilkerson got the money, but Kazinsky had the power. Must be a sticky arrangement.

But it was Brian Hecht who consumed most of Forbes's interest. The man owned no stock, seemed to possess no power, yet he ran the place. Apparently he had Laura Carlyle's ear. They met every morning for breakfast. She wouldn't make a move without consulting him, deferred to him constantly, and gave him full authority. There was no recorded instance of her countermanding anything he did. Forbes digested that information. At least he knew what he was up against. Hecht was Laura Carlyle's grandson-in-law, married to the granddaughter, known as Bobbi. Forbes had heard she was a real knockout, better-looking than most models or film stars.

He read the file on Jennifer Corban, his predecessor. Not much in it, but he got a pretty good overall picture. Efficient damned dame. He'd have to measure up to her. Raped, damned near killed, spent two months in the hospital, then took off for Buffalo a week ago. Files showed Riggins had investigated the rapist. Linked to Connie Payne. Police interested. *Maybe that's why Payne killed herself?* Forbes thought.

Forbes leaned back in his swivel chair, linking his hands behind his head, thinking. Hecht's wife was Connie Payne's daughter. Both Hecht and his wife were important to Laura Carlyle. He leaned forward and stood up, poured himself a cup of coffee. Lots to figure out there.

A little before four o'clock, Brian Hecht entered his office and asked how his day had gone. Forbes smiled. "I guess you could call it a typical first day."

73

He indicated the files on his desk. "I've mostly been catching up on my reading, Mr. Hecht."

"I think we can dispense with the 'Mister,' now," Brian said. "I'm Brian, you're Judd, unless you prefer something else."

"No, Judd's fine, Mr.—" He laughed. "I'm sorry. Brian. I'm a slow learner, I guess."

"You'll catch on. I saw your bulletin on Adriana Barre. It was first-rate."

"Thanks."

"But it may not be quite so easy tomorrow. It seems Miss Barre isn't here just for tests. She has a serious problem and may lose the baby."

"That's too bad."

"Isn't it? But that's what happens in a hospital. Let the current statement ride. We'll change it in the morning. Better consult with me about it. This could be a sensitive matter . . ."—he smiled—". . . not to suggest you aren't capable."

"I understand. I don't want to make any mistakes, either." Forbes hesitated. "Speaking of mistakes, I admitted Susan Raimond today. Hope it's okay." He saw the puzzled expression on the face. "Susan Raimond, the former child actress."

"Oh, yes, I remember now."

"Dr. Dodd wanted her in OB-GYN. Room two-twenty-six was available, so I put her in there."

"Has she been a patient here before . . . anyone in her family?"

"No."

"Did you check with the business office?"

"Should I have?"

"Ability to pay is important, Judd. Saves a lot of problems later. The business office keeps a Dun and Bradstreet, other information. They can do a financial check rather quickly."

"I'm sorry. I didn't know."

"My fault for not seeing that you did. Probably won't matter in this case. But now you know for the future."

"Yes, sir."

Brian smiled. "On a happier note, it's time for shift change and I've arranged a little reception in the cafeteria. You're the guest of honor. Just the key people. I want you to meet them and them to meet you. Put on your jacket and come on."

Forbes wished he'd had some time to prepare for it, but all in all it went pretty well. Ingratiating himself to strangers had long been a specialty of his. And he was good at remembering names and faces, having once taken a course to perfect those skills. The tone was informal, mostly light chatter. Lots of "welcome aboard" and "hope you like it here." Surprisingly, drinks were served. Forbes was careful to nurse only one.

One by one the names and faces were recorded in his brain, along with position and authority. He was pleased to meet McClintock and Kazinsky, noting that Wilkerson didn't show. Sheryl James just about knocked his eyeballs out. Then Hillary George entered. Heavens! He'd neglected to study up on her. Some woman!

A hush came over the gathering and Forbes turned. A petite, elderly woman approached, smiling. He knew who she was even before Brian Hecht introduced Laura Carlyle.

"So this is the newest member of our family. I'm pleased to meet you, Mr. Forbes. I hope you'll be with us a long time."

He was awestruck, but managed to accept the slender hand. He felt like bowing, kissing it, even kneeling, but found the poise to say, "I hope so, too, Mrs. Carlyle." As she engaged him in polite conversation, asking about his family, previous employment, he realized this woman was positively regal. Her mere presence commanded respect. And talk about elegant—appearance, manners, everything. And she was simply beautiful. It bothered Forbes that she unnerved him. Not many people could do that.

The real surprise was the appearance of Bobbi Hecht—a surprise to Brian, too, Forbes surmised. He had been favorably impressed with the women he'd met, notably Sheryl James and Hillary George, but Bobbi Hecht positively undid him. Her eyes, mouth, skin, that figure—everything about her seemed to strike right at his loins. She was a complete turn-on, and he hadn't even met her. If the rumors he'd heard about her estrangement from her husband were true, Brian Hecht had to be *crazy!*

Laura introduced him. "My granddaughter, Roberta Carlyle Hecht. I'm proud to say she is the newest member of our Board of Directors."

He mumbled something he hoped wasn't too inane.

"Such a pleasure to meet you, Mr. Forbes. I have an idea you and I may be working together."

Her smile devastated him. "I'm at your service." *What a stupid thing to say, Forbes!*

She laughed. "Hardly that. It seems Grandmother has given me a little task here at the hospital. I'd appreciate your help in handling the press."

"I'll be glad to do anything I can."

"Are you free a few minutes tomorrow? I can drop in at your office, or you can stop by mine." She looked at her husband. "Where did you put me, Brian?"

"There's an office on the second floor of the main building, just above this room, actually. It's near the out-patient office. Would that be suitable?"

He was putting her out of sight—out of *his* sight, at least. Better than the basement, anyway. She smiled. "I'm sure it'll do fine." She turned to Forbes. "Tomorrow, then? In the morning, if you can. I'll call you to set a time."

76

# Chapter 5

Maximilian Hill had just about had it. He was at the point of doing something, anything, even if it was wrong, not to mention atypical, rash, and disastrous. For a solid week now he had put up with Hillary George's silence and refusal to see him, all without explanation. She owed him one. He intended to get it if he had to kidnap her.

So agitated was he that petulant thoughts, the sort he normally exiled, crept into his mind and rummaged around as though seeking permanent domicile. There he was, Max Hill, one of the leading black actors in the country—hell, one of the leading actors, period—winner of an Oscar, about to be nominated for a second one, famous, handsome, sought after by women, with two marriages behind him, not exactly worried about where his next buck came from, and Hillary George was making him feel like a schoolboy turned down for the prom. Who did she think she was?

He poured himself a second stiff drink, walked out onto the deck of his beach house overlooking the Pacific at Malibu, and proceeded mentally to answer the question, as he knew he would. Hillary George was the most intelligent, companionable, beautiful, sexy, and desirable woman he had ever known, and he was madly in love with her and determined to marry her. She was also the most frustrating woman he'd ever known.

Never in his life had he wooed a woman like this—candy, practically a whole shop full of flowers until she begged him to stop, clever little gifts for her and her son, Tommy, sedate dinners, romantic dinners, dinners studded with his wittiest conversation. His hands had ached from wanting to touch her, but he hadn't. Her lips maddened him, but he resisted temptation. Her mere proximity aroused him physically to the point of pain, but he did nothing. Even when he realized how attracted she was to him, that she wanted him, too, he had kept his distance. She had suffered a lot from men. Max knew he was far from the only one to see her innate sensuality.

Slow and easy was the way. He sensed that, so he was a snail. Hell, a coral reef grew faster than he moved! When it finally happened, it was well worth the wait. Her sexuality, her unleashed sensuality, was awesome. Her passion, her need, was like a force of nature, burned in his memory forever. It had driven from his mind the thought of any other woman. No other women existed.

He had discovered Hillary's secret—actually, two secrets. One was that very passion he marveled at. Apparently she'd kept it under control, never giving in to it out of some misguided sense of shame. The second secret was that someone else had made the discovery before him. Max thought of him as her mystery lover, this man she saw only a few times a year. The thought of what happened during those infrequent get-togethers maddened him with jealousy.

He'd learned that this person existed and that Hillary was saving herself for him. Max had confronted her and she'd admitted it, even defended it as a happy life. He'd told her what a sap she was, finally convinced her that happiness and fulfillment for both her and Tommy lay with him, not the mystery guy. She'd asked him to wait until she could talk in person with "Arthur," the name she'd let slip once. Arthur had finally turned up and had agreed she should marry, something he couldn't offer for some reason. He'd bow out of the picture. Max had believed it would all be downhill then. Talk about a happy man!

Then something had happened. He didn't know what, couldn't even guess, except that it must have had something to do with Arthur. Hillary wouldn't answer his calls. Twice he'd gone to see her, and both times she wouldn't let him in, begged him to go away—forever. His brief glimpses of her convinced him she'd been crying her eyes out.

The phone rang. Max entered his cottage, turned right, and answered the wall phone in the kitchen. It was his answering service.

"Someone named Quentin Stillwell wants you to phone him. He says he knows you. At least you met a week ago."

"Yes. Give me the number." He jotted it down. Then, still holding the phone, he smiled, that famous boyish grin that lit up the screen and which was his trademark. He hadn't told the operator, though he'd been tempted, that "someone named Stillwell" was a very well known Catholic Cardinal. She ought to read something besides the funnies.

As he dialed, Max remembered meeting him around ten days ago at a Hollywood cocktail party for visiting celebrities. Max had been railroaded into going. Stillwell had sought him out, saying

79

he admired his work, wanted to meet him. The conversation was pleasant, much more so than was usual at such events. Stillwell had impressed Max. Something he'd said—Max couldn't remember it now exactly—had triggered a fleeting suspicion that Max had immediately dismissed as ridiculous. Why, he wondered now, did Cardinal Stillwell want to speak to him?

"This is Maximilian Hill. I'm returning Cardinal Stillwell's call. . . . Yes, I'll wait. . . ."

"Mr. Hill, thank you for calling. Quentin Stillwell here."

"Yes, Your Eminence."

"Please. I know we met only once, but I think of you as a friend—at least someone I'd like to know on a less formal basis. If you'll call me Quent, I promise to call you Max."

Max laughed. "An offer I can hardly refuse."

"Very good. I phoned in the hope that you might be free this evening. I've something to discuss with you."

Max hesitated, frowning. What was all this leading up to?

"Yes, I'm free." He was free *every* evening, dammit!

"Fine, fine. I'd like to buy you a drink and dinner, if I may. I don't know Los Angeles very well. What I want to speak to you about is rather . . . well, confidential. I thought perhaps you could suggest some quiet, private place where we might meet."

*Confidential. Private.* The forbidden thought again surfaced in Max Hill's mind. He did not dismiss it this time. "The most private and quiet place I know is where I am right now—my beach house. I live alone. Why don't you come over here? I have a bottle or two, and I can throw a couple of steaks on the grill."

Hesitation. "I suppose I could do that. Where do you live?" When Max finished with the address

80

and directions, he added, "If you'd like a private and confidential swim, that's easily arranged."

Stillwell laughed, but the laugh sounded hollow, forced. "I might take you up on that. See you in about an hour."

Brian had recently been elected to the board of the Metropolitan Hospital Association. He had spent most of the morning and afternoon in seminars and workshops concerned with upgrading hospital efficiency in the interest of cutting costs. Thus, he had been busy and surrounded by people, a welcome diversion from some rather unappealing thoughts.

Now that the reception for Forbes was over and nearly everyone had gone about their business, he sat behind his desk, hoping to work a little. In truth, all he was doing was dwelling on Bobbi's "bombshell," as he thought of it. So his wife was an heiress. Several million bucks. Face it, he was jealous and angry. Those were the thoughts he'd submerged all day. He didn't like himself for having them.

How would he have felt if this had happened while he and Bobbi were still in love and happily married? Tough question. How would he have felt? He wouldn't have touched it then, anymore than he would now. *Her* money. But it would have made everything so much easier. Financial security always did. He sighed. It might have saved their marriage. Bobbi would have felt more secure, independent, and important, as she surely did now.

No, that was nonsense. Bobbi would have done then what she surely was going to do now—go on a vast spending spree and blow every nickel of it. His efforts to talk sense into her would have resulted in more quarrels. It was worse than that. He'd have behaved badly, too. This day had taught him that he'd never make it with a rich

81

wife. Apparently he had to be dominant, responsible, providing everything in a marriage. He felt threatened if he wasn't. It was true, face it. "Great!" he said aloud. "You're a classic specimen of male chauvinism. Keep the little woman in her place—barefoot and pregnant."

As if that wasn't enough self-flagellation, Brian heaped abuse on himself for his attitude toward Bobbi's joining the staff. He didn't want her there and that's all there was to it. She was intruding on *his* turf. But there wasn't a blessed thing he could do about it. Bobbi and Laura were doing a number on him, apparently not realizing that he was being placed in an untenable situation. It was nepotism at its finest. And now that Bobbi was also a hospital director, he would never be able to supervise or control her. If he tried, she'd run straight to Grandma. Visions of imminent disaster filled his aching head.

Brian decided that what he really, truly wanted was to get drunk, hang a major one on. Abruptly, he left the hospital and drove to Westwood. He parked the car at Jenny's apartment—he still thought of it as that—and walked two blocks to a neighborhood watering hole. At least he wouldn't get picked up for DWI. Arrest for public intoxication might be another matter, however.

He sat at the bar, ordered a double scotch-and-water, then didn't touch it. Was Bobbi serious about moving out of the house? He went to a pay phone and dialed his own number, letting it ring a great many times. No answer. Apparently she'd turned off the answering machine. Maybe she had really meant it. Curiosity consumed him. He paid for his untouched drink, went to his little red Porsche, and drove to Bel Air. Deliberately he chose a route that took him past Connie Payne's house. Bobbi's Mercedes was there. *I'll be damned!* A few minutes later he unlocked the door to his house. Not really *his* house—the place where he supposedly lived. When Laura died it would probably pass to Bobbi, too. Nothing was changed inside, the furniture all in place. Somehow he'd visualized an empty house. He ran upstairs, taking the steps three at a time, and burst into Bobbi's room. The bed was made, the bureau, vanity, nightstands, mirrors were all there. He opened the closet, a huge walk-in affair. Empty, except for some hangers. He looked back at the vanity. Cleaned off. In a couple of strides he was looking in the bathroom. Cleaned out, too. By God, she *had* meant it! She had moved out, taking only her clothes, cosmetics and toiletries, and other personal items.

More slowly he ambled over to his bedroom, really the guest room which he'd moved into when their marriage had collapsed. His clothes were all there. He had taken only a few things to Jenny's. On the bed was a note in Bobbi's flamboyant scrawl:

I MEANT IT, BRIAN. MOVE IN IF YOU WANT. ENJOY.

He wadded it up and aimed it toward the wastebasket, missed. She knew he'd come and check it out. The knowledge didn't help his self-esteem. Apparently she could read him like a book.

He went back downstairs and poured a stiff drink from the tray of bottles on the buffet in the dining room, then wandered into the kitchen for ice. Move back here? He had always disliked the house. Built in the twenties, one of the original houses in Bel Air, Moorish style, he had always considered it dark and dank. Now it appealed to him more. Face it, he didn't care for apartment living, especially not Jenny's small place. He wasn't comfortable there—too full of memories and ghosts. And Westwood was surely a step down from Bel Air. Laura was right about the importance of a proper address for a man in his position.

By the time he'd refilled his glass, he'd made up his mind to spend the night. Yes, he'd move back. Made sense. Then he became aware of the drink in his hand, shook his head at it. Poison. The road to perdition. If he was going to live alone, he wasn't going to get drunk alone.

As he reached for the phone, he fished a piece of paper from his pocket—actually a cocktail napkin—dialed the number on it, and was rewarded with the recording on an answering machine. He hesitated. What the hell? He said, "Lorraine, this is Brian. If you're free tonight, give me a buzz." He repeated his home phone number, then ambled aimlessly into the living room.

Lorraine Paul was at home, using the answering machine to screen out those calls she didn't want to take, a necessity for someone who made her living as a very high-priced hooker.

"You must have made quite an impression on him."

She looked at the smiling face of Judd Forbes. "I usually do, thank you. It's my profession, after all."

"Just don't let him find out, understand? It'll ruin everything."

"Shall I call him back now?"

"No, let him stew awhile." He grinned. "Meanwhile, you and I can use the time to—"

"No way. I told you there'd be none of that. A deal's a deal."

He laughed. "Too bad." In truth, Lorraine Paul appealed to him, and blondes usually didn't. A really classy broad. You'd never guess she was a hooker. Dressed well, usually with eye-catching cleavage. Carried herself well, too, lots of poise and sophistication. She never came on to a man, just waited for him to react to her, and even then

84

she was very choosy. He had to have five hundred to spare, a thousand for an all-nighter.

She reminded him a little of Grace Kelly, blond, blue eyes, delicate, even features, aristocratic profile. The only major difference was that Lorraine Paul had a far better figure. But she had the same patrician quality as the late Princess Grace. Lorraine had class, no mistaking it.

"Are you sure I'm not wasting my time and talents, Judd?" she asked now.

"Positive." He hauled himself up from her white leather couch and went to the bar, pouring himself a drink. "I spent the whole day going over the books. The place is a gold mine, Lorraine. I'm talking big bucks."

"If you're going to drink, please don't sit on that couch. It cost a fortune."

He grinned. "If this works out the way it should, you can buy a dozen more."

"You'd better be right, Judd. I usually sell it, not give it away."

"Think of it as an investment for your old age." Now he laughed. "Hard to think of you as ever getting old, baby. Anyway, the only thing standing in the way of those bucks is Brian Hecht. If we can get rid of him, it's clear sailing."

Lorraine raised delicate, perfectly shaped brows. "I'm sorry, but I don't understand how fornication gets rid of anybody."

"Trust me, baby, it will—along with a few other goodies I have in store for him."

She looked at him sharply. "I still get my share?"

"As you say, a deal's a deal. You'll have big bucks as long as you live. Think of it as an annuity—insurance."

"How long will it take?"

"Not long. A few months—less if we're lucky."

Lorraine Paul had hesitated about going along with Judd Forbes in this scheme. She didn't really like him, and she didn't trust him any more than she did anyone else. But she told herself there was nothing illegal in what he planned to do. He was just playing both ends against the middle in order to gain control of a highly profitable business venture. If Forbes was lying to her, and there *was* something illegal, it wasn't apparent. All she was doing was sleeping with a very attractive man, giving away what she usually sold. She couldn't even be picked up for prostitution. She'd decided to go along with Forbes, for a while at least. She took no risks and there might just be a lot to gain. If Forbes held out on her, she'd know how to handle him.

"I think I'll phone him now," she said. "I want to appear interested."

Judd Forbes laughed. "You know, I really think you *are* interested. That Hecht is one lucky man."

Max Hill had showered and changed into white pants and a polo shirt by the time his visitor arrived. He was a little surprised to see Quentin Stillwell similarly attired, only in dark blue. His knowledge of Catholic prelates was limited, severely limited. He had vaguely assumed they wore clerical garb to bed.

"Good of you to let me barge in on you like this, Max"

He returned the firm handshake, smiling a little warily. "I'm trying to think of you as Quent, but it's going to take some getting used to—Your Eminence."

"Keep working on it. Can't be half as hard as it's been for *me* to get used to 'Your Eminence.' "

That helped break the ice, and Max relaxed slightly as he showed the older man around his place. Exchanging small talk, they made their way out to the deck amid deepening dusk. "Sure you won't change your mind about that swim?" Max asked.

86

"It's a temptation, but I'd better not."

"A drink, then?"

"Scotch with a splash, yes." As Max made the drinks, Stillwell said, "This is a beautiful spot, Max. I envy you. Must be a good life."

"Till the storms come in."

"You live here year round?"

"Yes, but I do a good bit of traveling when I'm filming on location."

They sat on deck chairs looking out across the water. Light from inside the house illuminated them both. Max deliberately lapsed into silence, hoping to encourage his guest to talk about the purpose of his visit. He felt the tension building again inside.

"It is . . . difficult for me to speak of what . . . I came for," Stillwell began at last. His hesitation left no doubt of that. "It is a private matter, confidential, highly personal—and extremely awkward to discuss."

The measured pace of the words was almost painful for Max to hear. "Would you be more comfortable inside?"

"Will we be overheard here?"

"No. The sound of the surf drowns everything."

Stillwell nodded. "Magical place here. Magical time of day."

"Isn't it?"

Another silence, even longer this time. Then: "I suppose the place to start is the beginning."

Max looked at him quizzically. "It usually is."

Stillwell smiled slightly. "The story I'm about to tell might make a good movie. I trust that will never happen, though."

Trying to keep things light, Max said, "If it involves you, I'm the wrong color to play the part."

This time Stillwell did not smile. "Some years ago I was a patient in a hospital out here—Bel Air General. For a long time I couldn't remember what I went in for, but it has come back to me.

Pilonidal cyst. The operation was a success, and I forgot about it."

"It also takes place on a part of the body a person doesn't get to look at too often." *Always leave 'em laughing, Max, my boy.*

"True. Never thought of it that way. Have you ever been in Bel Air General?"

"Once, some months ago."

"Then you know what a fine hospital it is. Splendid nursing care."

Max said nothing, knew he couldn't think of anything funny, couldn't think of anything at all. He waited.

"One particular nurse there was especially . . . attentive. Very fine nurse . . . very caring . . . compassionate. She was extremely intelligent. Great deal of character. A beautiful person . . . in the fullest sense of the word. Attractive, too . . . highly attractive."

Max looked away from him. He didn't want to hear what he knew was coming next.

"I was a Bishop then. She, of course . . . knew that." Still another sigh. "She had spoken of her childhood. Truly abominable. My heart went out to her. I—I wanted to . . . to help her cope . . . with all that had happened . . . to her." Suddenly Stillwell couldn't sit still anymore and stood up abruptly, crossing to the railing to stare out over the sea. "After I was discharged, I used to phone her . . . occasionally. When I was in the Los Angeles area . . . I'd see her . . . talk. Naturally, a . . . a friendship developed. I found her to be a most remarkable . . . woman."

Max could take no more. There was a hard edge to his voice as he said, "Excuse me for interrupting, but it seems to me I've heard this story before, from another point of view, Cardinal Stillwell. Or should I call you Arthur?"

After a long moment Stillwell spoke, his voice filled with pain. "You might as well. She does."

88

The silence stretched out endlessly until Stillwell finally turned to face him. "Why don't you just say it and have it over with? I deserve it. And it might make you feel better."

Another long silence. Finally, Max said, anger seething within him, "I've been thinking of what to say, but I can't find the words. And ranting and raving has never been my style. So I'll just say I think you are a *fucking bastard*—Your Eminence."

Stillwell did not flinch. "You are too kind. I deserve much worse. You are a fine man, Max. She is right to love you." He paused. "I've come to ask you to look after Hillie."

Still furious, Max said, "Do you know she won't let me call her that because it's your special name for her?"

"I'm sorry—for that and so many other things. I'll spend the rest of my life in atonement. I'm going away, Max. Neither Hillie—excuse me . . . Hillary—nor you will ever see me again. I'm here to ask you to help her, take care of her. I know how obscene it sounds, but I truly love her."

Max was unmoved by the confession. "I've been trying to take care of her for some time, but someone called Arthur keeps getting in the way. I thought I'd finally won. But now she won't see or talk to me. Cardinal Stillwell, whatever hold you have on her must really be something."

"You don't understand," Stillwell said heavily.

"I think I do."

"No, you don't, unless Hillie told you what happened a week ago. Did she?"

Max frowned. "No. What do you mean?"

Stillwell hesitated, buttressing his courage. For too long he'd relished his power and authority—abused it. God wanted him humbled. And humble he surely was. "A week, ten days ago, maybe a little more—I seem to have lost track of time—Hillary came to me. We met in a motel, as we

89

usually did. She told me of her love for you, that you and she had . . . slept together. She couldn't continue living a lie. She wanted to end our . . . liaison." Pause. "You must believe me, Max. I heartily concurred. Indeed, I had urged her, over all these years, to find and love a man who could offer her marriage and happiness, neither of which I could ever provide. She had spoken of you, your appeal to her. Believe me, please. I had urged her to accept you, to give your relationship every possible chance."

"She told me that. Go on."

"Again I ask you to believe me. Nothing happened that night. We just talked. I was so happy for her—and for myself. I guess I was . . . relieved. This . . . relationship with Hillie has been a . . . great burden as well as a joy to us both. She—you, too, I guess—was giving me the strength of character I . . . lacked, the strength to set her free. We talked about how she and I might assume a new relationship as friends. It was important to me that we pass into this new phase, of friendship, open, known to the world."

"You couldn't just let her go, could you, you bastard?" Max said through clenched teeth.

"I hadn't thought of it that way, but I suppose you're right. I arranged to meet you at the reception. I liked you, respected you. I knew then that we could be friends."

"You know, the thought crossed my mind that you might be Arthur, but I dismissed it as too incredible to be believed. Go on with your lousy story. What happened next?"

Stillwell sighed. "It was extremely important to me that the three of us be friends. I—I was . . . obsessed with the notion."

"I think you're obsessed with a lot of things. Go on."

"I asked Hillie to meet with me one more time to discuss . . . the future. Same motel. Might even

90

have been the same room. She . . . she wasn't very impressed with what I . . . wanted to do. Too risky, she said. You'd figure out who I was."

"Which proves she's a lot smarter than you. So you met her again. But I'll bet it wasn't just talk this time. You had to get her in the sack one more time, didn't you, you son of a bitch?"

Stillwell sank into a deck chair and covered his face with his hands until he could bring himself to reply.

"I'm sorry. The . . . physical attraction between us has always been . . . powerful. She didn't want to, I assure you of that. I—I was the . . . aggressor. I . . . forced myself on her. I am entirely . . . to blame. We undressed and—"

"Goddammit all to hell! Spare me the . . ." —Max suppressed a vulgarity—". . . details. What are you leading up to?"

"Suddenly the door burst open. I'd either neglected to lock it, or perhaps a key was obtained." Stillwell's voice trembled. "Anyway, the door opened and a flash went off. I've seen the . . . photograph. It—couldn't be . . . worse."

"Jesus Christ!" Max bolted to his feet. He wanted to punch Stillwell, maybe even throttle him. Instead, he stalked across the deck and poured a stiff shot of whiskey into his glass. He took a large swallow. In a moment he could say, "Blackmail?"

"Yes. A half-million dollars."

"Have you paid?"

"Not yet."

"Do you know who's behind it?"

"It seems it started with the three shift supervisors at the hospital. They wanted to get something on Hillie, force her to resign. The ringleader is a woman named Dana Shaughnessy. She had her son-in-law follow Hillie. His name is Wallace Dykes. Apparently he is an insurance investigator and has some . . . skills as a detective. I gather he even took photos of you and Hillie together on the beach when she visited here. I also gather that they were insufficiently . . . compromising."

"Son of a bitch! You've met with this Dykes?"

"Yes. He is not a very nice person."

"Blackmailers usually aren't. You say you haven't paid him?"

"I haven't got that kind of money, Max. It's impossible."

"The Church?"

Stillwell slumped in his seat, shaking his head. "I don't know. It is a decision I cannot make. Tomorrow I'm flying to Rome, to the Vatican. I have an appointment with the Holy Father. I'm going to confess everything. Then I intend to resign and enter a monastery, if the Holy Father will permit it."

"I don't care if you go to hell, which is where you belong! I ask you again. *Will the Church pay?*"

"It will be out of my hands." Pause. "The scandal would be . . . ruinous. I assume something will be . . . worked out to take care of . . . Mr. Dykes."

"Appeal to his better nature, no doubt. God! What a mess!"

"Indeed, it is. Oh, one other thing. Hillary says the Shaughnessy woman only wanted her resignation, no money. Hillie was going to speak to her, tell her what her son-in-law is doing. Something may come of that. I don't know."

Max drained his whiskey in one gulp, staring at the man seated before him. "You're still at it, aren't you? Still looking out for number one. *You're* going to confess. *You're* going to hide. You don't give a damn about Hillary, do you?"

"That's not true!"

"It sure looks like it to me. Listen, *Cardinal* Stillwell, man of the cloth, Prince of the Church, I don't give a damn what happens to you. Personally, I'd be delighted if your photo with your pants

92

down was spread across the front page of every newspaper in the country. But I'm not going to have the woman I love dragged through the mud with you. It's time you started thinking about *her*, dammit!"

"I do think about her—constantly."

"I'm sure I know what your thoughts are." In his anger, Max wanted to shout obscenities at him. Instead, he whirled and stalked into his house, muttering, "Let me think a minute." Inside he paced rapidly for a moment, then in the kitchen leaned over the sink, struggling to calm himself. When he returned to Stillwell, he had succeeded a little. "I don't know exactly what can be done, but there has to be something. I want you to stay here in Los Angeles, stall Dykes until I can figure this thing out."

"No. I have to go to Rome. Dykes wants his money by Friday night."

"Friday. That gives us three days. It ought to be enough time." He saw Stillwell shaking his head in weary denial and shouted, "Listen, you bastard, this is now out of your hands! You've caused enough trouble. You're going to do exactly what I tell you, nothing else."

"I've got to go to Rome," Stillwell droned, zombie-like.

"To make yourself feel better. You really are something else! Listen, it's all I can do to keep from punching your lights out. If you say one more word, I won't be able to restrain myself!"

Brian was surprised when Lorraine offered to come to his place. He had offered to take her out to dinner, spend some money on her, but she said she'd prefer to come over and have a late supper. Why not?

Brian had been half in the bag and deeper in the dumps last night, so he had no clear memory of exactly what she looked like, other than blond.

93

Thus, when she arrived at his front door, he was pleasantly surprised. Lorraine was a remarkably beautiful woman. She wore what he supposed was a cocktail dress, pale green, form .fitting, a little slinky. It showed considerable cleavage. His eyes brightened. "My, don't you look—I'm at a loss for a word. How about *smashing?*"

She smiled. "Just an old rag I found in my closet."

"Some rag!"

She laughed, a throaty, enticing sound. "Actually, I figure that if I'm to succeed in this town I ought to at least *look* like an actress. Am I over-dressed?"

"Hardly. But I think I'd better change into my tux."

Under other circumstances she would have said, "Why bother? It'll just be coming off." Now she said, "I'd rather you made me a drink."

"So would I." As he made it, he watched her stroll across the living room, into the dining room, where he was, as though making an inspection. Good posture. Carried herself well. Probably had modeling training. Then he realized something else. She had an unusual capacity to wear sexy clothes and still look positively demure—a lady, not a tramp.

"I like your place. Sort of Moorish."

"Yes. It took some getting used to, but it's growing on me. Here's your drink." As he handed it to her, he bent and kissed her on the lips, gently, lingering only a moment. Her lips were soft, responsive. He felt a stirring in his loins. Softly, he said, "Was I too bad last night?"

"You must not have been. I'm here, aren't I?"

"I wasn't exactly sober, I'm afraid."

She sipped her gin-and-tonic, maintaining eye contact over the rim of the glass. "Nor in the best of spirits." She smiled, reached up, and patted his cheek with long, slim fingers. "I got the impres-

94

sion it had been some time since you'd been with a woman."

Brian grinned, a little shamefacedly. "Yes, it had been. Did I act like a schoolboy?"

"A little." She smiled. "Graduate school, I think." Her light laugh was full of mirth, not at all nervous. "I liked it. Feels good to be really wanted."

"You were that, all right." He kissed her again, lingering longer, savoring the sensation. When they parted, he said, "Would you like to see the rest of the place?"

"Sure."

He put his arm around her and guided her through the downstairs, finally through the kitchen and all the way out to the pool. "How about a swim?"

"Some other time, maybe."

He really kissed her now, hotly, deeply, throbbingly. Her responsiveness engulfed him. His pulse pounded in his ears, especially when he thrust his hips against hers. He finally led her back into the house and paused in the kitchen. "Would you like something to eat first?"

"Second."

This was an interesting experience for Lorraine Paul, sort of refreshing. She was careful not to do anything that suggested she was other than what she appeared to be. She said none of the usual phrases, for example, the little lies that appealed to a man's vanity. Nor was she aggressive with Brian, avoiding much of the stroking and touching she utilized to turn a man on. She did not want to appear too experienced. Thus, she allowed him to make love to her, when in her profession it was usually the other way around. She actually enjoyed it. Yes, it was a refreshing change. Brian was handsome and had quite a good body. Kept himself fit. Clearly he wanted to make love, not just have sex. It was not a case of slam, bang,

thank you, ma'am. And nothing kinky. That was
nice, too. He concentrated on giving her pleasure.
Far more kissing than she was accustomed to.
Great foreplay. He was in no hurry like last night.
She managed to relax and enjoy it, something she
rarely did, and was rewarded with repeated or-
gasms, truly shattering. No faking at all, and faking was her specialty. Brian Hecht was indeed
something else.

Afterward, in the kitchen, he in pants, she
wearing his shirt sipping a fresh gin-and-tonic,
watching him scramble eggs, she heard him laugh
and say, "Do you realize I don't know your last
name?"

"I guess you *were* drunk last night. It's Paul."

"Lorraine Paul." He stopped stirring the eggs
and looked at her. "Pretty name for a pretty lady."

"Thank you, sir"—she smiled—"for everything.
You really know how to treat a lady."

He grinned. "I had a lot of inspiration."

She watched him return to the eggs, push the
lever on the toaster, trying to amalgamate what
Judd Forbes had said about him with what she
was beginning to find out for herself. Brian Hecht
was a nice man. She didn't catalog what made
him nice. She just knew he was from the way he
made love. Brian Hecht loved women, probably
respected them. He was unselfish, caring, giving.
He was also terribly frustrated and had been
hurt—a lot. Forbes said his wife was a real knockout, sexy as hell. In fact, Forbes had carried on
about her at great length. Obviously he had the
hots for Roberta Hecht. The girl friend, Jenny
Corban, had been raped, nearly killed, and had
left him. That accounted for the frustration.

It struck Lorraine as strange. Here was a legitimately nice man, good-looking, sexy, good job,
good money, nice house, who had all these troubles with women. It didn't make any sense to her.

96

As far as she was concerned, there were simply an awful lot of dumb women in his life.

He brought plates of eggs and English muffins to the table, kissed her lightly, gulped from his drink, and sat down. "Now, tell me about your acting career."

She laughed. "What acting career?"

"I know some people. Maybe I can help."

Even before she was fully awake, Hillary George heard the sounds, jumped out of bed, and ran to her son's room. Tommy's labored breathing was horrible. Not again! Not so soon! Cystic fibrosis was a ghastly disease.

At once she went to the phone, called the ambulance, then Bel Air General. Part of her deal with Laura Carlyle was that Tommy George received instant admission to the hospital whenever necessary and free medical care. How very much he would need it now!

# Chapter 6

Hamilton Dodd did not like Susan Raimond very much. It was nothing personal—she was probably an ordinary enough young woman. But he was disgusted that she was eight months pregnant and had not seen a doctor. It seemed to him incredibly stupid, not to mention selfish, callous, and cruel to the unborn. He had considered refusing her as a patient and turning her over to someone else. But he relented, telling himself it wasn't this frightened young woman's fault she was stupid. The mother was to blame. Again it was nothing personal. He simply knew Rita Farrell's reputation as the most overbearing stage mother in Hollywood.

"Dr. Dodd, I asked one of the nurses what *placenta previa* meant," Rita was saying now. "She said it meant 'placenta first.' I'm afraid I don't understand."

Ham Dodd continued to examine his patient.

She had a persistent trickle of blood from her vagina, confirming his diagnosis. He had ordered whole blood and IV to prevent shock, but there was no choice about what must be done, and the sooner the better. He finished his examination, covered Susan, then looked at Rita Farrell. " 'Placenta first' is the literal translation from the Latin. It also describes Susan's problem. Her placenta is in the wrong position. Ordinarily it is . . ."

As he had done with Adriana Barre, he found a piece of hospital stationery and made a quick sketch, showing it to both Susan and her mother as he explained.

"Ordinarily the placenta is here, to the side. It may be on the left or right, but in a normal birth it is on the side, nurturing the fetus through the umbilical cord." He added to the sketch with a few deft strokes. "In your case, Susan, the placenta is here, at the bottom or neck of the uterus, covering the opening called the os, through which the baby is to be delivered. Do you understand the problem now?"

"I—I'm not sure . . ."

"In a normal delivery, the baby emerges from the os through the vaginal area, and the placenta follows as the afterbirth. In your case this can't happen. The placenta blocks the way. It will have to come first; then the baby follows."

Rita Farrell, who, having had one child, considered herself an expert on childbearing, looked at him wide-eyed. "And what does that mean?"

"It means the baby will be born dead," Dodd said bluntly. He saw Rita's startled expression, the horror on Susan's face. "While the placenta is being expelled, the baby will be deprived of oxygen. Asphyxiation will occur rapidly and, subsequently, death."

"Heavens, Doctor! Can nothing be done?"

"Yes." He nodded his head a couple of times for

emphasis. "The baby must be delivered by cesarean section immediately."

"Cesarean? You mean cut—" Rita Farrell made a motion across her lower abdomen.

"Precisely."

"But isn't that dangerous?"

It occurred to Dodd that Rita spoke for her daughter so much that one would think *she* was having the baby. "It *is* surgery, Mrs.—I mean Miss Farrell. And of course there are risks in any surgery. But cesarean sections are considered routine these days. Hundreds of thousands—perhaps millions—of children have been delivered this way. Many women have had several cesarean deliveries." He turned to Susan. "Don't be alarmed. It will mean a couple more days in the hospital, perhaps, a little longer recovery period." He smiled. "But I can virtually guarantee that, barring unforeseen circumstances, you will be as good as new in no time." He patted her shoulder for assurance.

"Cesarean? I don't know, Doctor."

Dodd looked at the mother, blinked. He wanted to remind her that she wasn't pregnant and it really was not her decision. He wanted to express his irritation even more succinctly. But he only said, "What don't you know?"

Rita Farrell hesitated. "It's just such a . . . a *big step*. Susan is so young. Her whole life is ahead of her—her career." She shook her head, confused. "I—I have to think of . . . of Susan's welfare first. It is my primary concern, as always."

Ham Dodd hoped his absolute disgust didn't show. He honestly wished he had refused these two as patients—and there *were* two. He briefly considered doubling his fee.

"But, Mother, he says it's perfectly safe."

"I know, darling, of course it is. But . . . but there are . . . other considerations. We have to think about . . . *other things*." She looked at Hamilton Dodd. "May we do that, Doctor—think

100

about it? The operation doesn't have to be done
this minute, does it?"

"No, there is a little time. Do by all means think
about it." Abruptly he left. He'd had a bellyful,
and he wasn't even pregnant!

Adriana Barre considered herself something of a
mystic. She fancied that she had some Gypsy blood
in her veins, giving her a special relationship with
the occult. She had long practiced yoga. She believed in relaxation, breath control, and the ability of the mind to control the body. She was
capable of self-hypnosis and fervently believed
that one day she would have an out-of-body experience.

Thus, when she learned that her baby was in
danger, she gently sent Charles away and began
to practice mind over body, relaxing, breathing
deeply, finally entering a trancelike state in which
her agonizing pain even seemed to lessen. Using
the sketch Dodd had drawn, she visualized her
uterus, the ruptured placenta, the cord attaching
her to her infant son. She felt herself enter the tiny
body, helping him to breathe, to draw life from
herself through the cord. At the same time she saw
the dark area of blood, the hematoma, as an enemy she had to defeat, summoning all her anger
to command it to go away, to leave her and her
child alone.

Adriana had engaged in this process repeatedly
the previous day and frequently during the night.
Her pain had definitely subsided. She was sure of
it. And in the morning she had been rewarded
with an encouraging report from Hamilton Dodd.
"Whatever you're doing, Adriana, keep it up. You
do seem better. The baby's heart rate has stabi-
lized. Your pulse and blood pressure are im-
proved. The hematoma appears no larger."

Her smile was beatific. "I told you it would

work, Hamilton. I have special powers. Everything is going to be all right, you'll see."

"You're far from out of the woods," he cautioned.

"I'm going to have my baby the way a mother should. You'll see."

He did not see, but he was powerless to do anything but go along with her for the moment—and hope.

When he left, Adriana again closed her eyes, trying to focus her energies on her womb, but she was not entirely successful. Extraneous sounds and errant thoughts kept interfering with her concentration. Thus, when she heard the door to her room open, she opened her eyes and saw a very attractive young woman in a short white coat.

"I'm sorry," the young woman said. "I didn't realize you were sleeping."

"It's quite all right. I'm awake."

"Have you a minute to talk?"

Adriana's smile, so famous on the screen, irradiated her face. "I seem to have nothing but minutes just now." When her visitor came closer she read the name tag. "Dr. Sheryl James. You have extraordinary eyes, my dear."

Sheryl grinned. "Coming from you, Miss Barre, that is the most fabulous compliment I've ever received. How are you feeling?"

"Better than yesterday."

"So I just heard at the nursing station. That's good news."

Again Adriana studied the name tag. "Are you a medical doctor?"

"Doctor of psychology, clinical psychologist on the hospital staff. My job is to try to be available to those patients who—"

"I see—you're a shrink." The broad smile relieved what might conceivably have been an insult.

Sheryl laughed. "I can guarantee no brain has

ever lost volume or dimension from my ministrations. Dr Kazinsky asked me to visit you. I came yesterday but you were resting." She saw puzzlement on the actress's face. "I understand there may be problems with the birth of your baby. I thought you might like to share your feelings about it."

"My baby is fine. I will not lose him," Adriana stated calmly.

Sheryl's first thought was that the woman was refusing to accept reality. Clearly she would need help with that. "I certainly hope so, Miss Barre."

"It is not a hope, Dr. James. It is a fact."

"What makes you so certain?"

"He is *my* child, inside *my* body. We are as one. I *know* him, more completely than I have ever known anyone." She hesitated, feeling suddenly shy. "You wouldn't . . . understand."

Sheryl smiled. "Try me."

Adriana looked at her a long moment. "Very well. I lie here, very still, very relaxed. It may not seem possible to you, but I can feel myself entering my son's little body. I help him breathe, grow strong. I assure him all will be well. That blood clot or whatever it is—"

"Hematoma."

"Yes. I view it as an enemy. It will not harm my son. I will not let it. I will destroy it." She paused. "I'm sure you must think me very foolish."

"The term for what you are doing is *biofeedback*," Sheryl replied promptly. "It is of great interest to both psychologists and physicians. Some of the reported results are most interesting, even astonishing. No, I do not think you are foolish, Miss Barre."

The actress studied her for a moment, blinking the famous eyes. Then came the smile. "Please call me Adriana." She read the tag once more. "And I

103

will call you Sheryl. You are a very understanding person."

"Don't misunderstand, Miss—I mean Adriana. Biofeedback is not treatment, at least not medically accepted treatment. You must listen to your doctors and do exactly what they tell you. Only they can—"

"I am and I will, but I feel I've helped. My pain is less. The baby is doing well. The . . . hematoma has not grown any larger."

"I believe you *have* helped, yes."

"Do you mean that?"

"I will neither discourage nor disparage what you're doing. Keep it up. But remember, Dr. Dodd is the final authority here. He knows what's best for you and your baby."

Adriana reached out and took Sheryl's hand. "What a lovely person you are, my dear."

"I've always admired you, Miss—Adriana. No, I've *adored* you, I've seen all your pictures. Just knowing you were in a film was enough for me."

Adriana laughed. "Too bad there aren't more like you."

"But there are, millions more. It's a great privilege to meet you and to discover that you are as fine a person as I always imagined you were."

"You are too kind, Sheryl." She squeezed Sheryl's hand.

"I want you to know I am pulling for you. Everyone is—the doctors, the nurses, the whole staff."

"I will not disappoint them. I intend to give my finest performance for the sake of my little son."

"I'm sure you will." Impulsively, Sheryl bent down and kissed her cheek.

Judd Forbes was not exactly nervous as he entered Bobbi Hecht's office, simply conscious that anything he might hope to accomplish at Bel Air General would involve this woman. And he didn't

104

know her at all. He would have to be very careful in this initial encounter.

Bobbi had a swivel chair but no desk as yet. She sat in it, small and delicate, her fine, slender legs crossed. She wore a tailored summer suit, and Judd Forbes thought she was the most attractive woman he'd ever met. He was physically aroused just looking at her. *Careful. You're in trouble already.*

"Have a seat, Mr. Forbes. Seats seem to be all we have at the moment."

Her welcoming smile didn't alleviate his discomfort. He sat in a straight-backed chair opposite her and also crossed his legs. "I'll see what I can do about getting you a desk and anything else you need, Mrs. Hecht."

Again the red lips parted, revealing brilliant teeth. "I'm about as new here as you are, Mr. Forbes. But as I recall, there is a certain informality practiced at Bel Air General, at least among the administrative staff. Please call me Bobbi, and you will be Judd."

"Thank you."

"Is that short for Judson?"

"Actually, no. My birth certificate shows J-U-D-D. It's a family name." He smiled. "I've seen a photo of one of the Judds, a gent with a very long beard and a most severe expression."

She laughed. "Most inappropriate for you." Bobbi was uncertain of her reaction to him. He certainly was handsome enough, but then Southern California abounded in blue-eyed, blond men. She wondered idly if he lightened his hair. She felt immune to his handsomeness, but she also sensed that he was attracted to her. She was also immune to *that*, she felt. His next words confirmed her evaluation of him.

"May I say that Brian, along with his other sterling qualities, has excellent taste in wives. You are very beautiful." For a moment he thought he'd

**105**

gone too far. Her reaction was not at all what he had expected. She almost seemed to bristle. It flustered him. "I meant it only as a compliment, Mrs. Hecht," he added hastily.

"Bobbi, remember. I'm sure you did, but surely you know my husband and I are separated."

He'd messed up, all right. He took refuge in lies. "I'm sorry, I didn't know. It's only my second day here."

"Well, you do now. Brian and I have been living apart for some time."

He had gotten his feet wet. Might as well jump in. "Which, if I may say so, I find utterly incomprehensible."

Bobbi controlled an impulse to smile. The man was glib, all right. "Too bad my husband doesn't share your enthusiasm." She immediately changed the subject. "I asked you here to solicit your ideas and advice. After all, you're the new head of public relations. My grandmother has asked me to begin what she calls a Community Outreach Program. She wants Bel Air General to take a more active role in supporting various charities. . . ."

He really did listen, for he knew it was important, but a part of his mind kept evaluating her. There was a quality in her that he decided was toughness. Bobbi Hecht was no clinging vine. She had a strong sense of self and took pride in the person she was. Plenty of confidence, great inner security.

Outspoken, too. Lots of spirit. A fighter. Combine that with pride and she was probably a bitch to live with. It would take a strong man to stand up to her. Apparently Brian Hecht wasn't strong enough. . . .

"So what do you think, Judd?"

He made a motion. "Off the top of my head, okay?" He saw her nod. She was taking all this very seriously. "I like it. I mean that. I'm not

106

stroking you." *But I sure would like to.* "I think some of those charities you mentioned would leap at greater involvement from Bel Air General."

"But would they consider it just a public relations stunt? Would we be regarded as playing Lady Bountiful in order to get coverage in the press?"

"I don't see that as a problem at all, Bobbi. Why would we be undertaking such a project if we weren't sincere? Bel Air General isn't competing for patients with other hospitals. We turn them away. And from what I've seen, our profits remain excellent. Anyone who puts you or this hospital down for what you are trying to accomplish is unworthy of your consideration."

She stared at him, blinked long lashes over bright blue eyes. "That's very well put. Thank you."

He grinned in pleasure at having made points with her. "If you're worried about the reception you might receive from the charity boards, the way to avoid that is to have something specific to offer. That will settle any question of sincerity."

"You mean money?"

"That, yes, but also medicine, hours of staff time, whatever else you plan to contribute."

"I see what you mean. Get right down to brass tacks and keep the pious platitudes to a minimum."

"Exactly. Do we have such a program?" He deliberately used the word *we.* It was vital that he get involved in this.

"No," Bobbi admitted. Everything is nebulous at the moment."

"Still at the idea stage."

"Yes, but I will speak to my grandmother at once. We need a handle on what sort of funds, time, and whatever else we're prepared to invest." She smiled.

"Would you like me to draw up a list of poten-

107

tial charities we might approach? I could come up with names, addresses, phone numbers."

"I thought perhaps a press release first, announcing the program."

He shook his head. "If you want my advice, I think not. That will just encourage every kooky, off-the-wall charity racket in Southern California to come to Bel Air General, hat in hand." He laughed. "I don't need to tell you how many of those there are. I think we should deal only with the reputable, proven charities."

"No announcement, then?"

"To my mind, Bobbi, we should shun all publicity. That will certainly silence any criticism of our motives."

"I see what you mean."

"Another thing. Our silence, our modesty, will have the effect of putting the imprimatur of Bel Air General Hospital on those charities which we support."

The vivid eyes became even brighter. "I like your thinking, Judd."

"Thank you." Then he laughed, adding, "He said modestly."

"I'm serious. I *do* like it. And you're right. That's the way my grandmother would want it, I'm sure. She has never sought the limelight, or any recognition for her many private charities."

"A most gracious woman. It shows in her face."

"Doesn't it." Bobbi was immensely excited. She wanted to go to the Tower at once, but hesitated. "How soon could you get me that list of charities?"

"Shouldn't take long. Most are pretty well known." He glanced at his Rolex. "I should be able to have at least a preliminary list by late this afternoon."

She arose. "Do that, Judd. Maybe I'll even have a desk by that time."

"I'll see that you do, Bobbi."

It was an extremely self-satisfied Judd Forbes who left her office, whistling tunelessly under his breath.

Rita Farrell was so upset by the report from Hamilton Dodd that she made an excuse to leave Susan, went downstairs to the lobby, and had a Bloody Mary in the public dining room. She drank very little and hardly ever in the morning, but this excess was justified under the circumstances.

When she returned to her daughter's room, she was both calmer and thoroughly convinced of what she must do. From long experience in manipulation she began by discovering what Susan's attitude was. You couldn't change anything unless you first knew what had to be changed.

"That was dreadful news from Dr. Dodd, wasn't it?" she said sadly.

"Why did this have to happen to *me?*" Susan moaned.

Rita Farrell smiled, patted her hand in reassurance. "It's nothing personal, darling. I gather it happens every so often"—she laughed—"like having your luggage searched at Customs."

"We're hardly talking about luggage, Mother!"

"Perhaps it wasn't the best metaphor, Susan, but"—Rita sighed—I'm just suggesting you shouldn't feel . . . *guilty* or anything. It is hardly your *fault.*"

"I know, but Dr. Dodd is right. I should've gone to a doctor sooner."

"We all agree on that, Susan, but there's nothing to be done about it now."

"But my poor baby! That's all I can think about."

"Then you've made up your mind?"

"Yes. I'm going to have the cesarean. I have to. There's no choice."

Rita Farrell had feared this, but she was pre-

109

pared, determined, even adamant. "I certainly understand your feeling, dear."

"The baby must live," Susan said firmly.

"And so must *you*, darling."

Susan looked at her, a little incredulous. "You mean the surgery? Dr. Dodd said it's very common."

"He also admitted it is a risk. You are very brave, darling, but—" Sigh. "As for me, I'm frightened—petrified, in fact."

"Oh, Mother!"

Rita clutched Susan's hand. "Please try to understand, dear. You're all I have. Your father is gone. I have no other children, not even relatives. If anything happened to you, I don't . . . ." A sorrowful shake of her head finished the sentence.

"You're being silly, Mother."

"Am I? When you're a mother you'll think differently." It was a line she'd used so often in the past. This time it was a mistake.

"I *am* a mother, remember? And I do understand your feelings, which is why I must have the surgery."

"Oh, dear! This is so *awful*. Of course I share your concern for the child. What mother wouldn't?" Rita sighed heavily. "If I haven't said it before, let me do so now. I admire you so much—and love you so much. You are *so* caring, *so* unselfish." She patted Susan's unresponsive hand. "But I have to ask you to at least *try* to think of yourself and your future a little—just a little."

Susan looked at her closely. "What are you driving at, Mother? What are you trying to say?"

Rita conjured up her most frustrated, agonized expression. After all, she had once been some kind of an actress. "You're not planning to keep the baby, Susan."

"No, I guess not." She pursed her lips. "Part of me wants to, I suppose, but it would be better for the baby if I—"

110

"Gave him or her up for adoption." (She wasn't going to make the mistake of saying "it" again.) "I think it's wise, darling. I know *I* can't care for an infant at my age."

Susan knew her mother didn't want to, which was the same as not being able to.

"After all, you don't really know the father. He's not going to participate in the child's upbringing. Darling, darling, rearing a child is an awesome responsibility. And you're so *young*."

"I know, I know. Okay, I'll give up the baby."

"It is wisest, Susan, believe me."

Susan continued to look at her. She knew her mother so well. "What else do you have in mind for me, Mother?"

"Please, Susan, I'm not an *ogre*. I think only of you, your future."

"Think what?"

A long sigh. "It is just a *thought*, Susan, but"— Rita made a helpless little gesture with her hands—"since you aren't keeping the child, since it won't even be as though it were *your* child, maybe you ought to think about—"

"That's ghastly, Mother—contemptible! I can't *believe* you said it!" Susan cried.

Rita Farrell bristled. This was impertinence. "I haven't said *anything* yet."

"But you're *thinking* it. Let the baby die, that's what you're thinking."

Long, long sigh, full of anguish. "Susan, Susan, *my* baby, my love. Just think about it a minute. That's all I ask. You are willing to risk surgery for the sake of the child. I applaud you for that. I said you had courage. But even if the surgery is a total success, with no complications—even if you recover completely, there will never be an end to it. It will go on for the rest of your life."

"What are you talking about? *What* will go on?"

"The *scar*, darling, the *scar!* Do you have any

111

idea how it will limit your movie career? Think of the roles you'll be unable to play. After all, these days an actress is expected to appear nude occasionally—in good taste, of course, and only when it is appropriate to the part. You wouldn't even be able to wear a bikini. Have you really thought of what that scar will mean?"

"No, not exactly."

"Then do. And there's another thing. One day, hopefully soon, you will meet the man of your dreams, your Prince Charming. He will fall in love with you. He'll want to marry you. But what will he think when he sees that scar? Think of the questions he'll ask about whose child it was and what happened to the baby. Will he still love and want you then?"

Susan cringed. "Please, Mother, I—"

"I know. They're horrid thoughts. I hate them, too. But they must be faced *now*, Susan. You must think of yourself and your future. You face a momentous decision, my darling. You owe it to yourself and to me to give it *very careful* consideration." Rita Farrell, so experienced at molding her daughter to her will, could almost smell success. She didn't even need to read the expression on Susan's face. Gently, compassionately, she added, "All I ask is that you think about what I'm saying. Don't be hasty, child."

Susan Raimond nodded. In a small, barely audible voice, she said, "I'll think about it."

Hillary sat beside her son's bed, terrified, barely able to control her sense of panic. Tommy had had similar attacks before. With cystic fibrosis, the lungs tended to fill with thick mucus, and keeping the breathing passages open was a running battle. She had been waging it for most of Tommy's twelve wonderful years. Always she had won, although he had been hospitalized several times.

Now he was once more in a fight for his life.

112

His lungs had been suctioned and he was on a respirator, barely making it. He lay semi-conscious, struggling for every breath. The sound of it was horrible to hear. Pneumonia. Dear Lord! It could hardly be worse. Antibiotics had been given. Would they help?

Long ago Hillary had set her priorities. Tommy George was foremost in her life—no, he was her *whole* life. Everything else was secondary. This charming, intelligent, courageous boy needed her to help him live out the promise of his life. However long he lived, there was much he could accomplish. Now she felt she had failed him.

As she sat watching her son, unable to leave him even for a moment, she was agonizingly certain that all this was retribution for her sin. Didn't it say in the Bible that the sins of the parents would be visited on the children? The knowledge that her love had destroyed Arthur was almost more than she could bear. Because of her, this fine man, a Prince of the Church, a leader, a good man doing so much good to others, had been humiliated and disgraced. It was all her fault. Surely she had enticed him. She had known who he was and how wrong their affair was, the harm it could do him and his career. Yet she had gone on, overwhelmed by their passion, unable or unwilling to give him up. Knowledge of the magnitude of her sin had tormented her for days. And now Tommy lay there, possibly dying. Oh, God! The wages of sin were too high. Why did an innocent child have to pay? *Please, God, take me. Save my son.*

She felt a gentle hand on her shoulder, turned, saw Brian Hecht.

"I just heard about Tommy. I'm so sorry, Hillary."

She nodded. "Thank you for coming."

"It's bad, I hear."

"Yes." The distress in her eyes made the single word unnecessary.

113

"He'll be all right, Hillary. I know it. I'm certain."

"I hope so," Hillary whispered.

"Anything he needs will be provided. And don't worry about your responsibilities. Everything will be taken care of."

"Thank you." She turned back to her son.

Brian would have stopped by Tommy's room in any event, though perhaps not so soon, but Laura's recent expressions of concern for Hillary had motivated this trip. He had not expected Tommy to be in such critical condition. He had hoped to take a moment to question Hillary about anything that might be bothering her. That was impossible now. "I'm going now, Hillary," he said. "I just want you to know I'm with you. We're all pulling for Tommy."

Hillary nodded, unable to speak.

As he left pediatrics, Brian Hecht at least had an explanation for Laura. Apparently Hillary's distraction had been caused by her growing concern about Tommy's health, a concern that was more than justified, given the boy's current condition.

Max Hill laughed at the joke, but it wasn't genuine. Rather, it was one of his well-rehearsed movie laughs and had nothing to do with the joke. Humor was the last thing on his mind right now. All he could think of was what he called "the problem."

This was no casual meeting with Detective Lieutenant Frank Elgin of the LAPD, although Max had to pretend it was. Some years ago, when Elgin was only a detective sergeant, he had been Max's technical advisor for a film in which Max was to play a detective. He had followed Elgin around for a few days, learning how police detectives operated, to make his performance more authentic. He and Elgin had stayed in touch over the

114

years, mostly by phone calls, but they were hardly close friends.

Max had not exactly dropped in. He had phoned Elgin, saying he was downtown and wanted to drop by and "check up on him." Elgin told him to come on over. For the past twenty minutes the two of them had engaged in reminiscences, casual banter and joke swapping, reestablishing their old camaraderie.

Finally Elgin said, "I really don't think you just happened to be in the neighborhood, not this neighborhood anyway. What is it, Max? Come clean. You want a parking ticket fixed?"

Max grinned ruefully. "Sort of, in a manner of speaking. A rather large parking ticket, you might say. It'll take a lot of fixing."

"Want to tell me about it? What is it?"

"Blackmail," Max said without preamble.

Elgin gave a low whistle. "What exactly have you done now?"

"Me?" Max pretended injured innocence. "I'm an Eagle Scout. You know that. It involves friends of mine."

Elgin gave him a look. "That's what they all say."

Max was completely serious now. "It really *does* involve friends, but I guess it doesn't matter if you think it's me."

"Sex?"

"Yep."

"That shouldn't be hard. Just 'fess up and take your medicine. No jail time involved, after all."

"It's not quite that simple, Frank. The person being blackmailed is a priest."

"Roman Catholic?"

"Yes. Never thought of it, but I guess there are other kinds."

Elgin shook his head. "You're right. It isn't simple. How much money?"

"Half a mil."

The detective's eyebrows arched. "That much? Must be some priest!"

"The blackmailer figures the last thing the Church needs just now is a sex scandal." Max shrugged. "Good figuring, I suspect."

"What's he got?"

"Photo and negative. I haven't seen it, but I hear it's pretty damaging."

"Who is he?"

"The blackmailer? I don't want to tell you, Frank. Not right now. Not unless all else fails."

Elgin leaned back in his chair. "If you don't want to finger the guy, then what do you want from me?"

"Advice. How do I get this guy—and the evidence?"

"Without paying the dough or involving the cops?" He saw Max Hill nod. "Not very easily, unless the guy's a dummy. Is he a pro? What's he do for a living?"

"Insurance investigator."

"Too bad. Probably no dummy." He shook his head. "Looks like you got problems, Max."

"You can't help me?"

"Not as long as you keep talking in circles. You either trust me or you don't, Max. It's that simple."

The actor sighed, looked around the windowless office.

"What you say will stay here, between the two of us. I can promise you that," Elgin went on.

"Is that a promise?"

"Look, you S.O.B., I've thrown better men than you out of this office for saying less!"

"All right, all right. I guess I have no choice, but when I tell you, at least you'll know why I'm hesitant." He told the whole ugly story in a greatly expurgated form, identifying Stillwell, Dykes, and Shaughnessy, but not Hillary.

"Who's the dame?" Elgin wanted to know.

116

"Don't ask, Frank. Nobody important or well known. Just a nice lady who made a bad mistake. She's important to me—the real reason I'm trying to help that bastard in the red hat. I don't want her dragged through this."

"She may have to be, but okay—for now." Elgin sat forward in his chair. "Cardinal Stillwell, you say? Been going on for years? Since he was a Bishop? God almighty!"

Max grimaced. "I must say you express yourself with more restraint than I did when I learned of it."

"Did you know I'm Catholic?"

"I didn't, no."

"Baptized, confirmed, educated, married, all in the Church. My kids go to St. Ed's. How do you think this makes me feel?"

"I can imagine."

"You can't—can't even begin to."

Max saw the genuine distress on the detective's broad face. "Stillwell plans to confess to the Pope, resign, and enter a monastery, if that makes you feel any better."

"The bastard better!" He got up, went to a water cooler, filled a cup, gulped it down. "Okay, I'm gonna do what I can, but only because I got a lot invested in my religion. Can't see it hurt. I'm doing it for my kids and *their* kids and all their friends—also for some very fine priests I know who don't fool around. But you better believe I'm gonna hold out a couple bucks from the collection plate if we pull this off. I figure I got it coming."

Max was encouraged, but his voice was steady as he asked, "Then something can be done?"

"Maybe. Let me think about it, check on a couple things and get back to you. Maybe tonight. Okay?"

"Sure."

"Give me your phone and address."

117

As he fished out his card, Max said, "I can't thank you enough, Frank."

"Nothing's happened yet, you asshole. If we pull it off, *then* you thank me!

Laura Carlyle had mixed feelings. On the one hand, she was delighted that Roberta was showing so much energy and enthusiasm for her project. How like her father she was! Strong-willed, a little impetuous. No grass had ever grown under his feet. Like father, like daughter. Laura was positively thrilled to have her granddaughter at long last take such an active interest in Bel Air General, working beside her. Nothing must interfere with that. On the other hand—she sighed inwardly—all this was moving a little too fast. Only yesterday it had been nothing but an idea. Now she was being asked to commit herself. Far, far too much haste.

"Judd Forbes is right, Grandmother. I'm sure of it. The Community Outreach Program should be done with great dignity and reserve. There should be no question of our motives. And we must be prepared to offer a specific program. Don't you agree?"

Laura sought subtly to divert her. "Our Mr. Forbes sounds like an enterprising young man. What do you think of him, Roberta?"

"I think his ideas are most sensible and speak for themselves."

"But what do you think of him personally?"

Bobbi hesitated. "He seems pleasant enough. I think he's bright, informed. He wants to succeed here, I'm sure."

"Good-looking young man," Laura mused.

"I suppose. I hadn't noticed."

Laura doubted that. "Another sandwich? The pâté is quite good." They were having an English high tea, a ceremony Laura enjoyed whenever she had visitors. It was a point of pride with her that

118

Bel Air General was the only hospital she knew of that offered afternoon tea to patients, though not everyone partook.

Bobbi was not diverted by her grandmother's tactics. She was also characteristically outspoken. "I gather you don't want to discuss this just now, or make an immediate decision."

Laura's back straightened a bit. She blinked at her granddaughter. "I hardly think such a statement is called for, Roberta. Of course I want to discuss it. It *was* my idea, after all. In fact, I was just noting how pleased I am by your interest and energy."

"I'm sorry. I didn't mean to rush you. I guess I'm just so eager to get on with it, I—"

"Of course you are, my dear. It is to your credit. I'm impressed, believe me. It's just—" She chose that moment to sip her tea.

"Just what?"

"I'm an old woman, Roberta. I am unaccustomed to haste. I need to take time to think, evaluate, consult."

Whenever Laura spoke of being old or in poor health, Bobbi was suspicious. Laura Carlyle might be devious, but to her granddaughter she was quite transparent. "By consult, I gather you mean with Brian."

The immense blue eyes in the delicate face held hers a moment. "Of course. He is the administrator of this hospital. He must be—"

"Then we might as well forget the whole thing, Grandmother," Bobbi snapped. "You and I both know Brian is dead set against the project—indeed, against my having any role at all in *his* hospital. He's made that very clear, I think."

Again Laura offered a plate of tiny, triangular sandwiches, then helped herself and took a small bite. It was all designed to give her time to think. After all, she couldn't be expected to reply with her mouth full. Roberta was quite correct. Brian

119

would oppose the project, and probably for the reasons just given. But Brian was her right arm, her administrator, the person she depended on. For her to proceed independently of him, to make a major decision involving hospital finances without consulting him, was risky, to say the least. He might very well be insulted. On the other hand, Brian was being annoyingly willful, objecting to this project simply to spite his wife.

Bobbi gave up. "It *was* a good idea, Grandmother." She arose. "Something might have come of it. But we'll never know, will we?"

"Please be seated, Roberta. Indulge an old woman with a little moment to think." Laura watched her obey, however reluctantly. This might be her one chance to involve Roberta directly in the hospital's affairs. If she ignored her interest now, she might never get it back. Surely that overrode her concern for Brian's sensitivities. "My dear, I was thinking about a hundred thousand. Only to start, mind you." Bobbi's eyes widened. "A hundred thousand dollars?"

"It will hardly be in cash. That includes the cost of medicines and other supplies, as well as the salary of any members of the staff who may wish to become involved."

Now when Bobbi rose it was to cross to her grandmother, hug her, and kiss her cheek. "Thank you, Grandmother! You won't regret it. I'll make good use of the money and make you proud of me."

Laura patted her shoulder. "I already am, my dear." Indeed, Laura was pleased by Bobbi's spontaneous display of affection. It almost removed her doubts about her actions. She waited for Bobbi to sit again, then said, "I will want to see that list of organizations prepared by Mr. Forbes."

"Of course. It is to be only preliminary. I'll

120

make the final decision." At once she amended that. "With your concurrence, naturally."

"Yes. It should most definitely be interdenominational. All the major religious charities should benefit—Catholic, Jewish, Protestant. And as you know, I've always privately supported the work of the Salvation Army."

Bobbi nodded eagerly.

"I also think you should keep in mind that I already give generously to the United Way. All our employees do. I believe almost one hundred percent of the staff give. Since we are talking about an involvement in addition to money, we should evaluate—"

"I'm in total agreement, Grandmother," Bobbi interrupted. "I will proceed cautiously and carefully, never fear."

Max had met Brian Hecht only once, casually at some sort of social gathering, but he knew a lot about him from Hillary. Max's decision to phone him was motivated by desperation. Carmen Rodriguez, Hillary's live-in maid, had called to report Tommy's illness and to tell him that Hillary was staying at the hospital with her son. Her anguished voice, mixing Spanish and English, left no doubt about how serious it was. Max had to get into the hospital, which was impossible without prior approval, so he phoned Brian Hecht.

To Brian, the call was an annoyance, something his new assistant should have handled. Celebrities, real and imagined, phoned regularly, thinking their self-importance automatically granted them access or admission to Bel Air General. The phone calls were a constant nuisance. But Judd Forbes had left for the day, and Max Hill was not someone who could be turned away. Brian picked up the phone just as he was about to go out the door. "Of course I remember you, Max. How are you?" he asked with forced joviality.

121

"I was a lot better until I learned that Tommy George is a patient at your place. How is he?"

Brian was a little surprised at the famous actor's inquiring about the boy, but he accepted it. "Frankly, not too good. He has cystic fibrosis, you know."

"Yes. To get right to the point, Brian, both Hillary and Tommy are friends of mine—dear friends. I'm very upset. I've sent flowers and a gift, but I'd like to visit Tommy. I guess you know my problem—I can't get in."

Brian understood. No one walked into Bel Air General off the street. All visitors had to be on a list approved by either the patient, the family, or the physician in charge. "Have you spoken to Hillary?"

"Under the circumstances, it hardly seemed the time to bother her. I was hoping you could authorize entry for me and Carmen Rodriguez. She's the boy's nurse, Hillary's maid. Carmen is beside herself." Max heard the hesitation. "Look, Brian, I'm not BS-ing you. It's something Hillary would do herself if she were capable of thinking about it."

"Sure, I'll authorize it for you and . . . what was the woman's name . . .?" Brian wrote it down. "But I think it's pointless for you to come tonight. The boy is in critical condition. I'm not even sure visitors are allowed. Why not wait till tomorrow?"

Max sighed. "I suppose you're right."

"I'm sure of it." Then Brian remembered something. "Max, while I'm talking to you, could I ask a favor of you—I mean, a big, ugly, nasty, never-do-another-favor-again, cash-in-all-the-chips favor?"

Max laughed, the same one Brian had heard so often in the theater. "Since I just asked one of you, your timing is perfect."

Brian laughed, too. "I hoped it might be. I have

a friend who's trying to get into acting. I hoped you might give her a few pointers, steer her in the right direction."

"As you say, a big favor, but since you said *she* . . ."

"She's a *she*, all right. Quite ornamental, even stunning. As to her talent, that's an open question."

Unable to see a way out, Max said, "Why not? Sure, I'll talk to the lady. Where and when?"

"Are you free awhile tonight? She'll be at my place."

Max hesitated, remembering he was waiting for Elgin to call. "I'm not sure, Brian. I'm waiting for an important phone call. It might be possible later in the evening."

"Fine. Let's leave it that way. I'll give you my home phone number. I'd appreciate it if you'd call either way."

Max squelched a comment about how the two might be spending their time while they waited, but he didn't know the man well enough to kid around. "Fine. That's the way we'll do it." He jotted down the number.

# Chapter 7

After he left his office, Judd Forbes used the hospital switchboard to get through to Bobbi Hecht at her home. When she came on the line, he said, "I'm sorry to bother you at home, but I wanted to say I haven't forgotten my promise to get that list for you today. It took longer than I expected, but I've got it. I just wanted you to know."

Bobbi laughed lightly. "My, such dedication. I'd love to see it. Can you drop it off at my house?"

He hesitated. The length of the pause was carefully timed. "This evening?"

"I don't want to put you out."

Another hesitation. "Yes, I think I can do that." The invitation was precisely what he'd hoped for, the reason he had not given her the list earlier.

"Good. I've some wonderful news I think you'll be interested in hearing."

"Splendid. I might as well come right now." He

asked for and received not only the address but driving directions, both of which he already knew.

Bobbi greeted Judd in silky California-style lounging pajamas, loose-fitting and flowing, although belted at the waist. She looked both cool and quite beautiful. He was still wearing the suit he'd had on all day at the office.

"Good heavens, that will never do!" Bobbi said at once. "At least remove your jacket and tie, be a little comfortable in this heat." As he did so, she apologized for the appearance of the house with a wave of her hand. "Forgive this mess." There were many boxes and crates scattered around. "I'm busy moving some of Mother's things out and mine in."

"I haven't had an opportunity to offer my condolences on the death of you mother," Judd said, punctiliously polite, even formal.

"Thank you." Her brief smile dismissed the matter. "Now, where is that list?"

He pulled it out of the inside pocket of his jacket, which was now draped over the back of a chair. "It's preliminary, as I said."

She took it, unfolded it, started to read, then said, "I'm sorry. I'm a dreadful hostess. Would you like a drink?"

"Yes, I'd like that very much."

She pointed to the bar. "Help yourself, please. And scotch and a splash for me, if you wouldn't mind."

He went to the small but well-stocked bar and made the drinks, looking up occasionally to watch her read. Actually, he was watching *her*. Damned fine-looking woman. She could probably wear sackcloth and ashes and still look glamorous. Such self-possession. She was concentrating on his report, totally unaware of him for the moment. Nor had she paid particular attention to him this morning. Forbes had studied body language. This woman had yet to open up to him. He reminded

125

himself not to force the issue. All in good time. . . .

She looked up. "This is excellent, Judd. I think you've covered all the bases, including some I hadn't thought of. Thank you. There's just one thing."

He went over to her with the two drinks. "Isn't there always?"

She accepted the glass, tucking the list in an almost invisible pocket of her lounging outfit. "When I spoke to my grandmother, she reminded me that she personally—and most of the staff as well—gives to United Way . . . quite generously, I gather. There's no point in lavishing more on them, so I think we can move UW down from the top of the list."

Judd nodded. "I should have thought of that. We ought to deal directly with other individual charities. Did you notice I didn't include heart, cancer, lung, any of the national medical charities? I figured our efforts were to be directed more locally."

"Yes, I did notice. And I agree." She strolled past him. "Let's go out on the terrace. It's a nice time of the evening." The patio and pool comprised perhaps the most attractive area of the house—Connie Payne had certainly spent enough time there, soaking up the sun, and so had Bobbi, before she had fallen out with her mother.

"Very nice indeed," Judd said admiringly.

She saw him looking at the pool. "Would you like a dip? I can probably find some trunks somewhere. Mother was always prepared for company, especially male company."

He knew it wasn't yet time for skin. "It's a temptation, but I'm afraid I haven't that much time." He smiled. "You said you had good news."

"Yes, splendid news!" She sat gracefully at a white-painted wrought-iron table under an awning, motioning for him to do the same. "I spoke

126

to Grandmother this afternoon. She has pledged one hundred thousand dollars to start."

She said it so matter-of-factly he was unsure how to react. Perhaps to a woman like Bobbi Hecht, a sum like that was chicken feed. Still, she had said *splendid news.* "That's wonderful, Bobbi."

"It's not all cash on the barrelhead. It includes medicines and such, as well as staff salaries and expenses." Her smile was dazzling. "Isn't it wonderful?"

"I should say so. Congratulations! You're really in business now."

"So it would seem. I'm going to be a very busy girl. I think I'll approach Catholic Charities first. Tomorrow, in fact. Monsignor O'Reilly won't know what hit him!"

As he listened to Bobbi chatter on about her plans, he watched her closely. Legs crossed, elbows resting on the table, holding her drink in one hand and gesturing with the other. There was not the slightest hint of seductiveness in her manner, no awareness of him as a man.

"Would you like me to go with you when you meet some of these people?" Judd asked. "I don't know what Brian has planned for me to do and how much free time I'll have, but I'd like to." He saw her hesitation. "It'll be your show," he assured her quickly. "I'd be there solely for moral support."

"I might need that." Now she smiled and finished her drink. "How about another one of these, if you have time?"

Judd grinned engagingly. "You've twisted my arm."

They went back inside to the bar, and she sat on a stool while he made the drinks, deliberately not looking at her.

"Tell me about yourself, Judd," Bobbi said suddenly.

It wasn't much, but it was a start. "Let's see—
I was born at Cedars of Lebanon and weighed six
pounds, eleven ounces . . ."

She laughed. "Not quite *that* far back, please!"

When Frank Elgin phoned, Max agreed to meet
him at the detective's "local." It was charitably
called a neighborhood bar, although Max suspected it was more of a joint. No one paid any
attention to him, which was nice.

"I figured that lousy kisser of yours would go
unnoticed here," Elgin joked. Then he got down
to business. "I had that dude Dykes checked out.
You're right—he's a slime ball. He's also a pip-
squeak and a loser. No record, just a few shady
deals. He's a fringe player. This is his first attempt
at a big score."

"Is that good?"

"Maybe. He's probably nervous, antsy. Knows
he's in over his head. Maybe we can use that. The
important thing is to play *him,* not let him play
*us.* We've got to set the ground rules. He's got to
play on our terms or it's no deal. I figure he wants
the money more than the scandal. What good
would that do him?"

"He can sell the photo. There are any number
of rags that would snap it up."

"Probably. But that's peanuts—chicken feed,
like they used to say. He'll bite, if we bait the trap
right." Elgin shrugged. "If he doesn't, one very
high priest and your girl friend are in very big
trouble."

"What do we do?"

"Not we—*you.*"

"Me?" Max stared at him.

"If you want the police in on this, it's another
whole ball game. If it works, we'll do our part.
But it's all up to you to *make* it work."

Max sighed. "What do you want me to do?"

"That's better. The story is, Cardinal Stillwell,

128

being a big cheese, can't be expected to deal with the seamier side of life, so he's turned this over to a lower-grade priest who'll pay up. That's you."

"Me? That'll never play in Peoria!" Max scoffed.

"Yes, it will. Just listen. Dykes expects the money to come from the Church. Stillwell phones him, says he has the dough. But he's arranged it to look like a charitable contribution. The priest handling it has no idea of the real purpose. If Dykes wants his money, he has to go along with the scam. And believe me, he will."

"And I'm supposed to be the priest carrying the money? It'll never work, Frank. This face of mine is too recognizable. And Dykes already knows I'm involved with . . ."—he almost said Hillary—". . . with the lady."

"What are you—stupid or something? Didn't you win an Academy Award?"

"Yes, but . . ."

"With a beard, moustache, glasses, cassock, rosary, Bible, and a sanctimonious expression, your own mother wouldn't know you."

"Maybe."

"It's either that or give up acting, my friend."

Max raised his hands in a gesture of surrender. "Okay, okay. Go on."

"Dykes has to believe it's a charity scam. If you do it right, he will. After all, he's in the scam racket himself. Stillwell has to call him, tell him how it must be done. Then you phone him, lay it on thick about what a marvelous opportunity it is to help the poor and needy. . . . Look, I can't give you all the details, tell you what to do blow by blow. If you can't figure out something, then it's a no-go."

"I got it." Max thought a minute to make sure he did. Then, excitedly, he said, "AIDS! The Church wants to help the poor suffering homosexuals, but for obvious reasons they don't want the contribution made public. It has to be on the QT."

"Yeah, something like that might work."

"Sure it will. All in cash. No checks. It'll work."
Max was really into it now. "Okay, that's the scenario. Where do we go from there?"

"You arrange to meet him secretly, but not *too* secretly. Make sure it's a public place, like a park or shopping center. No back rooms. You got to be out in the open where you can be observed."

"Then what?"

"You give him a suitcase with the money."

Max slumped in despair. "But we haven't got the money."

Elgin laughed. "I wondered when you'd ask about that."

As he listened to Elgin revealing the details of his plan, Max began to grin. Then he laughed uproariously in delight. "I love it, I love it!"

"Don't love it too much. It all depends on how good a priest you are."

"Oh, I'll be good, I promise you that. I must have seen *Going My Way* at least six times!"

Brian was surprised that Lorraine not only agreed to play tennis, but played exceedingly well. He could have overpowered her, but if he eased up on his serve and volley, she could keep the ball in play. She moved well, had good form—tennis form, that was—played with stamina and energy and was competitive enough to give him an interesting game. What made it even more interesting was the fact that her brief tennis costume showed a lot of cleavage, as well as focused his attention on her long, slim, well-muscled legs. The sweat running down the valley between her breasts intrigued him. He pictured himself licking it off—and missed a ridiculously easy shot. A traitorous thought entered his mind, causing him to hit the next ball into the net. Bobbi's breasts were the standard by which he measured those of other women. Shaking his head violently to clear it, he

130

concentrated on his game, and barely won the final point.

She insisted on a second set, promising to get even, then ran out of gas the last few games, giving him an easy 6–2 win. At its end, shaking his hand across the net, she said, "I'm claiming it as a moral victory."

"You play well," Brian said. "You've had lessons?"

Lorraine smiled demurely. "I try to be good at everything I do."

Since they'd only done one other thing together, he laughed, then bent and kissed her salty lips. He put his arm around her sweaty back and led her in the direction of the house. "Sorry about the court. Haven't used it much." It was true. Bobbi didn't play, and she had been living here, not Brian. The clay surface needed a good bit of work.

"I was about to use it as an excuse for losing."

"Feel free. Want a drink first, or a swim?"

"Both!"

Brian carried both their tennis bags into the house and made two gin-and-tonics while Lorraine showered and changed. Her appearance in an all but nonexistent string bikini unsettled him. He exaggerated his reaction, grinning. She smiled, apparently pleased with her effect on him and his clowning. He came over to her with her drink, waited while she sipped thirstily, then kissed her with ardent enthusiasm.

"Swim, remember?" She patted his cheek and stepped around him, heading for the pool.

Lorraine Paul swam well, too, with long, powerful strokes. Obviously she'd gotten her second wind. Brian enjoyed watching her cut through the water, realizing that neither of the women he'd loved was athletic, although Bobbi swam fairly well. He and Jenny had never done anything athletic, unless one counted their activity in bed. Brian decided that didn't count.

131

Lorraine had hardly consumed his every thought during the day, but she had been on his mind. She represented a series of "firsts" for him. She was the first woman ever to go to bed with him on the first date and the first to do it again the next night. And here she was the third night. Strange. Brian certainly had no complaints. It had been a long time since he'd felt himself approaching sexual satiation. Readily available, enjoyable sex was a novelty, and it felt damned good. He wasn't going to analyze it. If there were strings attached, he hadn't discovered them. It bothered him vaguely that he was not in love with Lorraine. He was hardly being fair to her, loving Jenny as he did and screwing Lorraine. Yes, that was all it was. But, he told himself, since she didn't seem to mind, why should he?

As she climbed out of the pool ahead of him and reached for a towel, he said, "I suppose you're good at golf, too."

"Seven handicap. I'll beat you at the women's tees."

He laughed. "You probably would." When he climbed out and joined her, he said, "You're a good athlete. I like that."

Actually, Lorraine was exhausted, although she was determined not to show it. Judd Forbes had said Brian Hecht enjoyed sports. She figured it was a way to get to him, and so she had extended herself. "Any more fun and games?"

He got her meaning. "Maybe."

She smiled. "Too bad. I'd hoped the Olympics were over."

"All but the closing ceremonies."

"I see." She raised herself on tiptoes and kissed him lightly. "I just might be able to participate in that."

"Sooner or later?"

His mouth found hers, warming her lips. The kiss lengthened, deepened. At its end, she said

132

huskily, "It does seem a waste to get dressed twice, doesn't it?"

"Indeed." Carrying their drinks, arms around each other's waists, they walked toward the house. On the patio he heard the phone, excused himself, and broke away to go inside to answer. When he emerged, he said, "Better make it later. Max Hill is coming over."

Lorraine's eyes widened. "The actor? *That* Max Hill?"

"Yeah. I told you I'd try to help with your career."

"Thanks, Brian" She touched her wet hair. "I hope you have a dryer."

"Stay just the way you are. We need a new Esther Williams."

"Well, it's not *quite* a hovel, which is about the best I can say for it."

When Leon Kazinsky had phoned Sheryl at home to say he had something to talk to her about, she insisted on coming to his place, warning him not to touch a thing. She wanted to see how he really lived. "You cleaned it up while I was on my way over, didn't you?" she accused him now.

"Does it look like it?"

She laughed. "Hardly." The place was cluttered with newspapers, books, and magazines, mostly medical journals. Empty jackets from classical-record albums were another decorative feature. But she didn't see any discarded articles of clothing and there weren't any dirty dishes in the sink. "I'll bet you hid everything in the dishwasher."

"Use it once a week whether I need to or not," Kazinsky said virtuously.

She finished her tour, poking her nose into the bathroom, then the bedroom. The bed was made.

"I confess. I did that just before you came."

"You should've done the dishes instead." She laughed.

133

"So what do you think? Pretty bad, huh?"

It wasn't bad at all; indeed, just about what she'd expected. Leon Kazinsky was too involved in his work to give more than a passing thought to how he lived. "Bad? Bad as in bad, or bad as in good?"

"*Bad.*"

"No, it's not bad. But I wouldn't hire out as a butler if I were you." She moved closer to him and kissed him lightly. "The bed is sexy."

"You're incorrigible!"

"I know." She kissed him with greater intensity.

"Here I wanted to tell you something important, and all you want to do is go to bed." He sighed in pretended disappointment.

"That isn't bad, either." Sheryl smiled. "Okay, what's your news?"

"It's not exactly news. I've got a problem for you at the hospital."

"Now *you're* incorrigible! You're ignoring my most amorous advances to tell me that?"

"Yes. Her name's Susan Raimond."

Sheryl pouted. "I don't care what her name is. You could've told me about her at work, couldn't you?"

"I didn't have time."

"A likely story. You saved it for tonight and used it to lure me over here under false pretenses so you could have your way with me," she teased.

But Kazinsky didn't respond to her humor.

"I'm serious, Sheryl."

"I know you are, dammit!" She kissed him again, then stalked off and plopped down on his couch. "*Ouch!* I just got goosed by a spring!"

"Sorry, I should've warned you."

Sheryl gingerly shifted her position. "What about Susan Raimond? You do mean the child actress, don't you? Or she was, a few years ago."

"I didn't know that."

134

"You wouldn't. I saw her name in OB-GYN. She's across the hall from Adriana Barre. Are we talking baby?"

"Yes—or we should be. That's the problem—or, rather, the mother is."

"The mother? Oh, you mean Raimond's mother, Rita Farrell."

"You know her?"

"I know *of* her. Rita Farrell is one of the more famous—or maybe infamous—stage mothers in Hollywood. Susan Raimond can't . . ."—Sheryl hesitated—". . . break wind without her mother's permission."

He looked at her curiously. "How do you know these things?"

"Easy. I read something besides"—she made an expansive gesture to encompass his apartment—"medical journals. Leon, you have tunnel vision." She glanced in the direction of the bedroom. "Not that it's entirely bad."

Kazinsky didn't know what she was talking about, but let it go. "Susan Raimond is eight months pregnant and never went to a doctor till a couple days ago. Ham Dodd found a *placenta previa*. You know what that is?"

"Not sure." Actually, she didn't know at all, but as a Ph.D. psychologist in a medical environment she had learned never to reveal the extent of her ignorance.

"The placenta covers the os. Normally, it is expelled after the fetus. This time it's the other way around, which means the baby is certain to be born dead unless it is taken by cesarean. The mother won't allow it, and she's convinced the daughter."

"Why not?"

"Ostensibly it's a lot of garbage about the risks of the surgery. More likely the real reason is the scar."

"Is Raimond married?" Sheryl asked.

135

Kazinsky shook his head. "Father virtually un-known."

"So the scar would be a dead giveaway if she married a guy who thought she was a virgin. I see."

Again he stared at her. "You're very perceptive. Quick at figuring things out. That never occurred to me."

"I'm not surprised," Sheryl said airily. You're a little slow on the uptake. If you can't cut it, it doesn't exist."

"That's not fair." Kazinsky frowned.

"I know. I'm sorry, Leon. I gather you want me to convince Susan Raimond to save her baby's life."

"Either her or the mother."

"Thanks a lot." She stood up and walked away from him. "Wow! On one side of the hall is Adri-ana Barre, trying desperately to have a child . . ."

"And risking her own life, although she doesn't know that."

"On the other side is a spoiled brat, less than half her age, who's willing to kill off her kid. I wish I'd decided to enter some other profession. Life would be easier."

"Can you handle it, Sheryl?"

She shrugged. "Oh, sure. Duck soup." She sighed. "All I can do is try."

He came to her and kissed her. "That's all I ask. I know you'll succeed." He kissed her again, more earnestly, but Sheryl pulled away.

"You're dumb, Leon. If you want to get the lady in the sack, you don't lay a bad trip on her first. Sorry, but your bed no longer holds any fascina-tion for me—at the moment, anyway. I want a steak. You're buying."

"Really?"

"Really. It's time you took me out again, showed me off and spent some money on me." His

136

expression made her laugh. "Try to buck up. You'll get used to it!"

Charles Bridges had had his dinner served in his wife's room—beef Wellington, quite delicious, really, preceded by shrimp cocktail and consommé. He sat now, enjoying a glass of Zinfandel—California, but quite good. Adriana had eaten very little. She lay quietly now, eyes closed. He knew that she was concentrating all her energies on the baby, but he said, "Are you asleep?"

"No." She opened her eyes. "If you want to go, Charles, you may. I know I'm not very good company right now."

"I'd like to stay, darling, if you don't mind."

She looked at him, seeing him as though for the first time in a long while. He was her rock, her anchor. Such a fine, strong man, a man of integrity whose love for her had never wavered. "I do love you, Charles," she whispered.

The simple statement brought tears to his eyes, although he was not given to displays of emotion. He took her hand in his. "My dear, thank you. I feel . . . *privileged* to have such a miracle in my life."

Her beautiful face lit up with that wide, sweet smile. "I love you, among so many other reasons, because you pay the most outrageous compliments a woman ever received."

He smiled, too, as he squeezed her hand. "It's no empty compliment. Simple truth."

"Oh, Charles." Adriana sighed. "How can you put up with me?"

"With the greatest pleasure and pride." He changed the subject. "How are you feeling?"

"Fine," she said promptly. "Absolutely fine."

How like her. He'd never once heard her complain, though he knew how she had suffered. "The truth, Adriana. What about the pain?"

"Better, Charles, really."

137

"You think your . . ."—he never quite knew what to call it—". . . meditation is working?"

"I *know* it is. I learned the proper term for it today—biofeedback. A young psychologist on the staff here—quite beautiful, Charles, you'd love her—explained to me how it works. I really feel I'm accomplishing something. The mind truly *can* control the body. Many people think so."

"I hope you're right. You're a strong-willed woman, Adriana."

"I have to be, especially now."

She closed her eyes again, retreating into her inner world. Bridges sat silently for a while, sipping his wine, watching her serene face. Finally, "Adriana?"

"Yes."

"I love you, too."

"Oh, Charles." She smiled. "I know."

"I love our life together. You've brought me such happiness."

"Not nearly as much as you've brought me, but thank you for saying it."

"I mean . . . Adriana, we don't need a child to make our life together complete."

She opened her eyes, looked at him solemnly. "I know, but I want this child. I *must* have this child. I thought you felt the same."

"You know I do. A namesake, flesh of your flesh and mine." He sighed. "But Adriana, as much as I will love our child, I'll always love you more—always."

"What are you saying, Charles?" A tiny frown creased her brow.

"You and I were together before the child was conceived. We must still be together after he's born."

"Do you think I will love you less when I'm a mother?"

"Not at all. You misunderstand. I'm trying to

say that I don't want our marriage to be affected—if anything happens to the baby."

"Nothing is going to go wrong, Charles. I'm sure of it," Adriana said calmly.

But she had been sure before. "I just want you to know my priorities, Adriana—you and only you, first, last, and always. You are the most important person in my life."

She looked at his somber face a moment, then lavished the splendid smile on him. "You're being much too serious, Charles."

He hesitated. "Adriana, Hamilton explained to me that there is some . . . some risk to you if you go full-term with the child."

"There are risks to everything, Charles."

"True, but Adriana, my love, there are some risks I simply am not prepared to take. I want you to understand that."

Adriana laughed affectionately. "Oh, my dear, you're being much too solemn. Everything is going to be fine—the baby, me, our marriage. Trust me. I know what I'm doing."

He wished he could believe that.

The arrival of Maximilian Hill, somewhat earlier than expected, was slightly embarrassing to Brian. Lorraine was still upstairs touching up her make-up and fixing her hair, leaving him to explain what he was doing alone in the house with a woman who not only was not his wife, but quite obviously had the run of the place. He tried. "We played tennis, then swam. She's nervous about meeting you and wants to be at her best. Hopefully it won't take too long."

Max laughed. "I'm sure it'll be worth the wait."

They were in Brian's study, both of them holding tall drinks. Brian had showered and dressed hastily in slacks and a polo shirt. He'd shoved his bare feet into topsiders and his hair was still wet. "It's a lot to ask, Max, I know. This town is crawling with beautiful women who want to be movie stars."

"At least five thousand come to Los Angeles every day, I hear."

"So many?" Brian laughed. "They'd have better luck winning the lottery."

"Wouldn't they."

"Anyway, it strikes me that Lorraine has a certain quality that makes her a little different—I don't know how to express it. Class, maybe. She's blond, sort of patrician. Carries herself well."

"Another Grace Kelly? We could use one." He laughed. "Don't try to sell me on the lady, Brian. I'm happy to meet her, talk to her, do what I can, if it's only to point her in the right direction. I think anyone who's made it in this cockeyed business feels obligated to help out a newcomer."

"Thanks, Max. That's all I want to hear." Brian lifted his glass and drank, and Max did the same. To fill an awkward silence he said, a little too heartily, "So you're a friend of Hillary's."

"Yes—fortunately. She's a fine woman."

"Indeed." Brian was unsure what their relationship was, so he felt the need to tread lightly. "She's our Director of Nursing, as you know."

Max nodded. "As a matter of fact, I advised her to take the job. She wasn't sure she could handle it at first."

"Then you've known her awhile." Brian saw Max nod again. Casually, he added, "I gather you and Hillary might be more than just friends."

Max looked at him sharply. Brian Hecht looked like an upfront guy. Maybe appearances were deceiving, but in any event, what did it matter? He was determined to bring his affair with Hillary George out in the open. There had been more than enough skulking around—it was a major part of "the problem." "I love her very much. I hope to marry her," Max said.

140

Brian was surprised, but not too much. "Congratulations. You have excellent taste in women."

Broad, famous grin. "I like to think so."

"I guess you know her reputation." Brian saw the sudden tension and hostility in Max, and hastened to add, "Sorry—I didn't mean that the way it sounded. Hillary's an excellent nurse and a crackerjack administrator. She's also gorgeous. Many a man has come on to Hillary George, and many a man has been rebuffed. Among the hospital staff she's known as the 'praying mantis.' " He grinned. "It's not because she kills the man she mates with, but that a man would happily die to have the opportunity. If you've won her love, I congratulate you. I wish you both nothing but happiness. She certainly deserves it."

When Brian had begun talking about the praying mantis, Max had thought it stupid and tactless of the man, yet it came out all right because Hecht was obviously sincere in his admiration of Hillary. "I gather you're fond of her," Max said.

"I am indeed. I have the greatest respect for her. And please believe me when I say that I'm not one of the guys Hillary has had to fight off."

Max studied him closely, wondering how far he could trust this man. At last he said, "I'm going to take you at face value."

"I don't know any other way to be, Max."

Max nodded. His mind was made up. "Can I tell you something in strictest confidence? What I mean is, Hillary has a problem—therefore, I do, too. It occurs to me you might be able to help."

"Are you talking about Tommy?"

"Oh, his health is a problem, no doubt about it—probably her biggest one right now. Lord, I hope he'll be all right! Actually, I was speaking of something else."

Brian frowned. "Involving the hospital?"

"Yes, in a way. That's why you might be able to help."

141

Brian frowned. "You asked for confidence. I gather it's something Hillary wouldn't speak of."

"Never. But I think it's something you ought to know."

"I'm beginning to think so, too. Go on."

Max paused, getting his thoughts in order. "I'm not a hundred percent certain of all the facts—you will know better than I—but when Hillary was appointed Director of Nursing, I gather she passed over other people—senior people."

"Yes. She went from, I believe, floor nurse. She was promoted over head nurses and supervisors of nursing. That's the way Laura Carlyle wanted it. Is there a problem with that?"

"I think so. In fact, I know so. Most of the nursing staff accept her, but three don't—I believe you called them supervisors?"

"Supervisors of nursing, one for each shift." Brian thought a moment. "Dana Shaughnessy, Kathryn Quigley, and Barbara Brookes."

"That's right. It seems they've formed a . . . what's the word? Cabal, I guess. They want to force Hillary to resign and are apparently willing to do anything to accomplish it."

Brian laughed. "They can try all they want, but I guarantee there isn't much chance of it. Laura Carlyle has the greatest affection for Hillary, and Laura is the one who decides these things, not me. And if it *were* up to me, I can guarantee whose side I'd be on."

"I'm glad to hear it, but that's also part of the problem, I gather. To get rid of Hillary, they feel they have to pin something really heavy on her."

"Are you talking about moral turpitude?" Brian laughed. "Forget it!"

"She's been seeing me, Brian."

"Forget that, too. Hillary has every right to her own private life." He saw the grim expression on the actor's face. "What's going on, Max?" he asked quietly. "There's more to it than that, isn't there?"

142

"They hired some sleazy detective. He's been hanging around my place when Hillary's there, taking photos."

"You're kidding!" Brian was outraged.

"I wish I were. Hillary plans to resign."

"But why, in this day and age? I don't get it."

"She just is, Brian. Believe me."

It didn't make any sense to him. "Because of how this might affect Tommy?"

Max was relieved by Brian's assumption. He'd hoped to avoid mentioning Stillwell; in fact, knew he couldn't. "I think so."

"Yeah." Brian nodded. "It figures. She'd do anything for Tommy. If this detective sold the photos to some of those sleazy publications—we both know what they are—she'd figure the publicity would ruin both their lives. That about it?"

"Close, anyway." The remark was Max's way of avoiding telling a total lie.

Brian stood up and strode across the small study to stand behind his desk. "Thanks for telling me. Hillary never would have. She'd never come to Laura or me with a problem like this. I'm glad to know it. I'll get on it right away."

"Brian, Hillary'd kill me if she knew I'd said a word," Max put in.

"She'll never know, believe me."

"What are you going to do?"

"Not quite sure at the moment. Some subtlety is required—maybe a lot of it. But I guarantee you that if a choice is to be made between Hillary George and those three broads, there will be absolutely no contest."

"I love her very much, Brian," Max said.

"Good for you!"

A movement at the door attracted Brian's attention and he looked up. Lorraine Paul stood in the doorway, looking merely ravishing. She hadn't been wearing that low-cut dress when she'd ar-

143

rived. Apparently her tennis bag held more than rackets and balls.

"Sorry to keep you waiting," she said, moving gracefully into the room.

Brian grinned. "Some things are worth waiting for." He turned to his other guest, who had stood up. "Lorraine Paul, Max Hill."

As he took the hand she extended to him, Max was impressed. Beautiful woman. At once he agreed with Brian's description, classifying her as the epitome of elegant sexiness. But could she act? As they sat over drinks he asked tactful questions designed to elicit information about her training and experience.

Lorraine had been through all this before. She recognized that she would gladly give up her "profession" if she could make the same amount of money or more doing something else. That was extremely unlikely. At least Max Hill, whose talent she greatly admired, was treating her with respect, and it wasn't just a pretense designed to lure her into bed for a freebie. She didn't lie too much, for she had indeed studied acting—it was something to do—and had worked in summer stock in Connecticut before coming to Hollywood.

Max did the best he could. He recommended a couple of coaches and also volunteered to mention her name to some casting directors. If he heard of any part she might be suitable for—unfortunately, he was between films and didn't know of any at the moment—he'd certainly let her know.

When the evening was at an end and Max rose to leave, two thoughts flitted across his mind. One was that Brian Hecht had a good thing going with this chick. The other was that he had a vague feeling that he knew her from somewhere, but he couldn't pin it down.

At the door Brian said, "I appreciate your telling me about Hillary's problem. I mean that. And I promise I'll take care of it immediately."

144

"I know you will. And thanks. I mean that, too." Max felt he and Brian Hecht were on the same wavelength, so much so that he motioned with his head toward the study, where Lorraine was sitting, grinned, and said, "Have a good time."

And Brian did. Lorraine was so appreciative of his modest efforts on her behalf that she actually introduced him to several variations on the act of love that he'd never known existed. All in all, a most satisfactory evening.

# Chapter 8

Hamilton Dodd was incensed, Brian knew. He could see it in the man's eyes, his exaggerated, abrupt gestures. Words were not needed, but Dodd raged on. "I'm not going to have it, Brian! I should never have accepted her as a patient. If anyone thinks I'm going to stand still for the deliberate, needless death of a child, I have news for them!"

It didn't happen every day, thank God, but it was not unprecedented for Brian to be confronted by an irate, fuming doctor before breakfast. He applied his usual technique, an attempt at calm reasonableness, tinged with a certain amount of ignorance. Doctors were sometimes prima donnas, after all. "I know *you* understand the situation, Dr. Dodd, but I'm not sure I do. Explain the problem, please."

"That misguided brat, Susan Raimond, is eight months pregnant. She has a *placenta previa*. Unless the baby is taken by cesarean, the child will die! She refuses to undergo surgery—or, rather, her blasted mother won't let her. It is that simple."

"I see."

"No, you *don't* see, Brian! I regret more than I can say that I ever saw her as a patient. I won't be a party to this, not on my life. I want to get rid of her."

Brian sighed. "But you *did* see her as a patient, Dr. Dodd."

"I had no idea this would result! I cannot—will not—contribute to the death of a living fetus. Third-trimester abortions are not my thing."

"I understand, believe me. And I'm sympathetic. You want to be relieved of a difficult patient." Long pause. "I have to ask, Dr. Dodd. Will another physician take her?"

Dodd scowled. "No. No one would." He accompanied his words with a characteristic gesture of rubbing his nearly bald head. His frustration was most apparent. "What you're saying is that since I made the gross mistake of seeing her in the first place, and since no other obstetrician in his right mind would touch her, I'm stuck with her—and her blasted mother."

"I'm sorry."

"Look, Bel Air General can hardly want to be a party to this . . . this *murder*."

"Hardly," Brian agreed.

"Then throw her out. Dump her somewhere else, some charity hospital, some fly-by-night clinic where I don't practice medicine."

"And leave this hospital open to a suit? With that mother, I guarantee there will be one. No way, Dr. Dodd. I'm as stuck as you are. Besides, what hospital would take her?"

"Oh, God!" Again the characteristic gesture.

"What's the law on this?" Brian asked.

"You must know, Brian. The patient is seven-

147

teen years, eleven months old. She is not at the age of consent in California. Therefore, her mother must consent to the surgery. If she won't, we're up the creek."

Brian smiled, hoping to alleviate Dodd's agitation. "That's a Midwest expression, and you did say *crick*."

"Yeah, I'm from Ohio, little town called Gamble's Mills. Maybe we could send her somewhere where the age of consent is sixteen."

"I know you're kidding. Anyway, she's going along with the mother, isn't she?"

"Yes, unfortunately, although I think she could be reached."

Brian raised his eyebrows. "Ward of the court? Is that what you have in mind? Have some judge declare the mother incompetent, unjust, un-everything? Have a judge save the baby?"

Dodd managed the semblance of a smile. "Would be nice, wouldn't it?"

"I just can't see Bel Air General getting involved in an action like that. We have to think of something else." Brian frowned. "Is there no way to convince the mother?"

"Go ahead and try. Be my guest. I can tell you I really dumped on her. I pulled out all the stops." Dodd made a gesture. "Zilch."

"How about waiting a month until the girl reaches eighteen, the age of consent? If we can convince her, then—"

"Touch and go at best, Brian. Turning eighteen and having the baby will occur at the same time— I should say, having the stillbirth. Besides, if this thing goes on much longer, we're talking about a substantial risk to both mother and child."

"Really?"

"The girl is bleeding persistently from the os and vagina. We're giving her whole blood, but how much of that can a person take?"

"Have you told her that?"

148

"No, I've been saving it for the clincher. If all else fails, maybe it'll change the mother's mind." Dodd stroked his pate. "Look, it *could* happen, but chances are it won't. The kid is just young and healthy enough to lose a lot of blood and blunder through."

"And you're talking lawsuit if you exaggerate or lie. I understand." Brian pursed his lips in thought, then said, "Let's try another approach. There's a person on our staff—Sheryl James, staff psychologist, Ph.D. She's good with women patients. They relate to her. I'll sic her on the girl and her mother. Maybe she can do something."

Hamilton Dodd sighed. "Okay. I'll try anything. At the moment I feel like I live under a little black cloud."

Brian laughed. "And it's always raining. I read *Li'l Abner*, too."

When Brian discussed the problem of Susan Raimond with Laura Carlyle at their breakfast meeting, she kept saying, "Oh, dear, oh, dear." Then she added, "How disreputable!"

"Isn't it."

"How did this dreadful person ever become a patient here?"

"Apparently the problem is not the patient, but the mother. In any event, it was a mistake." He thought of telling her Judd Forbes had made it, but thought better of it. The responsibility was his own. "But there's a lot of hindsight involved here. No one could have foreseen—"

"Quite. I agreee. She's actually going to let her baby die." It was an expression of disbelief more than it was a question. "That simply cannot be allowed, Brian—not in my hospital."

"I know."

"Might it help if I spoke to her?" Laura said after a brief pause.

"It might." It was indeed a possibility. Laura

149

Carlyle was at her best handling delicate situations. "But not just yet. I'm going to ask Sheryl James to talk to both the girl and her mother."

"Sheryl James? Oh, yes, the staff psychologist."

"She's an excellent counselor, Laura." He hesitated. "She helped Jenny. Also Allison Boushay." He noted her puzzled expression. "You remember—the young actress whose face was so badly broken in an auto accident?"

"Of course. How is she?"

"Well enough to go home. Ben Singleton, her plastic surgeon, anticipates an excellent recovery."

"Very well. I'll stay out of it for the moment. Give your Miss James a chance."

"*Dr.* James."

"Of course." They ate in silence for a minute or two, finishing their ham and eggs. Suddenly Laura said, "Brian, are you convinced of my regard for you?"

He glanced across the table at Rosella Parkins, as though her impassive black face could give him a reading on what this was all about, but Laura's secretary-companion offered no help. "I was until you asked that question." He did not smile.

"I'm serious, Brian. You know I trust you implicitly. I have *complete* faith in your good judgment."

"Which means you really don't," Brian said flatly. "Why not just spit it out, Laura? Tell me what's on your mind."

Laura patted her lips delicately with her napkin. "A most vulgar figure of speech, Brian. I wish you wouldn't use it." She sighed. "I am in a most difficult position. I love both you and Roberta. I need you both. I want to please you both. It is not altogether easy sometimes."

Brian waited a moment, looking at her. When she did not continue, he said, "I do not want to place you in the position of making choices,

150

Laura—whatever is going on. Bobbi is your granddaughter, your only blood relative. If a choice needs to be made, it should be easy. I know it is the one I would make."

She was touched. "Thank you, Brian."

"Now what the hell is going on?"

She looked down at her hands, fingering the huge diamond Oliver Carlyle had given her. "Roberta has moved quite rapidly on the Community Outreach Program—more rapidly than I had expected or"—sigh—"I guess wanted. She is very enthusiastic." She looked at him now, the huge blue eyes possessed of almost immeasurable depth. "I can't discourage that, Brian. You know how much I want her—"

"Go on. What happened?"

"She asked me for a commitment of funds for the program. When I told her I needed to discuss the matter with you, she became . . . well, upset. She believes you disapprove of the program and—"

"She's right there!"

"—her involvement in hospital affairs."

"Right again."

"Brian, I *want* her involved in hospital affairs. She is my *granddaughter*."

"How much did you give her?"

"A hundred thousand, which includes medicine, supplies, and personnel services." Laura lowered her eyes. "Please, Brian, don't be angry with me. I know I should have talked to you first, but"—she made a gesture of futility—"there wasn't time. I—I didn't want to . . . to lose Bobbi—again."

It was one of the few times he'd heard her use the name "Bobbi." He was angry and more than a little hurt at being ignored. It turned his worst fears into confirmed certain knowledge. His wife was going to prove a disaster for him in this hospital. He couldn't control her. She would run to

Laura, whenever she wanted anything, go over his head. He'd lose the respect of his staff. His administration would soon be a shambles. This he had to prevent right now.

But when he spoke, his voice was level, soft, giving no hint of his anger. "Very well, Laura. It's done and can't be undone."

"Are you angry with me, Brian? Do you understand why I had to do what I did?"

"I do, yes. But I want to make my position absolutely clear to you. I want nothing to do with this community outreach nonsense—nothing at all. I don't want to be consulted about it. I will approve or disapprove of nothing. I don't even want to *know* about it. It is between you and her."

Laura was astounded. "That's impossible, Brian, and you know it. At the very least, your approval must be given for supplies, staff time."

"Then have her work with Judd Forbes. I'll tell him to account for the money up to a hundred grand." He saw her start to protest. "I mean it, Laura. I'm out of it. That's the way it is going to be."

"Oh, dear!"

"And one more thing. This is as far as her authority goes." His voice rose, took on an edge. "If she does one other thing in this hospital, gives one order, interferes with *anything* in the slightest way, unless it relates directly to her personal project, then you have my resignation. I mean it, Laura."

"Oh, dear, dear. How did you two ever reach such a state of antipathy?"

"It has nothing to do with antipathy or any other personal feelings. A hospital can have only one administrator. If another person—and it doesn't matter who it is—can run to you behind my back, about *anything*, it doesn't matter how picayune and insignificant, then I might as well close up shop. Do you understand?"

152

"Yes, of course. We've always worked this way."

He wanted to say *until now*. Instead, he abruptly changed the subject. It was what he'd planned to speak to her about before she'd put him off stride. "What do you think of Dana Shaughnessy?"

"Think of her?" Laura frowned. "I don't know that I think anything. She's been with us a long time. I've always considered her competent, if a bit severe."

"What about Kathryn Quigley? Barbara Brookes?"

"The other supervisors? What do I think of them?" She saw him nod. "About the same, I suppose. Why do you ask?"

"Why did you pass them over and appoint Hillary George Director of Nursing?"

"I think you know. You concurred in the appointment."

"I did indeed. I thought it brilliant. But for my own reasons. I've never been quite sure what yours were."

"For choosing Hillary?" Laura pursed her lips, patted her hair as she thought. "I wanted a fresh start, a new point of view, someone not encumbered by the past. That's basically it, I think."

"To do what? Accomplish what?"

"Well, I can tell you what I told Hillary. I was a nurse here once, you know. If there is one aspect of this hospital I know inside and out, it is nursing. I told Hillary I wanted discipline among the nursing staff, application of the highest standards, but administered with a lighter hand. I wanted the nurses to be motivated by pride in their professionalism and loyalty to this hospital and its goals, rather than—"

"Fear."

"Exactly." She looked at him quizzically. "Why are you asking me all this, Brian?"

153

"You asked me to discover what, if anything, was bothering Hillary, remember?"

"Yes."

"It seems the three supervisors are having difficulty in accepting Hillary as their superior."

"She told you that?"

"No, Hillary would never speak of such a thing. She would try to work out her own problems, not run to me or you. I found out from another source."

"Precisely what is going on?" Laura asked.

"I'm uncertain of the details, but apparently there is some insubordination going on, some"—he smiled grimly—"lack of enthusiasm, shall we say, in carrying out her orders. I believe the usual term is *foot dragging*." He didn't want to tell her more, not yet anyway.

"Goodness! I had no idea."

"Nor I until yesterday."

"Where did you get this information?"

"I'd rather not say, if you don't mind. But I consider it an unimpeachable source."

Laura accepted that, but said, "The supervisors seem fine to me. I see at least one of them nearly every day."

"Apparently they're rather clever. They do nothing overt. Theirs are more sins of omission than commission."

"What do they hope to accomplish?"

"For Hillary to fail, for you to lose confidence in her, replace her with one of them, as they felt should have occurred in the first place."

"I see." She looked away a moment—at Rosella Parkins, actually—dumbfounded by this startling news. "Do you know anything about this, Rosella?"

Rosella, impassive as ever, shook her head. "No, I don't, Laura."

She turned back to Brian. "Do you want me to

154

speak to the supervisors or to Hillary—although now hardly seems the time, with Tommy so ill?"

"I want this to be kept in the strictest confidence among the three of us, Laura, for the time being. Say nothing to anyone. Let me handle it, please. When I've ascertained all the facts and decided what course to follow, I will seek your concurrence."

"Very well. So be it." Considering how much she'd interfered with his administration already, she had no choice.

Brian's secretary had phoned to say he'd be dropping by, so Sheryl James was prepared. She offered him a seat in the leather chair across from herself in her little consultation area.

Brian Hecht began by grinning and saying, "I think I've been doing very well, don't you?"

She looked at him in puzzlement. "In regard to what?"

"Staying away from you."

She felt uncomfortable at first, then laughed. "Don't be too proud of yourself. It's only been a little over a week."

"Seems longer."

Sheryl had counseled Jenny Corban after she had been raped, which automatically meant involvement with Brian Hecht, Jenny's lover. He had been dissatisfied with the result of the couseling—Jenny's leaving. He had not liked being informed by Sheryl that he was part of Jenny's problem, not the solution, as he had hoped to be. Since Brian Hecht was Sheryl's boss, the big boss at Bel Air General, it had been a delicate, difficult situation, in the midst of which Brian had astonished her by impetuously sweeping her into his arms and kissing her. She had responded, couldn't seem to help it. Then he'd come to her place late at night. She had been tempted—oh, so tempted—but she'd sent him away, thank God!

"Time's relative, Brian," she said now.

"Relative to what?"

She shook her head. "We're both adults, Brian—in this case, *unconsenting* adults. Look, I feel strongly attracted to you, as I suspect you are to me. I could easily —but I won't. It would be an unnecessary complication in both our lives. Besides, as I told you, I don't get personally involved with my patients or with people who are important to them. It's a matter of professional ethics, which I'm sure you understand as well as I do. I like, respect, and admire you. I know you're going through a difficult time, but believe me, I'm not what you need. I'll be your friend. I'll talk to you till my tonsils fall out, and listen until my ears fall off. I'm available any time of the day or night. But on a purely professional basis. Agreed?"

"Agreed."

She was relieved at his prompt concurrence, and smiled. "Now, what do you want to talk to me about?"

"A patient named Susan Raimond. It seems she—"

"I know," Sheryl interrupted. "Leon Kazinsky told me. Isn't it ghastly?"

He blinked. "Leon told you? This situation only developed last night."

"I know." Her smile widened. "That's when he told me. Leon and I have been seeing each other."

"Really? *Leon?*" Brian was frankly incredulous.

"What a thing to say! I like Leon very much."

"But *Leon*—" Sheryl had turned him down in favor of *Leon?*

"I don't want to discuss him just now, if you don't mind," Sheryl said calmly. "As a matter of fact, I'd rather not discuss my personal life at all."

Bemused, Brian said, "Sounds serious."

"Maybe it is. Time will tell. You want me to talk to Susan Raimond?"

"And her mother. I guess you know she's the real culprit."

"Yes, but it's not going to be easy. There's not a whole lot I can do if neither of them is actually in favor of the idea. People have to want counseling for it to work. I don't see much hope of that in this case."

"Do your best. I just want you to know the hospital has a major stake in this." He explained briefly the problems he'd discussed with Ham Dodd.

"I can't make any promises, but I'll try," Sheryl said.

As Brian stood up, preparing to leave, he asked, "Have you heard from Jenny?"

"Yes. She phoned once. She seems to be doing all right." Pause. "She was wise to ask you to stay away for three months. That *was* her idea, you know, not mine."

"I realize that. But it's very hard."

Longer pause. "May I give you some gratuitous advice?" Sheryl asked.

"That means free."

"And therefore of little value," she replied, smiling.

"Shoot."

"Find someone else, Brian."

He nodded. "I'm working on it." Then he grinned. "But I can't help wishing it could be you."

Sheryl laughed. "I'll remember that on long, cold winter nights."

"If Leon doesn't distract you," he couldn't help adding.

"That's a distinct possibility," Sheryl purred.

Hillary could hardly bear it, but she forced herself to watch as her son's lungs were suctioned. The long, yellowish strings of thick, sticky mucus that

157

were removed sickened her. This was the enemy, insidiously draining the life from her beloved son.

The suctioning did help. Tommy was breathing a little easier now and was asleep, the mask over his handsome little face providing a fifty percent oxygen mixture, as well as Alupent, a drug that was supposed to keep the mucus loose.

Such a terrible disease! Relentless. And there was no cure, just regular physical therapy, that horrible pounding on the chest to loosen the mucus so it could be coughed up. The dreadful coughing that claimed so many young lives. The child simply became too tired to cough anymore, and the mucus built up, harboring pneumonia germs. That was what had happened to Tommy. To *Tommy!* If only she'd paid closer attention to him, been aware he wasn't coughing. It was all her fault. She had been too involved in her own problems. Never again, Hillary swore. Tommy was going to be her whole life from now on.

But for how long? Maybe not even through this day. *Oh, Tommy! Please live!* With proper therapy and care, Hillary knew that some cystic fibrosis patients were living into their twenties—even thirties—now. Oh, he'd get proper care from now on. She'd see that he did. Whatever was required, she'd do to stretch out every precious minute of life for him. Again she mentally cursed the disease. It affected the pancreas, too, interfering with digestion. It was so hard for him to eat. Terrible diarrhea. How small and thin he was!

Hillary was somewhat cheered by a visit from Laura Carlyle. The old woman, almost like a mother to her, simply hugged her close, saying nothing. There were no words. While Laura went to stand by Tommy's bed, looking down, shaking her head, Rosella Parkins clasped both of Hillary's hands, her soft brown eyes enveloping her in silent sympathy and encouragement.

After a minute or so, Laura turned back to Hil-

158

lary and hugged her again. Now she said, "I stopped at the chapel on my way down and will again this evening. I will continue to pray until he gets well." As though not even God could resist the will of Laura Carlyle.

Her eyes filled with tears, Hillary said, "Thank you."

"I believe in the power of prayer, Hillary."

"So do I. I'm praying, too."

"Just ask God to give your boy strength to fight this disease."

"I will." Impulsively, Hillary kissed her cheek. "God bless you, Laura." But would He listen to her, she who had caused one of His priests to forsake his vows? *The sins of the parents . . .*

First thing in the morning, Max had gone to the studio to pick up a priest's cassock from wardrobe. The wardrobe mistress was one of his most devoted fans and didn't even make him sign for it. In a public men's room, he applied a black moustache and small, neat goatee, just covering his chin, then donned steel-rimmed glasses. When he was admitted to Stillwell's office, he was relieved that the man didn't recognize either him or his voice until Max said his name.

Despite his distress, Stillwell managed to smile. "Most impressive. But why the disguise?"

"Two reasons. In case Dykes is following you, I want him to see you talking to a priest, not to Max Hill. Then I have to rehearse my role. I've never played a priest. If you have any suggestions for improvements, tell me. I want to be convincing."

Completely at sea, Stillwell said, "I don't understand."

"You will. Just listen. We are about to do a number on one Wallace Dykes."

As he told Stillwell the plan he'd worked out with Elgin, he was annoyed by Stillwell's repeated

159

shaking of his head. When he said, "I don't like it; I don't want to get involved in this," Max's anger flared.

"I don't care whether you like it or not! I care even less what happens to you, Your Eminence. I'm doing this for Hillary. Elgin's doing it to try to save the Church from a scandal you instigated. You're going along with it whether you like it or not!"

"But it's not right."

"The hell you say!" Max yelled. "Where was your great sense of right and wrong when you were screwing Hillary every chance you got?"

"Please, don't raise your voice." Stillwell sighed in defeat. "All right, I'll do whatever you say."

"You damned well better! Hillary has to get out of this mess you created, and this is the only way."

"All right. I told you I'd cooperate."

"Damned right!"

Roughly half an hour later, having rehearsed what he was to say several times, Stillwell had Dykes on the phone. Max listened on an extension, ready to prompt the Cardinal if necessary.

"Quentin Stillwell here."

"Oh, yes, Yer Eminence, to be sure." Dykes's voice was filled with contempt.

"We are interested in making a contribution to your organization."

"We?"

"Yes, a contribution from Church funds."

"It figgers that's what they'd be." His laughter was gleeful.

Stillwell glanced at Max on the other phone, shaking his head in dispair. Into the receiver he said, "It would be most helpful if you would treat this matter with greater seriousness."

"Oh, I'm serious, Yer Eminence, *real* serious. Where and when do I get this *contribution*, as you so aptly put it?"

160

"That is the purpose of this phone call. In the next few minutes you will receive another call, this time from Father Jackson. He will arrange to meet you. At that meeting he will talk to you about making a large, *anonymous* cash contribution to help relieve the suffering of AIDS victims."

"AIDS?"

"That is correct, Mr. Dykes."

Long pause on the line. "I don't like this, not a'tall. I'm dealing with *you*, buster, not no Father Jackson."

Stillwell saw Max nod encouragement to him. "I'm afraid you're going to have to, Mr. Dykes. Father Jackson controls these particular funds, the only ones immediately available in such a large amount. If you want your . . . what you want, then I advise you to go along. Believe me, there is no other way."

Silence, studded by an exasperated sigh. "But AIDS? I ain't no fuckin' queer!"

"Whether you are or not is immaterial, Mr. Dykes. But, believe me, it is vital to your self-interest that Father Jackson be convinced that you are a bona fide representative of an organization helping AIDS victims. Father Jackson knows nothing of the real purpose of the money. He is sincere in wanting to make a substantial contribution toward the care of AIDS victims. If you will permit me, Mr. Dykes, I suggest you clean up your language, put on your better suit, and try to act respectful, polite, sincere, and grateful when you meet with Father Jackson. If he has any notion that the money is not going to be used for the desired purpose, I'm afraid you are entirely out of luck."

"And so are you and yer lady friend, Yer Eminence."

"Agreed," Stillwell said coolly. "But my disgrace will not enrich you by one red cent."

Very long pause. "I still don't like it. Why can't ya just hand over the money to me in person?"

"Because it is completely out of the question." He saw Max mouthing some words at him. "There are certain procedures that must be followed, accepted practices in any large organization, especially one as large and *wealthy* as the Church."

Long sigh, followed by a muttered obscenity. "Okay, I'll go along with it, at least long enough to check out this Jackson dude."

"May I respectfully suggest, Mr. Dykes, that he will also be checking *you* out—most carefully, I assure you. I believe the expression is: *Don't mess up.*"

Sheryl had no particular strategy for confronting Susan Raimond, other than a conception of the mental attitude she wanted to project. She would play it by ear, ask questions, react to the patient's replies. All standard technique.

She had hoped to be alone with Susan, because she knew it would make her initial task easier. But what was the use? Even if she convinced Susan, the girl's mother would overrule her. Rita Farrell was the nut that had to be cracked. A hard nut, too.

Susan Raimond was not alone, of course. Her mother was there, looking very chic in pale green, her red hair immaculately coiffed. She also looked very uptight, even hostile, to Sheryl. Susan was about what she had expected—a worried, intimidated young woman. She also looked quite different than Sheryl remembered from her early films. Such a darling she'd been on the screen. But she had not matured well. Sheryl introduced herself.

"Now it's a shrink, is it?" Rita snapped. "This hospital seems to have an unending supply of people determined to make Susan do something that is not in her own best interest."

The occasional lie never hurt. Sheryl addressed

162

it to Susan, smiling as she said, "Actually, I came to see how you're feeling—if there is anything I can do for you, anything you want to talk about."

"I'm fine." The words were automatic, but clearly Susan Raimond was hardly fine.

Standing by the bed, Sheryl sought a diversion. "I saw many of your films, Miss Raimond. You were so precious—I especially liked *Summer Rain*."

"Thank you. It was my favorite, too." Her round face did seem more attractive when she smiled.

"And *Dragon Weed*. That must have been a hard part to play—the deathbed scene and all. And you were so young! Not more than six or eight."

"Actually, I was ten, but they made me up to look younger."

Sheryl smiled. "You certainly convinced me." Now she deliberately turned her attention to the mother. "It must have been a tremendous challenge to you, Miss Farrell, keeping Susan on an even keel while she was making such a difficult film. Susan played a little girl who dies. How did you explain the role to her, keep her from being upset?"

Rita Farrell was surprised. This was hardly the approach she had expected from Bel Air General's shrink. "I talked to her, told her the difference between play-acting and real life. Susan and I have always had an honest relationship."

"I'm sure. But weren't you concerned that the death scene might traumatize Susan? After all, most children of ten have no conception of death, particularly the death of a child."

"I know what you're getting at," Rita accused.

Sheryl spoke calmly. "I see what you mean. But actually I was only making conversation. I had not made the connection you apparently have." She wanted to say to Susan that this was not play-

163

acting anymore. This was a real, live human being she was carrying within her, but Sheryl did not want to antagonize Rita Farrell unduly, so she said to Susan, "I understand you are having some problems with your baby." The frightened expression in the big brown eyes provided the answer. "Do you want to have the baby, Susan?" she asked gently.

"Yes!"

The answer surprised Sheryl and obviously shocked Susan's mother.

"What are you saying, child?" Rita said.

"What I mean, Mother. I want the baby—I mean, I don't want anything to happen to the baby."

Rita Farrell seemed relieved. "Of course you don't, darling. No one does." She moved her hands in a gesture of futility, sighed. "But it is in God's hands. This . . . this *unfortunate* location of the placenta is something no one could have foreseen."

Now Sheryl was shocked. This woman had worked it out in her own mind so that everything was God's fault. God had created the problem— let Him solve it. Sheryl wanted desperately to argue with her, express her outrage, but it would be a violation of professional ethics to do so. Instead, she said mildly, "I see what you mean, Miss Farrell."

"If you do, then you're the only person around this hospital who does! Everyone else seems perfectly willing to put my daughter at great risk, both to her life and future, just so they can say they changed what Nature intended. They all seem terribly eager to play God!"

Sheryl hoped her amazement didn't show. This woman could enter the psychological Olympics and win a gold metal for rationalization. She turned to the girl. "How do you feel about it, Susan?"

"As I said, I want the baby to be born . . . okay,
but . . ."

Sheryl ignored the "but." "Do you want to keep
the child?"

Sigh. "I'd like to, but I can't. It's impossible."

"I understand. You'll give up your baby for
adoption?"

"Yes."

Sheryl smiled encouragingly. "That's a very
wise decision. There is such a shortage of healthy
babies and so many parents eager to love them. I
know you'll make some deserving couple very
happy. Have you spoken to anyone from an adoption agency?"

"No, not yet."

"I'm sure the minute the baby is born they'll be
beating a path to your door . . ."—she laughed—
". . . or bedside, in this case. The hospital will
help you deal with them, if you wish."

Susan glanced at her mother and saw a puzzled,
wary expression on her face. "Thank you. I might
want to do that."

"Has Dr. Dodd told you whether it will be a
boy or girl?"

"He thinks it's a boy, but the baby wasn't turned
quite right for him to see for sure on ultrasound."

"Would you prefer a boy?"

Susan shrugged. "It doesn't matter."

Sheryl smiled. "Not much to be done about it
one way or the other. If it were a boy and you
were able to keep him, what would you name
him?"

"I—I hadn't thought about names." Pause. "I
always sort of liked David."

"Me, too. One of my favorites. Davids are al-
ways thoughtful, sensitive people." She laughed.
"I believe there's a lot in a name, Shakespeare to
the contrary. Mike Royko, the columnist from
Chicago, insists that if you call a boy Bronco or
Rocco, he'll grow up to be a football player."

165

Susan smiled. "Maybe there's something to that."

"I've never had a child, although I want to one day—very much," Sheryl went on.

"Are you married?"

"No. But I'm working on someone. He's a doctor here at the hospital. I don't see much of him, though. I think he's already married to Bel Air General."

Susan laughed, feeling comfortable and relaxed for the first time in months.

"It's very nice of you to drop by, Dr. James." The voice of Rita Farrell, saccharin and syrupy, broke in. "I'm sure Susan's enjoying your visit, but I think she ought to rest now."

"Of course." Sheryl patted Susan's hand. "Maybe I can stop by and talk with you again."

"That would be nice. Thank you." The smile on Susan's face proved she meant it.

Rita Farrell stood up, accompanied Sheryl to the door, then outside into the corridor, closing the door behind her. Her voice when she spoke was hardly more than a whisper, but a venomous one. "I know what you're trying to do, Dr. James. Believe me, it won't work!"

Sheryl raised her brows. "I have no idea what you mean, Miss Farrell."

The sharp, agonizing pain stabbed at Adriana, and she cried out, but not too loudly. Fortunately, she was alone and unheard. She brought her hand to her mouth, covering it tightly with her fingers to prevent a recurrence. *God, help me, please!* Then she closed her tear-filled eyes, trying desperately to increase her mental efforts to subdue whatever was raging inside her. But the pain made it so terribly hard to concentrate. . . .

166

# Chapter 9

St. Bonaventure's in Watts was perhaps the least of the parishes in the diocese, not so much in terms of the faithful, who loved and supported it as best they could, but in terms of the physical plant. The church building was old, not well built to begin with, and currently in a state of disrepair that made it hopeless. It had been condemned and was slated to be abandoned and torn down. Only the great need of the parishioners kept it still in use.

The rectory was as run-down and dilapidated as the church, though it was scrupulously clean. The furniture, what there was of it, was polished, though the wood was scarred, the upholstery worn to the same degree as the threadbare carpet. This was the place Cardinal Stillwell—after inquiries, for he was not familiar with Los Angeles—had recommended as a meeting place. He had also arranged for Father Norris, the parish priest, to vacate the premises for an hour.

167

Max thought it would do. The church and the rectory looked precisely like the place where a priest would reside if he was so much involved in charitable good works and the task of uplifting social consciousness. It was the perfect setting for the scene he was about to play—Max had even thought to bring framed photos of his own mother and father to put on the desk. He was ready to play the most important role of his life.

He met Wally Dykes on the steps of the rectory, greeted him enthusiastically, and escorted him inside, talking nonstop in a hearty voice about "St. Bonny's." Then he led Dykes into the study and offered coffee—wine, perhaps? They both had a little red wine.

Dykes had put on a suit, however rumpled, and was trying to act like a representative of a reputable charity. Clearly, though, he was on guard, and mystified as well. This broken-down church and this black priest hardly looked capable of coming up with half a million bucks.

Max had elected to use a Southern drawl, knowing that a bigot like Dykes would expect it of a black priest. He was familiar with it, having used it in his last film.

"The Auxiliary Bishop himself phoned me to tell me of your excellent work, Mr. Dykes. I can't tell you how much I admire what you're doing. Such courage surely will have its reward in heaven, if not on earth."

"How's that?"

Max shook his head. "You're too modest, Mr. Dykes. The whole country—the whole world—is scared out of its wits about AIDS. They'd rather pretend it doesn't exist. But here you are, doing all you can to raise money to help those poor suffering men—and women and children, too. They're the most unfortunate of all, aren't they?"

"Yeah—I mean, yes, they sure are."

"The disease is so terrible, a regular scourge.

168

Some people believe it is God's punishment for . . . for licentious behavior. But I don't believe that for a moment, do you, Mr. Dykes?"

"No—no, Father, of course not."

"Our poor brethren in Africa are suffering terribly. Quite dreadful outbreaks there, I understand. And there is no more homosexuality practiced there than anywhere else, which just goes to show that no single segment of the population can be singled out as being particularly depraved or especially licentious."

"Sure, I think so, too."

"Is your organization hopeful of finding a cure?"

"Cure? For AIDS? Oh, sure. No doubt about it."

"Soon, do you think?"

"Oh, yeah. I was talking to a doc just the other day—I mean a research scientist." Dykes shook his head. "I don't pretend to understand it, not being in that . . ."—he started to say *racket*—". . . that *business* myself, but—"

"I know what you mean. Science is so . . . well, scientific." Small laugh. "But this scientist you spoke to felt progress was being made toward discovering a cure?"

"Oh, yeah, he sure did."

Max smiled, feeling the false moustache pull at the skin of his upper lip. "That's wonderful news. Most encouraging. Did he say anything about progress in creating a vaccine to immunize people against this awful disease?"

Dykes hesitated. "He did mention it, but—" He let a shrug finish the statement.

"More difficult. I understand. I must say, Mr. Dykes, I am impressed with the dedication and energy you devote to your cause. God bless you, my son." Max's smile could not have been more beatific. "I want you to know that we intend to help you continue your good work. God knows

169

the suffering victims need all the help they can get. It's all so very sad."

Dykes felt he was getting a little more comfortable with his role. "That's so true. We do need help. Tough to find volunteers. Nobody wants to get near those—"

"The victims. How well I know! And that is saddest of all. We must attempt to alleviate the public's fear of the disease."

"Yeah, but everything costs money, you know, Father. The bottom line is money."

A gentle nod. "Isn't it always."

"Are you talkin' money—a contribution?" Dykes burst out.

"Hopefully quite a generous one, Mr. Dykes."

"How much?"

"We'll discuss that in a moment. First, I have to explain something about a little . . . problem we have." Max assumed a most somber expression as he pushed his spectacles up on his nose. "The very fear of which we just spoke—and like all fear, it is based upon ignorance, as you know—makes it difficult for the Church as a whole to be instrumental in helping AIDS victims. We have found that as soon as we announce a concern for the victims themselves, not research, which the public approves—our level of contributions drops off. Quite dramatically, I might add. We have considerable difficulty in overcoming many of our parishioners' prejudice and hostility toward AIDS victims. They are mistakenly convinced that the disease is the victims' just deserts for the sins they have committed."

"Yeah, it's a crying shame," Dykes said piously.

"We who do God's work have a responsibility to help the suffering physically as well as spiritually, and that, of course, means financially. If we cannot do so aboveboard, we intend to do it *below* the board—if I might coin an expression." Max allowed himself a slight smile. "The Church in-

170

tends to make a donation to help AIDS victims. To avoid publicity which might affect our regular contributors adversely, we propose to make the donation in cash, which is, of course, untraceable, and even more important, anonymously. I'm sure you understand." He waited for Dykes to make some sort of comment, but he did not. Dykes was a clod, Max thought. How did he ever get into the blackmail racket? "What we need to know, Mr. Dykes, is how your organization would make use of our funds."

"Use?"

"Yes. How would our money be spent?"

"Oh, *used*. I get it." Pause. "It would depend on how much money there was."

"A substantial amount. At least, it is to a parish priest like myself. I am, you understand, only the Church's agent in this transaction. I know the need is so great that no sum is sufficient. I assume you have hospitals—clinics you support?"

"Oh, yeah, we got 'em. Lots of 'em."

"What are some?"

That stopped him. "Well, let me see. . . . There's . . ."

In spite of the seriousness of the situation, Max was having a hard time keeping a straight face. He was thankful for the beard and moustache. Leaning back in his chair, he said, "Well, it doesn't really matter, Mr. Dykes. I understand why you don't want to reveal specific details. You're trying to keep the victims under wraps, so to speak, to protect their privacy."

"Yeah, that's it, Father. They don't like publicity."

"I'm sure. Do you do counseling to help the patients cope with what has happened to them?"

"Oh, sure, we do lots o' that."

"And social service work, no doubt. The effect on the families must be dreadful."

"It sure is. Yeah, you can say that again."

Broad smile. "Well, I am impressed, Mr. Dykes. I've heard what excellent work your organization does and I'm discovering how true that is. I will recommend that the contribution be made without delay." Somber hesitation. "Do I have your personal word that you will honor the anonymous nature of the gift?"

"Oh, sure, you betcha!"

"I don't mean to belabor the point, but if any word about the source of the funds leaked to the press, it would be *embarrassing*, to say the least."

"I unnerstan', Father. You can count on it. Mum's the word."

"I can tell you're a man of discretion. Very well. I will so recommend to my superiors."

"You haven't said how much," Dykes prodded.

Max feigned surprise. "Haven't I? We are discussing half a million dollars, I believe. At least that's the figure that has most often been mentioned."

Dykes grinned from ear to ear. "That has a nice ring to it."

"We want to be generous. We are sincere and we want our money to be put to good use, have an impact on the welfare of mankind."

"Oh, it'll have an impact, all right! When do I get it?"

"I must talk to my superiors. Then the cash has to be assembled. No more than a few days, I should think."

Dykes's grin faded. "Not sooner?"

"I understand your urgency. The need is so great." Max smiled. "I'll do what I can to speed things up." He stood up. The interview was over. "It has been a pleasure to meet you, Mr. Dykes. Men like you are few and far between." *Thank God!* "By the way, are you Catholic?"

"Yeah, but I don't get to Mass as often as I'd like. Busy, you know."

"I see." Dykes had made no move to leave. "Is

172

there something else, Mr. Dykes?" Max asked pointedly.

"Yeah, Father. I got a question. How come a deal like this—half a million bucks is a lotta dough—is being made in, no disrespect intended, in a little place like this?"

Max looked at Dykes severely. "Appearances can be deceiving, Mr. Dykes. I asked for St. Bonaventure's because this is where my people are and where the need is greatest. My true interests lie here. I would not be happy in a more affluent parish. Do you understand?"

"Sure, sure, but—"

"You wish to know how I happen to be involved in allocating such large sums of money? Quite simple, Mr. Dykes. I have certain duties in the diocese—Catholic charities, to be precise. I try to be useful where I can. It is sometimes more convenient for me work from the rectory here rather than in the offices downtown."

"Okay, sure, makes sense."

"I should have made that clear in the beginning." Max went to the study door. "I don't want to keep you any longer, Mr. Dykes. As you say, you're a busy man."

Dykes now stood up and followed Max down the hall. "What happens next?" he asked.

"About the contribution? As I said, I must make my recommendation and then—"

"I mean, when do I hear from you?"

Big smile. "Oh, I understand. I'll phone you in a day or two, Mr. Dykes. We'll set a time to meet again. It's quite simple."

"A day or two, huh? No sooner than that?"

"As soon as possible—ASAP, as they say." Max's smile was benevolence itself. "I realize you're in a hurry, but remember, patience is a virtue. I guarantee, Mr. Dykes, you'll get what's coming to you all in due time."

\* \* \*

Though Adriana Barre would not admit her pain, Hamilton Dodd knew her pregnancy was in serious trouble. The numbers left no doubt. Most alarming was the heart rate of the fetus. It had varied all over the place, shooting up close to one hundred eighty at one point, but was now consistently low—one hundred twenty, sometimes falling a little below. Adriana's pulse was rapid, consistently one ten, sometimes higher, and her blood pressure never dropped below one sixty over a hundred. All this indicated hypovolumia—reduction in her blood supply. No wonder. She continued to pass bright red clots of blood in spite of the enforced bed rest, medication, and transfusions. It was a case, Dodd thought wearily, of putting the whole blood into a vein in her arm, then watching it run out her vagina.

Most worrisome to Dodd were Adriana's blood-fibrin levels. Normally between one fifty and four hundred per hundred ccs of blood, they were now below a hundred. The continued bleeding was exhausting her blood-clotting mechanism. She was being put at an intolerable risk.

Dodd did not talk to Adriana first, but to Charles Bridges—privately, in the lounge behind the nursing station. He began by explaining the significance of the numbers, then said, "We must operate at once—*now*, Charles. If we do not, I cannot be responsible for either the baby's welfare or Adriana's."

Bridges's eyebrows raised. "Are you saying Adriana's life is in danger?"

"I am, yes. Adriana's continued bleeding is exhausting her blood fibrin, the ability of the blood to clot. This also means that if we perform the cesarean now and take the baby, the results are difficult to predict. With her reduced clotting, there is a risk of continued bleeding after the surgery."

"You're saying—"

174

"I am saying just that, Charles. I have to be honest with you. Adriana is in danger right now. I don't want to be an alarmist. Hopefully it will work out. But I must tell you there will be difficulties. The longer we wait, the greater those difficulties will become, and the greater the risk."

"Oh, my God!" Charles Bridges leaped to his feet and went over to the window behind the coffeepot, staring out, seeing nothing. "The baby?" he said without turning around.

"Right now the baby is in extremis. It is being starved both of food and oxygen because of that hematoma behind the placenta."

"Can the baby be saved?"

Dodd sighed and shook his head. "I honestly don't know."

"Odds?"

"Not very good, Charles. A betting man wouldn't take them."

"Christ!" Bridges covered his face with his hands, held them tight against it. His whole body trembled as though he were crying. But when he turned back to Dodd there was no evidence of tears, only grim determination. "All right. Let's go talk to her."

But Adriana Barre refused to accept what they said. "It is *my* baby and *my* body. I will not let either or both of you decide what is to happen to me and my child!"

"Listen to me, Adriana, please—" Dodd began, but she cut him off.

"No, *you* listen, Hamilton. You said all this to me the other day, that I needed an immediate cesarean. I didn't believe you then, and I don't believe you now."

"But—"

"Did I not improve, Hamilton? Did I not help the baby?"

Dodd was puzzled, but only for a moment. "You're talking about that damned biofeedback?"

"You may damn it if you wish, but it works. I *know* it does."

"It obviously isn't working anymore, Adriana. Your condition is worsening by the minute."

"That's because I haven't been concentrating properly. There have been . . . distractions, too many of them. If you and Charles will just leave . . . I'll do what . . . must be done."

Both Dodd and Bridges realized she was in such pain that she could hardly speak. "As your doctor, I cannot allow this, Adriana," Dodd said flatly.

"You don't know everything, Hamilton. One of the other doctors here said biofeedback . . . would work. That is . . . correct. I'm . . . sure of it."

Dodd was incredulous. "Who told you that?"

"A doctor. I—I can't . . . remember her name . . . Oh, yes—Dr. James."

A furious Hamilton Dodd went to the phone at once.

Hillary George looked up from Tommy's bed at the sound of footsteps. Tears filled her eyes at the sight of her visitors. She hugged short, buxom Carmen Rodriguez, speaking to her softly in Spanish. When Carmen went to stand at the bedside, weeping softly, Hillary looked at Max Hill.

"How is he?" Max asked.

"Not very good. His fever is still over a hundred and five. Breathing is an ordeal."

"He'll make it, Hillary."

"I hope so."

Max felt so awkward, so helpless. He wanted to take her in his arms, comfort her, but he felt constrained, among other things by the large box containing a ship model he carried. "I—I phoned Brian Hecht to let us in," he said.

"I'm glad you did. I should have . . . I haven't been able . . . to think of—"

"I know." He put down the box, stepped forward, and put his arms around her, holding her

176

close, her head against his shoulder. They stood there for a long time. Then Max said, "You look so tired, Hillary. Have you slept at all?"

It felt so good to be held in Max's embrace. It was almost as though some of his strength seeped into her. "A little, I think. In the chair."

"Have you eaten?"

She raised her head, looked at him, eyes searching his handsome face. "Eaten? I don't know. I guess. I—I can't remember."

"You won't be any good to Tommy if you're exhausted."

"I'll be all right, Max."

"Yes, and I'm going to see that you are." He went over to the sleeping boy, gently patted his leg. Then, in Spanish, he asked Carmen to remain with Tommy while he took Hillary downstairs for something to eat. When he turned back to her, he saw her hesitation. "I won't take no for an answer. Tommy'll be all right with Carmen."

They had to go to the public dining room because Max was not an employee. He ordered chicken soup and a roast-beef sandwich for her, coffee for himself.

The hot broth made her feel better almost at once. She even tried to smile. "Thank you. I guess I was hungry."

Max grinned. "I guess I don't need to tell you about the therapeutic benefits of chicken soup."

She looked at him, great intensity in her gold-flecked eyes. "Thank you for coming, Max. I'm so glad to see you."

"I couldn't stay away any longer, Hillary. I love you—and I love Tommy."

She bit her lower lip, hard. Tears filled her eyes. "I don't deserve it," she whispered.

"Allow me to decide that, please. Now eat."

She obeyed—a few spoonfuls of soup, a bite of sandwich—then wiped her lips with her napkin, staring down at her plate. "I've been so awful to you, Max."

"I think so, yes."

"It's all so . . ."—a despairing shake of her head—". . . so dreadful."

"It's going to be all right, Hillary. Believe me, everything's going to work out."

She gaped at him. "How do you know?"

He didn't want to tell her what he and Stillwell were doing, but he wanted to reassure her. "Don't worry about it, Hillary. I mean it. Just trust me."

Still she stared. "I asked how you know."

He leaned across the table and took her hand. "Would you like to know how I know I love you? Let me tell you. When a man loves a woman, *really* loves her, he wants to protect her. After two wives and assorted supremely cunning girl friends, I finally learned that from you. I suppose it's some kind of primeval, primordial instinct having to do with preservation of the species."

"All that?" She had to laugh, in spite of herself. "Protect me from what?"

"From anything and everything," he said quietly. "Anything that might harm you or Tommy."

She narrowed her eyes. "What exactly are you up to, Max?"

"I dislike women who poke their noses into a man's affairs."

"Who have you been talking to?" Hillary persisted.

"Who I talk to or don't talk to is entirely my business."

"Oh, God! Arthur? Have you talked to Arthur?"

Max squeezed her hand. "Right now your priorities are to eat, get some rest, and look after Tommy."

"You know who he is. He came to you, didn't he?" She shook her head, stunned. Max said noth-

178

ing. "You know everything, don't you?" she whispered.

"I know you are a woman with more than enough on her mind, really important stuff, without taking on anything else. Everything is under control."

"I'm sorry, Max—so very sorry." Hillary's eyes filled with tears and she lowered her head.

"Will you stop, *please!* Everything works out, somehow—sometimes when it seems impossible and we least expect it." He saw her start to protest. "Let it be, Hillie. I mean it."

She heard the nickname but made no comment.

Brian chose the four o'clock shift change to visit the nursing supervisor's office. Dana Shaughnessy sat at Hillary's desk; Barbara Brookes, just coming in for the second shift, was seated across from her. His ostensible reason for coming was to inquire how things were going with Hillary off duty, looking after her son. Did they need anything?

"We have everything quite under control, Mr. Hecht. Thank you," Shaughnessy replied.

Brian felt he was seeing her for the first time— mid-fifties, square, fleshy face, salt-and-pepper hair drawn severely in a bun, cold, gray eyes. No wonder the staff called her "the battle axe." He smiled. "Such competence is greatly appreciated."

He turned to Barbara Brookes. Twenty years younger than Shaughnessy, or nearly so, dyed blond hair, ripe mouth. Pretty, he supposed, opulent breasts well displayed in the Empire-style uniforms, which were de rigeur at Bel Air General, supposedly designed by Laura herself back in the days when she was attracting the attention of Oliver Carlyle. Brian knew Brookes's reputation— considered herself irresistible and didn't resist much. He thought of her as merely obvious. "Any problems for you, Barbara?"

"Not that I know of." Her smile was lavish, pure

179

invitation. She would happily disrobe for Brian Hecht in a second, sure she could thereby cement a relationship between them, much to her own benefit.

"I assume Kathryn Quigley is coping similarly."

"We've heard nothing to indicate otherwise, have we, Barbara?"

"No, indeed."

Brian nodded. "Glad to hear it. It's comforting to know we have three such competent people backstopping Hillary during her time of crisis. The reports on Tommy are not very good, as you know."

"Most unfortunate," said Dana Shaughnessy.

After a deliberate pause, Brian said, as though as an afterthought, "While I'm here, I'd like to ask you both what you think of Hillary's performance as Director of Nursing. I mean, professionally speaking—I know how fond you both are of her personally." He waited for a response, and when none was forthcoming, went on. "All staff are evaluated regularly. I'd appreciate any input you care to give. It will be in the strictest confidence, of course."

The two women looked at each other, obviously uncertain of their ground. Barbara Brookes, always impulsive, spoke first. "I really don't know what to say, Mr. Hecht. She has not been here long—I mean as Director of Nursing."

"But you surely have formed *some* impression."

"I have, of course, but—"

"In strict confidence, as I said."

"Well-l . . . to be entirely honest, I keep thinking of the word *distraction* in regard to her. I feel she is *distracted* by her . . . her *personal* life."

"You feel she is not attentive to her duties?"

"That's one way of putting it, I suppose. She seems a little . . . well, like I said, *distracted*, lately. And, if I may say so—in confidence, of

180

course—Miss George is *distracting* to the staff and patients."

"Distracting? In what way do you mean, Barbara?"

"As I'm sure you must realize, Mr. Hecht, she is very . . . very—"

"Attractive?" Brian suggested.

"Yes. She commands a lot of attention from the male staff and patients, and I don't mean for her nursing care. I . . . well, I hesitate to say it, but I think sometimes she isn't taken *seriously.*"

"I see. Thank you." He turned to the older woman. "Dana?"

She had had plenty of time to consider her words. "My real complaint is that she is lax about discipline. We must have discipline, you know. I fear that sometimes she is hesitant about cracking down on . . . on *loose* behavior. This may be a result of her . . . her . . . I'm not sure how to express it."

"Personal predilections, perhaps?"

"Yes. Perhaps."

"Thank you very much." He nodded at them both. "I appreciate your candor. I will keep your comments in confidence, but I'll consider them at evaluation time."

On his way back to his office, Brian made up his mind. Those two biddies would have to go. And he suspected Kathryn Quigley was no better.

Sheryl had heard of Leon Kazinsky's temper, but not seen it, not directed at herself, anyway. But the moment he stormed into her office just as she was preparing to leave for the day, she knew she was about to have the experience.

"How *could* you, Sheryl!" he shouted after he had slammed the door behind him.

She stood her ground—literally, since she was erect behind her desk, Leon opposite her. She had the sudden impression that the desk had become a barricade separating two warring forces, one which the attacker was about to breach. Puzzled, she tried a smile. "What am I supposed to have done?"

"Adriana Barre. Didn't you tell her to continue with that stupid biofeedback?"

"Yes, I did. And it is *not* stupid."

"God, Sheryl! Hamilton Dodd is livid!"

"And so are you," she pointed out.

"Yes, I am! What the hell possessed you to interfere with the practice of medicine? You know better than that."

She bristled now. He was treating her like a child—an idiot child, at that. "What's happened? Or am I supposed to guess?"

"Adriana Barre is a *very sick woman*. She desperately needs a cesarean to save her life and the life of her child. But she won't agree to surgery because *you* told her that ridiculous biofeedback would work." He scowled at her. "I'm extremely *disappointed* in you."

Sheryl was now thoroughly angry. His tone, his words, his entire belligerent attitude were extremely offensive to her, to make an understatement. She was wrestling to control her temper, telling herself that Leon was simply exercising his authority as Chief of Surgery, upholding the highest standards of medicine. And he was obviously very concerned about Adriana Barre, as she was herself.

"You have no right to inject psychological mumbo-jumbo into a purely medical situation," he continued.

That did it. "Fuck you, Dr. Kazinsky!" The expression, so uncharacteristic of her, shocked him. It shocked her, too, but she brazened it out. "How does that phrase sit with you?"

"You will not talk to me that way. I'll have you—"

"You'll have me what? Disbarred? Tarred and

182

feathered? You barge in here, jump all over me without asking for an explanation from me. You attack not only my competence as a psychologist and my professional ethics, but *me* as a person. Did you ask me what I actually *said* to the patient? Hell, no! Well, Mr. Chief of Surgery, as far as I'm concerned you can go . . ."—she fought for and found a little control of her tongue—". . . give yourself a proctology exam!"

Kazinsky thought about it for a moment, then said mildly, "What *did* you tell her?"

"*Now* you ask, do you? The hell with you! I'm invoking patient confidentiality."

He looked down at his feet, sighed. "Perhaps I didn't . . . handle this very well—"

"That's one way of putting it!"

"Did you tell her to practice biofeedback?"

"Yes, I did—on the theory it couldn't hurt anything and might help the patient's state of mind. For your information, I also emphasized how important it was to follow her doctor's orders to the letter."

"I hadn't realized that."

"Of course you didn't. And you didn't ask. You just came on like Dr. Atilla the Hun and did a number on me." She marched to the door, flung it open. "I believe you were just leaving."

He looked at her, unsure of himself now. "I apologize, Sheryl."

"Good!"

"I mean it. You're right—I did come on too strong." He paused "Can I . . . see you tonight? Make it up to you?"

But Sheryl was unmoved. "Not on your life!" She marched over to the desk, snatched up her purse, then brushed past him, saying over her shoulder as she went out the door, "*You* may not be leaving, but *I* am. I trust you can find your way out!"

# Chapter 10

Charles Bridges paced the floor of the hospital corridor outside room 227. He prided himself on his self-control and on the ability to maintain at least the appearance of calm in particularly trying circumstances, so his pacing was an aberration, evidence of just how upset he was.

He knew his problem. All his married life he had deferred to his wife in everything. It was part love, part indulgence. She was an artist, while he was merely a builder, a person who liked to work with his hands, although he had deep appreciation for art, letters, music, sculpture; certainly architecture. His admiration for Adriana was boundless. Therefore, he had always given in to her temperament, her nature, her desires. His greatest accomplishment in life, he was convinced, was to have won the love of Adriana Barre and to help make it possible for her to practice her art.

184

Now, because he loved her, he was being forced to make a decision that was contrary to her wishes. It should have been easy, he knew. Adriana was more important to him than anything in the world. The thought of losing her was—he refused to contemplate the possibility. He couldn't bear it. Then why didn't he simply give his consent for the surgery and have it over with? The answer to that question made him sigh as he paced the floor. If she lost the child, she would never forgive him. It was that simple. The baby was paramount. She loved him, he knew, but he also knew at this point he was secondary to the child. If the baby died, it would create a permanent wedge between them, and Charles feared they would never find a way to repair the rift. Always she would feel—probably say—that if he had just stayed out of it, let her deal with things her own way, she would have achieved what she'd longed for these many years— to be a mother. Yes, he—and he alone—had denied her happiness and what she wanted most in life. He mentally swore, something as uncharacteristic of him as his endless pacing.

"Would you like some juice, Mr. Bridges?"

He turned and saw Nurse Tawari. "You're working late," he said.

"Yes, just helping out." She offered him a glass of tomato juice. "Here—it's on the house."

"No, thank you." He was still looking at her, thinking, Japanese extraction, not truly pretty, but so nice, so caring. He asked, "Are you married, Ms. Tawari?"

"Very much. Three children ago."

"Do you love your husband? Does he love you?" Charles asked abruptly.

"Yes." She smiled. "To both questions. My husband is a fisherman. He's away a lot."

"I see." Still he pondered her. "What is love, Ms. Tawari? Do you know?"

She thought a moment.

"I don't *know*, but I have an opinion. I think, Mr. Bridges, love is sacrifice."

"Sacrifice?"

"Oh, yes. When you truly love, you love enough even to give up the person you love if you must. That's how I endure my husband's long trips at sea."

He stared at her, bemused. Then he said, "May I use your phone, please?"

Judd Forbes had just called in a debt. Years ago he had done a favor for Raleigh Scott, and now he wanted it returned. Raleigh Scott, a stage name coined when he was an aspiring actor, had given all that up and accepted respectability and a regular paycheck as executive director of the Abrams Foundation. The foundation was not well known in Southern California, but Forbes had included it on his list for Bobbi because he knew he could count on Raleigh Scott.

As he hung up the phone, Forbes knew he now had his ducks in a row. Bobbi Hecht was delighted at the idea of meeting the executive director of a charitable foundation. She understood that it was just a preliminary meeting, a sort of test of the waters, but it would produce useful information for the future. She had thanked Judd profusely for moving so quickly.

Forbes turned to Lorraine Paul. "All set. The country club. Can you get him there?"

"Should work. He's on the golf course right now. I'll be there when he arrives at the clubhouse. I assume he'll buy me a drink, at least, maybe dinner."

"He can't hide you away forever, the cheap bastard."

Lorraine gave no visible reaction, but she had a sense that the pot was calling the kettle black. Brian Hecht was a far better person than Judd

186

Forbes would ever be. "He's talked about taking me out, spending money."

"Tonight's the night." Judd chugalugged his drink. "I'd better run, let you get dressed. Knock his eyes out, honey."

Lorraine watched him leave, making a face as the door closed behind him. She didn't like this thing. Why was she doing it? She sighed. Doing what? All she was doing was hoping to run into a man she knew at his club. Nothing wrong with that.

Kazinsky stayed cooped up in his office, trying to catch up on his paper work, but his mind remained on Sheryl James. He'd made a fine mess of things. She was right, of course. He should have asked her what happened instead of confronting and accusing her on the strength of Ham Dodd's accusations. "Kazinsky, you're a sap," he told himself.

Then he began to consider why he was so upset about the incident. He'd blown up before. It was inevitable, given the tensions of the OR. He could think of a couple of interns so terrified of him they tried to stay out of his sight. That was all to the good, he figured. Kept them on their toes. Then why did this thing with Sheryl bother him? Had she gotten to him so much? Did she mean more to him than he realized?

Always the realist, Kazinsky figured the answer just might be yes. He was thinking about her more than he should. Their lovemaking, her body . . . Damn! Double damn! He wasn't ready for this sort of complication. He had all he could handle as Chief of Surgery—there simply wasn't time for a romantic entanglement. And where could it possibly lead? As far as he was concerned, Sheryl James was utterly unobtainable. Yet they had made love several times. Memories of her softness, the passion of her response, drifted across his

187

mind. What could she possibly see in him? Nothing. And after today, *absolutely* nothing.

The ringing phone was a welcome intrusion into what were becoming blacker and blacker thoughts.

"Glad I caught you in, Leon. Ham Dodd here. I just got a call from Charles Bridges. He's Adriana Barre's husband."

"I know."

"He's authorized her cesarean. I want to proceed immediately. I just hope it's not too late already. I'll want OR Two, I think—your best people. If you want to assist, I'd be honored."

Kazinsky only half-heard him, his mind zeroing in on an immediate problem. "Did you say the *husband* authorized the surgery? What does the patient say?"

"She's dead set against it, but she's being stubborn and foolish. Her life is in danger. Thank God her husband has the good sense to see what must be done."

Kazinsky hesitated. "Is that legal, Dr. Dodd? Can a husband approve surgery the patient does not want?"

"I don't know or care at the moment, Leon."

Kazinsky exhaled in a long sigh. "Maybe you should. Have you ever known of an instance like this?"

"No . . ."

"Me, either, though I've had the exact opposite. As a matter of fact, when I did the heart transplant on Gregory Claiborne, his wife opposed it. Did she ever! But Claiborne approved and the wife couldn't block it." He paused, thinking. "Is Adriana Barre of sound mind?"

"She's not crazy, if that's what you mean," Dodd snapped.

"Does she know the risks? Have you explained the need for the surgery to her?"

"I have, most carefully. But she insists on persisting with that stupid biofeedback, thanks to that James character."

"By the way, I spoke to Sheryl—Dr. James. She apparently told Miss Barre the biofeedback couldn't hurt, but that she must follow her doctor's orders. I don't think Dr. James is at fault in this."

"Okay, okay, but the bottom line is that Adriana Barre may die if we don't get that baby out of there *right now*. I'm going ahead, Leon, regardless of what you say. The legal niceties be damned!"

Kazinsky understood and approved. That had been precisely his attitude when he'd done the Claiborne transplant. The needs of the patient overrode every other consideration. "Very well, Dr. Dodd. I'm with you. I'll get OR Two ready and I'll try for Horace Black as anesthetist. I'd be happy to scrub with you."

"Good. I'm coming right over. Tell them to start prepping the patient. I'll want an epidural—Zylocaine, I think."

"Very well."

Kazinsky severed the connection, then quickly made the necessary calls to OB-GYN and the surgical office. Yes, Horace Black was available. Then he paused for thought, and finally made another call. No answer. Through the hospital switchboard, he reached Addie Weickel, Hecht's secretary, at home. She thought he was playing golf at the country club. No, he didn't normally carry a beeper, but if the club was called and told it was an emergency, a phone would be taken out to him. Kazinsky told her it was indeed an emergency. It seemed to him he waited forever.

Brian was on the sixteenth tee when the phone was brought to him. He listened to Kazinsky's apologies for disturbing his game, said, "What's up?" and listened with great interest. Kazinsky was very good at explaining complex matters succinctly. "I never heard of a case like this, either. Is it purely a medical decision?" It was. "Time is of the essence?" Yes. Brian thought a moment. If he insisted on legal opinions and consultations, it might mean the end of Adriana Barre. He made his decision. "Do what you have to do, Leon— Ham Dodd, too. We'll worry about the fallout later." He heard thanks from Kazinsky. "And thank *you* for calling me. I need to know these things in advance. . . . What? Oh, my game is lousy. You didn't interrupt a thing."

He turned to his good friend and partner Darryl Feinsinger, a lawyer who coveted Maurice Edgerton's job as legal counsel to Bel Air General. "I got one for you, old buddy." He told him the situation. "What d'you think?"

Feinsinger shrugged. "I only offer opinions on screwball situations like this on the basis of a big fat retainer."

Charles Bridges was dismayed. He had naturally assumed the surgery would be performed under general anesthetic. Adriana would be out of it, unable to protest. Indeed, she would know nothing about it until it was all over. Now Dodd was telling him that general anesthesia was impossible. The baby would also be anesthetized, ending any chance whatsoever for life. Cesareans were always performed with a spinal block. The mother felt no pain, but she was awake during the procedure.

"I'd better talk to her, then, Hamilton," Bridges decided. "I've got to get her to agree to it."

When he entered his wife's room, preparations were already under way. She had been scrubbed, shaved, and painted with iodine. She had also been given a diuretic to empty her bladder.

Adriana was not only in great pain—so much that she could no longer even attempt to mask it— but she was frightened and alarmed about what was happening to her. "Charles, what is going on?"

He nodded to Jane Tawari. She understood immediately, and with another nurse and Dr. Shedd, left the room. Alone with his wife, he said, "I've authorized the cesarean."

"No!" Adriana cried. "I won't permit it! I will not risk our baby's life!"

"The child is already in danger, Adriana. And so are you. I cannot permit that."

She looked at him beseechingly, gasping from the pain. "I'll be all right, Charles."

"I know. I'm going to see that you are."

"Please. Let me . . . do it my way," she begged.

"I'm sorry, my dear. I've tried to please you always—whenever I could. I hope you know that."

"Yes, Charles . . . you're a . . . good man, which is . . . why—"

"I love you, Adriana. You are my whole life. I simply cannot let . . . anything happen to you. You must have the surgery."

"But, Charles, our . . . baby. I want him . . . so much!"

"I know. So do I."

"It'll be . . . all right, Charles. It's only . . . a little pain."

"So little you are in agony." He tried to smile, patted her cheek. "Your problem, my dear, is that you suffer from an excess of virtue. I've always admired your courage, but right now you have an excess of it, and excess in anything is a fault."

"Oh, Charles, please listen . . . to me! Hamilton said . . . the baby might not . . . live . . . if he does the—"

"There is a chance it will. There is no chance at all unless the cesarean is done at once. Can't you understand that? Or are you just being stubborn?" He made an attempt at humor. "I didn't know muleheadedness was a particularly Italian trait." He saw her shake her head. Was it a negative or a reaction to the pain? "We must get on with our lives, Adriana. We must do what is necessary, hoping for a happy ending. If not, we still have the future. We can try again to conceive a child—I would like that very much." She smiled tentatively. She was wavering. He knew he was winning. "In any event, Adriana, I have made the decision and I am prepared to live with the result. You must, too." He kissed her pale cheek, then went to the door and motioned for Nurse Tawari to return.

Judd Forbes thought things were going quite well. Bobbi Hecht looked smashing. She wore a simple black dress that fit her to perfection, befitting a woman on a philanthropic mission. Then why did he have such a sense of her nakedness under it? This woman was really getting to him.

She was getting to Raleigh Scott, too, Forbes could tell. Scott was a considerable womanizer. Indeed, the favor Forbes had done for him was related to that tendency. In the full heat of the chase, Scott sometimes forgot to use discretion. He was in his early fifties, but looked younger thanks to a full head of dark hair, year-round suntan, and natty attire.

"If you want my opinion, Mrs. Hecht, I think what you are proposing will be warmly received." He smiled, showing straight, white teeth. "One might even say you will be welcomed with open arms."

From across the dinner table Forbes shot his friend a warning glance, together with a nearly imperceptible shake of his head.

"Do you really think so, Mr. Scott?" Her smile of delight was truly ravishing. "I want—rather, Bel Air General Hospital wants—our program to be accepted."

"And appreciated. It will be, believe me.

192

There's an unlimited need for charity funds, especially since the government has cut back its welfare appropriations so drastically." He glanced at Forbes, seeing no disapproval now. "If I may, I'd suggest you refrain from letting any one organization know the full extent of your generosity. That will just"—he smiled again—"whet their appetites. You might end up—"

"Being talked into contributing it all to one organization," Bobbi finished for him.

Scott nodded. "Which I gather you don't want to do."

Forbes interrupted. "Mrs. Hecht's aim is to discuss specific areas, perhaps those which have been somewhat neglected for lack of funds, then choose those which are suitable for her program and—"

"Amenable to solution utilizing our means. Yes, you've said it very well, Judd." Bobbi really was enjoying herself. She liked this man Scott. The Abrams Foundation—she knew of its work, and Judd knew Scott as a friend. He really was bending over backward to help her. To Scott she said, "Do you have any ideas about the specific areas I should consider in relation to your organization?"

Forbes tuned out Scott's reply, for he had just seen Lorraine Paul enter, attracting a great many appreciative male eyes. Couldn't blame them, for she was stunning in ice-blue linen, cut low to reveal the curve of her breasts. He focused on her cleavage. The valley of the shadow of death. Damn near everybody at the bar would happily enter it. He looked around, but saw no sign of Brian Hecht. Where was he?

Lorraine slid onto a bar stool and ordered a gin-and-tonic. She was not in the least nervous. Making an entrance, being ogled, was all in a day's work for her. Nor did it bother her that she saw at least three men who were her "clients," one of them a regular. That happened a lot. Couldn't be avoided. She just ignored them unless they ap-

193

proached her, which virtually never happened. Most had too much to lose by admitting their liaisons with a call girl, however high-class and high-priced.

She saw Judd at a corner table. He was studiously ignoring her. The woman with him must be Bobbi Hecht. Lorraine was impressed. She knew a really beautiful woman when she saw one.

Lorraine's biggest problem was thinking of a reason for being alone in the bar. She'd made no date with Brian, not even hinted that she might be there. She decided to say she was just circulating, hoping to be noticed by a producer or director. That was what she'd said the night she first met him. Among aspiring actresses, circulating, being seen, was virtually a national pastime. . . .

Hamilton Dodd carefully noted everything before he began. Kazinsky and young Shedd were across the table. Horace Black, the able anesthetist (as they insisted on calling them at Bel Air General, rather than the more common *anesthesiologist*), was at his patient's head. Charles Bridges stood by, masked and in a scrub suit, holding Adriana's hand. He had asked if he might be allowed to do so, and Dodd figured he might comfort his wife or at least distract her. He did not know the scrub and circulating nurses by name but was certain they were competent. Leon Kazinsky had really shaped up Bel Air General's surgical department in an amazingly short time. Perhaps it was because he either operated or assisted so much of the time that no one could screw up and hope to avoid him.

Also present were Dr. Edward Randall, a pediatric resident on the hospital staff, and one of his nurses. They would receive and tend to the infant—if it survived.

"Scalpel, please."

He began with a Pfannenstiel's incision, named

for the German gynecologist who first used it. It was much favored now, for it made it easier for women to hide the cesarean scar in bikinis and such. Thus, he made a transfer incision approximately six inches long across the lower abdomen, about an inch above the pubes. Once under the skin, he switched to a vertical incision, slicing through the muscle wall from the navel to the pubes. This exposed the now empty bladder, which was quickly pushed upward out of the way and held by Shedd.

Now came the incision into the uterus, again done quickly. His gloves, scrub suit, Adriana—indeed, everything was covered with blood, but no effort was made to tidy up. There was no time, for this was a race to release an infant struggling for life. His uterine incision was horizontal, about four inches long, and cut into the lower uterus. Blood and amniotic fluid spurted. Dodd put his hand inside, groping for any body part he could find. His fingers closed on what felt like a leg and tiny hip. He pulled Adriana Barre's child out of the uterine opening as fast as he could, feet first.

He made no examination of the infant, noting only that it was small, more blue than normal— oxygen-starved, no doubt—as he laid it on a towel held by the pediatric nurse. Quickly Kazinsky applied two clamps to the umbilical cord, and Dodd severed it between the clamps. At once the infant was placed into the hands of the pediatrician.

"It's a boy," Randall said.

Adriana Barre had only one question. "Is he alive?"

Dodd's concern was elsewhere. "One cc of pitocin by injection, Dr. Black." As that was done, he again reached inside the uterus, pulling out the placenta, which had caused so much trouble, dropping it in a bucket. While the nurse suctioned out excess blood, Dodd ordered a second cc of pitocin injected. It was a drug natural to the body that induced shrinkage of the uterus. That shrinkage, more than anything he could do, should stop the internal bleeding that threatened the life of his patient.

"*Is my baby alive?*" Adriana tried to sit up to see for herself, and had to be gently restrained.

"Please, Adriana," Bridges said. "We'll know in a minute."

"Yes, Adriana, lie still," Dodd said. "We've important work to do. It's not over, not by a long shot."

"I want to know if my baby is alive!"

Dodd glared at the pediatrician. "For God's sake, man, tell her something!"

"Yes, he's alive, Miss Barre." He held the infant up for her to see. "And he has all his fingers and toes. He's whole."

This brought forth cooing sounds from Adriana. "Isn't he beautiful, Charles?" She sighed, despite the fact that the baby was blue, wrinkled, and still covered with a cheesy-looking substance from its interuterine life.

Dr. Dodd was already closing, using catgut, in three layers, the wall of the uterus, the vertical incision in the abdominal wall, and finally the Pfannenstiel's incision. The catgut would be absorbed by the body. When he finished, he ordered whole blood and continued IV of .5 percent glucose and water, to which was to be added pitocin as a drip.

Only then did he become aware of Adriana's happy chatter. She felt no pain from the surgery, and was overjoyed to have given birth to a healthy son. When Dodd came within her line of vision, she smiled radiantly and said, "See, I told you everything would be just fine!"

But Dodd knew better. This woman was far from out of the woods—the next few hours would be crucial. Still, there was no point in alarming her. "We'll see how fine you think everything is when the spinal block wears off," he warned.

"Oh, Hamilton." She even laughed. "I'll love the pain because it gave me a son—" She squeezed her husband's hand. "Our beautiful, wonderful, utterly delightful son!"

Bobbi saw her husband emerge from the locker room with his friend Darryl Feinsinger. Though she and Brian were estranged, she still considered him the handsomest man she knew, rugged, wholly masculine. He carried himself so well. One would swear he had no awareness of how attractive women found him. A thought crossed her mind. Yes, they were estranged, separated. But whereas that had originally been her fault—she knew she had driven him away with her bitchiness—the animosity between them was now caused by him. No matter how much he professed to believe it, she had had no part in the rape of Jenny Corban.

Brian didn't see her, intent as he was on his conversation with Darryl. She thought of calling or waving to him, then lost her chance as Brian reacted to someone he saw at the bar. His smile was a positive beam. She turned her head and watched him approach a blonde on a bar stool. Her back was to Bobbi, so hair color, blue linen, and slimness were all Bobbi could see of her.

"Oh, there's Brian," Judd Forbes said.

She glanced at him. "Yes—his golf day, I believe." She did her best to ignore her husband, turning her attention to Raleigh Scott and the dinner they had ordered—escargots for her. But she swore she could hear Brian's laughter behind her. It unnerved her a little, and she doubled her efforts to block it out.

In a few minutes she was aware of Judd Forbes rising. Raleigh Scott stood up, too. She looked up

197

to see Brian standing by their table. The blonde was at his side.

"Judd, how are you?" Brian said.

Forbes grinned. "Mixing business with pleasure. May I present Raleigh Scott, executive director of the Abrams Foundation. He's been giving us some pointers on the Community Outreach Program."

Brian said hello and shook Scott's extended hand. Then he nodded at his wife, who was still seated. "Bobbi." What more was there to say? But he did feel a little like a boy caught with his hand in the cookie jar. Throughout their estrangement, Bobbi and he had kept up at least the appearance of being man and wife. They attended social functions together when necessary and behaved in a reasonably civil manner. As far as he could remember, this was the first time he'd ever had to introduce his wife to another woman.

"Lorraine Paul. My wife, Bobbi; my assistant, Judd Forbes; Mr. Raleigh Scott."

Bobbi tried not to stare at her, but couldn't help it. The girl was simply gorgeous, no two ways about it, a walking butter-cream bonbon. No, not that. Bobbi immediately revised her initial impression. She was no wide-eyed ingenue, but a very sophisticated, chic, and self-confident young woman. She'd have to be to expose her breasts that way. *Why not? If you got 'em, flaunt 'em*, Bobbi thought acidly.

"Mrs. Hecht, it's a pleasure to meet you."

Bobbi was not without poise, so her hesitation was imperceptible as she shook the proffered hand. "Miss Paul." As the slender hand was offered in turn to Forbes and Scott, she saw the possessive way Brian held his hand at the small of her back. She was with *him*. He was *with* her. This was no casual pickup, a friend of a friend, a business acquaintance. The two of them were obviously see-

198

ing each other. Her anger flared. The bastard! First Jenny Corban, now this!

No hint of Bobbi's emotional reaction showed in her words, however. "I must say you're quite lovely, Miss Paul."

"Thank you." The smile was modest, yet self-confident.

Brian knew he had to say something. "Lorraine is an actress."

Lorraine laughed lightly. "*Hoping* to be is more like it."

Scott, who was considerably impressed, contributed. "Well, you certainly do look the part, Miss Paul."

Brian applied gentle pressure to the small of Lorraine's back. "We'll leave you to finish your dinner. We're just going to catch a bite ourselves." He led her to a table, as far away from his wife and her companions as he could possibly get. But there simply was none far enough away for Bobbi's peace of mind. Elegant meals were unfortunately not yet being served on Mars.

Pediatrician Ed Randall said nothing until he had a chance to consult Dr. Dodd. He had not lied in the OR. Baby Bridges was alive, had all his fingers and toes. But Randall was worried. A certain amount of blueness was common in newborns. The trauma of birth frequently caused oxygen deprivation. But this infant was much too blue. Randall was prepared to attribute it to the difficulties associated with the *abruptio placentae*. Still, he worried. The baby was having difficulty breathing.

He put the child in natal intensive care, in an incubator at fifty percent oxygen, then found a tiny vein for an IV drip of glucose and water.

When he told Dodd what he'd done, the obstetrician said, "It sounds to me like you're on top of things, Doctor."

"I hope so . . ."

Dodd eyed him a moment. "What are you thinking?"

Randall pursed his lips, shook his head, then finally said, "Hyline Membrane Disease."

"God, Doctor! If you're ever going to be wrong about anything in your life, now's the time."

"Isn't it?" Randall sighed.

Kazinsky phoned Sheryl James to report the successful result of Adriana Barre's surgery. He was aware that she said all the right things and seemed genuinely pleased for Adriana, but he could still detect cool distance in the tone of her voice. She offered nothing to make it easier for him.

Finally, after much hesitation and a little stammering, he said, "I've been reading through the latest medical journals trying to discover the most professional way to make an abject apology." He'd hoped for a laugh at that. None came. "I couldn't find any articles on the subject," he continued. Still no reply. "Would you have any ideas how I might go about it?"

Long pause. Then, sharply, "No apology is necessary, Leon."

That was something, at least. She'd stopped calling him "Dr. Kazinsky."

"Oh, I think so. Have to disagree with you there. I acted like a sap. I also jumped to conclusions." Silence. "If it helps any, I told Dr. Dodd what you had said to Miss Barre, and I also told him it wasn't your fault."

"Thank you."

Sigh. "Let me try again. I'm really sorry, Sheryl. It was rotten of me to confront you—no, *accost* you—that way without even trying to find out what had actually happened."

"No more, Leon. You've apologized and I've accepted your apology. That ends the matter."

"I wish I thought so. You've said all the right

200

words, but I gather I'm not on your list of favorite people just now."

She sighed. "Oh, Leon, I don't know what I think. Let me sleep on it. Maybe in the morning . . ."

"Are you always this slow to get over anger?" he asked.

"I don't know. I don't get angry very often." A pause. "You hurt me, Leon. I don't like being made to feel like an unprofessional nincompoop by someone I respect and admire."

"You know you're not, and I don't think you are. I just shot from the hip, that's all."

She laughed a little. "You *did* sort of do that."

"I've been reviewing my whole life to see if I've ever done that sort of thing before."

"And?"

"I'm going to invest in a new, longer fuse to allow me more time to consider the feelings of others."

"Now that's the best apology I've heard yet."

"Thank God! Still friends?"

"Still friends. See you tomorrow."

The warmth in her voice came as a huge relief.

Bobbi's immediate reaction to Brian's appearance with the beautiful Miss Paul was numbness. She was so surprised she was literally stunned. She couldn't seem to think. As soon as she could, she excused herself and went to the powder room, not using the facilities, simply standing at the sink, staring at her image in the mirror.

She wanted to weep, to dissolve in a spate of hopeless, bitter, desperate tears. The need almost overwhelmed her. Her throat tightened until she could not swallow. Breath came painfully and her eyes filled with tears. But she fought against it as hard as she could, and finally succeeded. Bobbi Carlyle Hecht had not indulged in a hysterical fit of sobbing in so long she couldn't remember it.

201

And now was no time for one. Red eyes would cause too much curious comment at the country club, not to mention the reaction of Scott and Judd.

The need to cry surprised her. She had first felt anger—indeed, rage. Throwing a few things, even screaming, was certainly in order. God knew she'd done it often enough in the past, especially when her anger was directed at Brian. Where was that anger now? She needed it badly. Why had she turned into a quivering blob of jelly?

Bobbi looked at the face in the mirror—dark, expensively styled hair, vivid blue eyes, ripe lips, flawless complexion. A pretty face—no, more than pretty. Beautiful, even eye-stopping. Many men had said so. She appraised her figure, knowing what lay beneath her dress. A good figure, better than good, enough to drive a man wild. It had happened many times, often with Brian.

Memories flooded over her—Brian's eyes and hands, his body. And now she understood why she was so upset. The one great accomplishment of her life had been the captivation of Brian Hecht. She had seen the passion in his eyes, felt it in his hands, knew it fulsomely in his repeated lovemaking and her own ecstatic response. Brian Hecht had left her with no doubt, actions making words unneeded, though they were uttered, that she and she alone was the most beautiful, desirable, and passionate woman he had ever known, would ever want to know.

That knowledge had been a certainty in her life. No doubt she had abused it, giving in to tempers and vituperation, abusing him, because of her certainty of her attraction for him and the absolute knowledge that she could always win him back in bed. Such a mistake. A horrid mistake. She had driven him away. The physical attraction might still be there, but it was not worth everything else he'd had to put up with.

And so he had fallen in love with Jenny Corban. How she'd hated that! The knowledge that Brian was in Jenny's bed drove her wild—and to the arms of a succession of her own lovers. No, not lovers—studs, servicemen. But deep down, Bobbi had always been convinced that Jenny was not a true threat to her. Jenny was nice, sweet, accommodating. She was also intelligent, highly competent, a soulmate whom Brian had learned to admire and, yes, love. But Jenny Corban had posed no threat to Bobbi's own ultimate security, or so she'd thought. Jenny was pretty, winsome, appealing to a man like Brian because of her sweet nature and proximity. But Brian could never find in her what he did in herself. Bobbi had proved that, seducing him anew. Oh, God, their lovemaking had been so wonderful, titanic, two starved people drinking at an endless well of passion! He had stayed with her rather than return to Jenny on the night Jenny had been raped. Brian had blamed her. She'd lost him again.

Bobbi realized that this new woman, Lorraine Paul, was quite different from Jenny Corban. Brian had chosen someone so beautiful, so stunning, so sophisticated that Bobbi knew she was overmatched. Depression weighed on her heavily. Until now, she'd hoped he might come back to her. Had she truly lost Brian for good this time?

She fixed her face, put on a smile, even the appearance of brightness, and returned to the table, ending the dinner meeting with as much dispatch as possible. All she wanted was to be alone, but this turned out to be impossible, at least for the moment. Judd Forbes had picked her up at her house and she had to ride home with him. In the darkness of the car he talked on about Raleigh Scott, their meeting, the project. Her answers were few and hardly enthusiastic. She didn't want to talk. She just wanted to be alone.

"You seem a little down, Bobbi," Forbes said at last.

"I am, a little. Sorry."

"Nothing to be sorry about. Happens to the best of us." Forbes laughed. "You should see my funks. Better yet, *don't* see one." He drove in silence for a while. "Forgive me for butting in, but I gather it has something to do with seeing Brian with another woman."

Bobbi glanced at the outline of his face in the semi-darkness. She nodded. "Yes, it did upset me."

"I know you and Brian are having . . . troubles."

"That's a mild way of putting it. We're separated. Have been for some time."

"Still, seeing him out with another woman upset you."

"He has a perfect right to do as he pleases. It wasn't the first time."

"But it still was something of a shock." When he earned no reply, Forbes ventured, "I know it's none of my business and I'm probably skating on thin ice, but if you were *my* wife, I'd never so much as *look* at another woman." He gave a small, deliberately nervous laugh. "I meant that to make you feel better. Besides, it's the truth."

"It does. Thank you. Always good to have a second opinion." They stopped at Bobbi's house. She opened the car door to get out, immediately illuminating the interior of the car. "Thank you for the ride, dinner, introduction to your friend, everything. We'll talk about it tomorrow."

Forbes put a hand lightly on her arm.

"Look, Bobbi, I don't think you ought to be alone right now."

"I'm fine," she assured him.

"I'm sure you are, but a little company, diverting conversation, might cheer you up."

"Would you like to come in?" She looked at the

204

handsome face a moment, knew the answer, shrugged. "What the hell? Maybe you're right."

Inside what she still thought of as Connie Payne's house more than her own, Bobbi wandered through the sliding-glass doors into the night air at poolside, looking up at the stars as Forbes made drinks. The vast night sky made her feel small, comforted her a little. The scotch he brought her was strong. She made a face when she tasted it. "So much?"

"I figured a good belt couldn't hurt you." He grinned.

"Maybe not, but I learned awhile back this stuff really doesn't help. Oh, it does at the moment, sometimes, but the fallout later is dreadful—at least for me." Nevertheless, she raised her glass, sipped, and saw him do the same. She looked up again at the stars. "Do you like me, Judd?" She said abruptly. "No, strike that. 'Like' has nothing to do with it. Do you really find me attractive?" She said the words to the stars.

"Extremely."

Now she looked at him, at least at his shadowy form, in the dim light. "I mean, if you were walking down the street and passed me, would you turn around for a second look?"

"I already have." He smiled. "When I first saw you at that reception the other day, I was stunned. I felt like a schoolboy with his first crush."

She smiled slightly. "I noticed. It made me feel good." Without hesitation she asked, "Do you want me, Judd—I mean physically?"

"I think I'm suffering from terminal lust."

"Really? That's nice." She took two strides toward him, raised her head, found his mouth, kissed him. His lips were soft, warm, nice, but she felt nothing.

He did. The kiss was electric, shooting right to his loins. He let her move away, surprised both by her action and his response. He stood looking at

205

her a moment, then pulled her close, as close as he could with each of them holding a drink. His kiss was harsh, demanding, full of desire.

Bobbi felt it now, as though from far away, like a breath of wind fanning the ashes from not quite dead embers. She felt the importunate pressure of his mouth, the thrust of his tongue, the intensity of his passion. She responded, at first automatically, then out of sudden, sharp need. She felt shivers of desire throughout her body. So welcome! How long had it been? She backed away, shaken, and raised her glass to take another sip. "You did say terminal?"

" 'Fraid so."

She heard the huskiness in his voice. An image crossed her mind—Brian in the silken arms of his blonde. She forced it away. Softly she said, "That sounds very serious. I can't have your death on my conscience."

As Bobbi slipped out of her dress, she only dimly understood why she was doing it—or perhaps she understood fully but didn't want to let it into her consciousness. It was an ugly thought. She was trying to prove her worth to a man she hardly knew. Worse, she was sober and not even particularly turned on by him. With the other men she'd had, she'd always been drunk or worse, certainly in a who-cares mood, certainly self-destructive. She wasn't any of that now. She simply wanted— no, *needed*—to be admired, desired.

Judd Forbes certainly did that. When he saw her naked body in the faint light that came from the house, he was so aroused that he felt like a kid with his first woman, actually trembling as he touched her. Her coloring was so dramatic, luxurious black hair against snowy skin. Her breasts seemed to leap toward him, her nipples luscious strawberries against the snow. Never had he seen such breasts. She had prominent nipples, so very ripe for the picking.

206

To her dismay, then ultimately her pride, and finally pleasure, Bobbi became aroused by him, welcoming, then being thrilled by, his passion. They made love on the living room floor, something she'd done only with Brian—and even then, never on this particular floor.

Forbes was at first stunned, then driven wild. She was wild, uninhibited, accepting him, then sliding out from beneath him and rolling away, to rise to all fours, sometimes on her knees. He'd reach for her, find her breasts, pull her down on top of him, enter her, only to have her escape once more, taunting him, teasing. She was the ultimate temptress, untamable, enflaming him, yet unobtainable. He had never in his life been with such a woman. When at last she allowed him to overcome her with his greater strength, he pinioned her and forced entry, feeling her nails raking his back. He plunged wildly into her and knew the victory of her coming and his own. The only trouble was, he felt the victory was hers. He had overpowered but not dominated her.

Bobbi Hecht had the same feeling.

# Chapter 11

Everything including X ray confirmed his diagnosis, but Dr. Edward Randall continued to consult every doctor on the staff about the Bridges infant. Dr. Sean McClintock, Director of Medicine, Dr. Leon Kazinsky, Chief of Surgery, and a pair of attending pediatricians who happened to enter the nursery all agreed with him, shaking their heads sadly.

The final person consulted was Dr. Hamilton Dodd. He said, "Lord, we're talking snakebite. Of all the rotten luck!"

"How about calamity, Doctor? Shall I tell the parents?"

Dodd looked at Randall. "I know it's your responsibility as the baby's pediatrician, but since I've known them both so long it might be a little easier coming from me."

"I agree," Randall said promptly and with relief.

208

Dodd stroked his pate in frustration. "If there *is* any way to make it easier. Right now I wish I'd become a plumber!"

Brian felt a little depressed and he wasn't sure why. It wasn't alcohol. He'd hardly had any all day yesterday. And it certainly wasn't a dearth of sex—he was getting plenty of that. Too much? Lorraine had returned to his place and spent the night. No question about it, she was terrific in bed. She turned him on when he thought he'd never rise again. And she was certainly beautiful. It had felt good to be seen in public with such a gorgeous blonde on his arm.

It had gotten to Bobbi, all right. Sure had. That expression in her eyes . . . She was suprised, hurt. Probably mad as hell right now. Too bad. She'd had her chance.

Such soul-searching was not normal for him, especially not first thing in the morning. He usually got right down to work. He tried to concentrate for a minute or two, then sighed, gave up, and leaned back in his chair. Why the hell did he feel so rotten? Probably had a lot to do with Jenny. He couldn't seem to get her out of his mind. Brian stood up, went out to the reception area, and poured himself a cup of coffee, returning with it without speaking to Addie Weickel or Raf Spina. Now he sipped it, staring out the window.

*Jenny.* He conjured up a visual image of her. Clearly she was more than a sex object to him. He had a sex object very much at hand, yet his mind kept dwelling on the one woman he probably was never going to have. Was that it? Was absence making his heart grow fonder?

He needed to *talk* to Jenny, really *needed* to. The communication between them had been the basis of their love. She had been his sounding board, the one person with whom he could discuss problems and share ideas, certain she would lis-

209

ten, understand, and help *him* understand if only by disagreeing with him. Yes, the one person in the world.

He had no one now, and that was his problem. Oh, there was Laura, but he never had talked about his personal problems with her if he could avoid it. Even in their discussions of hospital affairs, she tended to live in a dream world of gentility, seldom getting down to the blood and guts of hospital problems. Jenny had. And Jenny was gone—at least for a while. He sighed. Better not to think of her as really gone.

This frustration, he now knew, was due to the huge void Jenny had left in his life. He was alone, making decisions unaided. Judd Forbes? It would take some time, if ever, before he developed the sort of working relationship with him that he'd had with Jenny.

Brian drained the Styrofoam cup and tossed it in the wastebasket. Judd Forbes. Out with Bobbi last night on that damned outreach project. Well, there was nothing to be done about it. He swore under his breath. Bobbi was going to be nothing but trouble now that she was a hospital director, claiming office space and the time of his new assistant. Soon the doctors and nurses would be asked to take care of . . . shit! It was going to be a mess. It already *was* a mess.

Suddenly Brian knew what was really bothering him. He felt like a eunuch, or maybe a marionette hopping to strings pulled by others. Yes, that was his real problem. He turned and stared at his cluttered desk, as though the answer lay buried there somewhere under stacks of paper. Maybe it did. He was damned if he was going to be a eunuch! He was administrator of Bel Air General. He was going to exercise his authority. Suddenly Brian felt better. He knew just what to do. He was either the boss or he wasn't

At once he began to draft a letter in longhand,

his usual custom, for Addie Weickel to type. Actually, it would be three letters, all saying the same. Then he began to draft an administrative order.

It was perhaps the least pressing of all Hillary's immediate problems, yet it made her weep. When she thought about it rationally, she knew just how stupid she was being. Tommy was failing, just sinking away from her, but she wasn't crying over that. The magnitude of the possibility of actually losing Tommy had not yet reached her. What she was crying about was not knowing who to ask to give him last rites.

Hillary considered herself fairly religious. She believed in God, often prayed for guidance, and she believed her prayers were sometimes answered, often mysteriously. But she was unchurched. As a child she'd hardly known what a church was, other than a forbidding-looking building. Later, she had made her own faltering way to God. Now all of a sudden, she didn't know where to turn. She was neither Catholic nor Protestant, Jewish nor Moslem. That sense of helplessness, of rootlessness, brought tears of frustration. What a wasted, sinful life she'd led.

Finally, in desperation she had invited both a Catholic priest and a Protestant minister to give the last rites to her son. Making that decision had helped her to feel better at the time. But now, as she listened to their prayers at Tommy's bedside, she began to weep again, silently, her anguish seeming to tear her apart. Tommy was dying. *Oh, God, why him? It was my sin—take me!*

Ham Dodd first checked on Adriana and did not like what he saw. But he had no real chance to do anything about it immediately because Charles Bridges entered. He signaled to Bridges, then led him to the nurses' lounge.

Once there, Bridges said, "I think I'll always associate this room with bad news. What is it now?"

Dodd shook his head slowly. This was going to be very hard. He had gone into obstetrics originally because he hated illness, death, and dying. It didn't happen too often in childbirth anymore. His efforts usually produced a happy event. Everyone was joyful. Again he shook his head. Not this time, that was for sure. Without preamble, he said, "your son has Hyline Membrane Disease."

Bridges looked apprehensive but puzzled. "What is it?"

"It's an uncommon disease, usually seen in premature babies. I could go into technical details, explaining the inability of the infant to handle certain proteins, but the bottom line is that respiration is affected. Your son cannot make use of the oxygen entering his lungs. His breathing is very labored, the chest indrawn, and this is occurring while he's in an incubator with fifty percent oxygen. The chest X ray confirms the diagnosis. I'm sorry, Charles. There is no doubt it's Hyline Membrane Disease." Dodd paused, sighing heavily. "Again, I'm sorry."

Charles Bridges was staring at him. "What are you saying? That my son is handicapped?"

Dodd looked away. "I'm saying worse than that, Charles."

"Oh, my God!"

"Your son probably will not live through the day, Charles," the doctor told him gently. "Certainly not another." He saw the shock in his friend's face, the sudden slump of his shoulders. "It's the same disease which took the life of Patrick Kennedy, the infant son of John and Jacqueline Kennedy shortly after Kennedy was elected President."

"I remember." Bridges, stunned, clung to the

piece of information as if it were a touch of normalcy in a lunatic world. "Can nothing be done?"

"Nothing."

"What causes it?"

"We really don't know, except, as I said, premature birth, when the lungs are not fully developed."

"Oh, God!" Bridges turned his back on Dodd, lowering his head. His entire body shook with sobs, but he made no sound. Dodd went to him, put his arm around him. There was nothing to say. "Hamilton . . . is it my . . . fault? Is there . . . something . . . wrong with . . . me?"

"No," Dodd said firmly.

"All this . . . tragedy. So many . . . miscarriages and . . . deaths. I'd never be able to face Adriana again if . . . if it was something in me that caused it."

"No, Charles, it is *not* you. You've been tested. Your sperm is healthy, completely normal."

"Oh, God!" Bridges struggled to regain control, and succeeded to an extent. He pulled a linen handkerchief from his breast pocket, wiped his eyes, blew his nose. When he turned to face Dodd, it was as though his breakdown had not occurred, except for the redness of his eyes. "I have to think of Adriana. This is just about going to destroy her."

"I know. That's why I spoke to you first," Dodd said.

"She won't be . . . prepared for it. She thinks everything is fine. She's . . . so happy . . ."

"I'm sorry, Charles, but there was no way to tell anything was wrong at first. The baby was blue, but we all thought it was just the usual trauma of birth, aggravated by the *abruptio placentae.*"

Bridges, haggard, looked at him. "You know what this means, don't you? Adriana will say that if we hadn't taken the child so early—"

213

"There is no way to know that for sure," Dodd interrupted. "And the baby most definitely would have been born dead if we had waited any longer. Then there was the considerable danger to Adriana."

"I know that and *you* know that, but will she understand?"

"Charles, I don't know for certain—no one may ever know—but it is reasonable to speculate that the hematoma causing the *abruptio placentae* also caused the malfunction of the baby's vital organs. The fetus was starved for oxygen, nutrients, unable to eliminate its own wastes. This must have interfered with normal development. It certainly is something we can honestly encourage Adriana to believe."

Bridges rubbed his red-rimmed eyes. "This is going to be a terrible blow to her. I don't know if she can take it. She doesn't seem very strong as it is."

Dodd considered and immediately rejected telling this man of his new fears about Adriana. Enough was enough. "She doesn't have to know this minute, Charles."

"Yes. I want to think about the best way to tell her."

"That's wise. And please let me be with you. We'll do it together."

Bridges nodded, all he could do, for his eyes suddenly filled with tears again. Finally he could say, "You know, all this . . . time, it has been . . . Adriana's child. But when . . . the boy was . . . born, I suddenly . . . well, it was *my* child, too, my *son*." His face screwed up into a grimace and a sob tore from him. "Now he's . . . *dying!*"

Dodd was so choked up he couldn't have spoken even if he could have thought of anything to say. All he could do was turn away, pour coffee in a cup, and bring it to the suffering man.

214

Finally Bridges asked, "Will Adriana be able to have another child?"

Dodd had been dreading the question. "I don't know. It's too early to tell."

"Why?"

Dodd didn't want to answer, not yet, not now. "Her age is a factor that must be considered, Charles. I'm sure you understand."

Bridges only nodded.

Sheryl James had asked the nurses in OB-GYN to phone her the first time Susan Raimond was alone. When the call came, she rushed for room 226. Just outside she encountered Dr. Dodd emerging from Adriana Barre's room.

"Dr. James, isn't it?" he said.

Her reaction was immediately guarded. "Yes."

He eyed her for a moment. "Dr. Kazinsky has explained to me what really happened between you and Miss Barre. I'm sorry I blew it up. It was unwarranted."

She relaxed, smiled a little. "Thank you. Believe me, I would never countermand a doctor's orders. I just wanted—"

"I understand. You needn't explain." He hesitated. "Adriana seemed to like you, Dr. James. You gave her confidence, and she badly needed that."

"It's part of my job, Dr. Dodd. I can only try."

Another hesitation. "Perhaps you may get a chance to try again. She's going to need all the help she can get." He told her briefly of the situation.

Sheryl was shocked. "How terrible!"

"Yes. She may need a shoulder to cry on, and any good advice you can give her."

"I don't think of it as giving advice. I just let the patient's own good sense and strength of will exert themselves. I'll visit Miss Barre, of course, but perhaps not until . . . the worst is over."

215

"Yes. Thank you." He saw her turn toward room 226. "Visiting that brat?" The tone of his voice had changed completely.

Sheryl was greatly surprised by his attitude. "Yes. I'm trying to help her see—"

"The error of her ways. Good luck! We're all going to need it. As a matter of fact, I plan to have a few words with her and that blasted mother a little later on."

Sheryl really wished he wouldn't, but she knew it wasn't her place to tell him so. She pushed open the door to Susan Raimond's room.

The girl was awake when she entered and seemed glad to see her.

"How're you feeling?" Sheryl asked.

"Okay, I guess."

"Do you have any pain?"

"Not really, I just feel weak—loss of blood, I guess."

"No doubt. And how are you mentally, emotionally?"

Susan looked at her a moment. "Sad, depressed, scared."

Sheryl firmed her lips, nodded. "That's only understandable, under the circumstances." Then she smiled, deliberately brightening her voice. "Do you know who's across the hall from you?"

"Who?"

Sheryl now hesitated. It was a hospital rule that patients were never to be discussed with other patients—indeed, with anyone. But if she was to have any chance of helping this girl, that rule had to be broken. "Adriana Barre."

"Really?" Susan perked up considerably.

"Do you know her?"

"Yes. I was in a film with her once, years ago. I was very young and it was one of my first pictures. But I remember her so well. She was so very nice, and so beautiful. I loved her—or I would have if I hadn't been so in awe of her."

216

Sheryl smiled. "That's understandable. Miss Barre is what they call 'a legend in her own time.' "

"What's she in for?" Then Susan giggled. "That's a silly question! This is obstetrics and I remember reading she was expecting. Has she had her baby?"

"Last evening. A baby boy."

"How wonderful! She must be so thrilled."

Again Sheryl hesitated. She was taking a terrible risk. What she was about to say could be the end of her job at Bel Air General and might well jeopardize her whole career. But she had to speak. "I don't think so, Susan. It's all terribly sad—dreadful, couldn't be more so."

"What happened?"

There was concern in the young face. That was a good sign—Sheryl was counting on the finer instincts of this girl. "Miss Barre was eight months pregnant, like you. She had a condition called *abruptio placentae*, which is very serious and threatened both the baby's life and her own. Dr. Dodd took the child by cesarean last night."

The young actress was affected by her somberness. "The baby was okay, wasn't it?" she asked anxiously.

"At first. But the little boy has a disease which interferes with his breathing. I'm afraid he's going to . . ."

"Die?"

"I'm afraid so. Very soon."

"How awful!" The girl was very upset, genuinely so.

Softly, Sheryl said, "Isn't it?"

Then Susan Raimond was staring at her. "Why are you telling me this?"

"I think you know. Across the hall is a woman you know, admire, and respect. I believe you even said you loved her. She has been desperately trying to have a child for years. So much courage, so

217

many disappointments. In the last few days she has endured agonizing pain, trying, hoping to carry her child to term. Finally, under doctor's orders and at the urging of her husband, she had the cesarean. The baby appeared normal, at first, but then . . ."

"It's going to die." Susan looked away, toward the window and the sunshine outside. Finally, she said, "Meanwhile, here I sit, prepared to let my baby die rather than have a cesarean."

"I don't think that is really your decision, is it, Susan?" No answer. "If it were up to you, wouldn't you let your child live?"

"It is *not* up to her!"

Sheryl turned to see Rita Farrell standing in the doorway.

"I will thank you to leave at once, Dr. James, and not return to this room ever again."

Sheryl met the woman's eyes. They were blue ice. Sheryl felt like shivering.

"The fact remains that Susan cannot make the decision. She is a minor. She is *my* daughter and *my* responsibility and *I* have decided what is best for her—something you wouldn't possibly understand. Therefore, there is no need for you to waste your *valuable* time *counseling* her. Go, this instant!"

Sheryl saw the door open wide. She had no alternative but to pass through it.

Max waited, heard Wally Dykes come on the phone. "Ah, Mr. Dykes. Good to hear your voice. How are you this fine day?"

"Who's this?"

Max heard the guarded tone. "This is Father Jackson. I hope you remember me—St. Bonny's?"

"Oh, yeah—sure, I remember ya."

"I have splendid news for you, Mr. Dykes. I think you'll be most pleased. I know I am."

"Ya got the dough?"

218

"Dough?" Hearty laugh. "Oh, you mean money."

"Yeah, sorry. I meant to say *contribution*." Titter. "Just a little joke."

Max intensified his laugh. "With the work you do for all those poor suffering people, a person just has to hold onto a sense of humor, doesn't he?"

"Yeah, sure. Have you got the contribution?"

Prolonged pause. "I'm happy to inform you, Mr. Dykes, that I have met with the board. The vote was unanimous to make an anonymous contribution to your cause."

"That's great! The amount ya mentioned?"

"Oh, yes, indeed. In fact, the board went along with all the terms we discussed."

"Cash?"

"Oh, yes."

"Small bills?"

Long pause. "I don't believe we discussed that, Mr. Dykes. I'm sure you understand. That amount is quite . . . large. To be honest, I don't think either one of us could lift half a million dollars if the bills are too small." Laugh. "I know I couldn't."

"Never thought of that."

"I've asked the bank for smallish bills, shall we say—nothing larger than hundreds. Will that do?"

"Sure, sure."

"I believe it will all fit in a small suitcase. I hardly thought you wanted an armored truck." Hearty laugh again.

"Good thinking, Reverend—I mean, Father. When do I get it?"

"I was thinking about late this afternoon. Would five-ish be acceptable?"

"Sure, I'm free then."

*I bet you are!* "Then it's all set. See you then."

"Wait! Where? I don't know where to meet you."

"Oh, I'm sorry. St. Bonaventure's, of course.

That seems like a suitable place, don't you think—
a church in which to do God's work?"

"St. Bonaventure's. The same place as before.
Okay, I'll be there."

"How nice of you." Pause. "Oh, Mr. Dykes, I
almost forgot. I'm to remind you to bring your
little gift."

"Gift?"

"Yes, surely you remember. The Cardinal told
me he'd spoken to you directly about the contribution after I did. As a matter of fact, he mentioned how impressed he was with you and your
desire to make good use of our donation. You *do*
remember talking to the Cardinal?"

"Oh, sure—sure, the Cardinal."

"He said you wanted to make some sort of gift
to the Church in thanksgiving for our donation.
Nothing lavish, I understand. Just some sort of
memento enabling the Cardinal to remember you
and our most pleasant dealings with you in his
prayers. It was to be something private, personal.
He wouldn't tell me what it was"—laugh—"but
I'm sure you know. I suppose it must be some kind
of a surprise?"

"Surprise?" Dykes sounded surprised, all right.

"Well, he did say it was to be sealed in a manila
envelope. You are to give it to me when the contribution is made. You *do* recall all that?"

Long pause. Then light apparently dawned.
"Oh, yeah, of course! Manila envelope."

"Very well, Mr. Dykes. It'll be a pleasure to see
you again—at five. Good-bye."

Laura Carlyle accepted the phone call only because Rosella Parkins said it appeared to be ur-
gent, that Dana Shaughnessy seemed extremely
upset and was demanding to speak to her. Laura
was a great believer in the chain of command. She
issued orders only to Brian as administrator, the
Director of Medicine, the Chief of Surgery, and

220

Hillary George, Director of Nursing. Subordinates were spoken to on her daily inspections, which she called "rounds." Her only other contacts came via her famous "memos," which sometimes fell like confetti over the hospital staff. But since Hillary was with her son and Dana was for the time being acting director, she accepted the call.

"Why have you done this to me, Mrs. Carlyle?"

Laura, astonished, heard the tears and outrage in the woman's voice. Deliberately, she made hers as soothing as possible. "Done what, Dana?"

"I've been here practically my whole life. I've always done everything you asked of me. Why have you stabbed me in the back?"

Thoroughly puzzled, Laura asked, "Is there some sort of emergency I'm unaware of? I don't know what you're talking about."

"What do you mean, you don't know? You just fired me, Kathryn Quigley, and Barbara Brookes, too!"

"*I* fired you?"

"Don't pretend, Mrs. Carlyle. You've never been two-faced with me before. Why are you now? What have I done to deserve it?"

Laura bristled. "I will not be spoken to this way, Dana! Now just calm yourself and tell me what on earth you are talking about."

An audible, quavering sigh was heard over the phone. "This letter I just got, eliminating the position of Shift Supervisor. That's what it *says*, but I know what it really means. I'm fired, Mrs. Carlyle."

"A letter? Who wrote it?"

"Well, it's signed by Mr. Hecht, but I know it had to come from you."

"Just a moment, please." Greatly mystified, Laura held her hand over the mouthpiece and turned to her secretary. "Do you know anything about a letter from Brian firing the Supervisors of Nursing?" She saw Rosella shake her head slowly, as puzzled as she. Back on the phone, she said, "Dana, will you be so kind as to come to the Tower and bring that letter with you?"

A few minutes later, a weeping Dana Shaughnessy sat across from her in Oliver's study while Laura read in utter amazement. The letter addressed to all three supervisors was brief:

I believe the enclosed administrative order to be self-explanatory.

I am sure you realize I take this step with a heavy heart. Your long years of dedicated service are most appreciated. To help you with the transition period, please find attached a check representing your accrued salary as of this date, accumulated vacation pay, and one month's salary as severance pay. You will receive shortly a statement of the cash value of your pensions.

We will, of course, do all we can to assist you in finding other employment, including providing you with a letter of recommendation.

Again, I regret being forced to take this action, but I am sure you understand why it is necessary.

It was signed "Brian Hecht, Administrator." Without even glancing at Shaughnessy, Laura immediately began to read the attached administrative order.

For some time a study has been in progress with the dual aim of increasing the efficiency of nursing care at Bel Air General Hospital and reducing costs, an important aim in all major hospitals today.

After thorough and prolonged study, the decision has been reached that the best way to implement these two goals is to reorganize the nursing staff.

222

As of noon today, the position of Supervisor of Nursing has been eliminated.

The duties of Supervisor will now be assumed by floor nurses and head nurses who will assume direct responsibility, under the Director of Nursing, for the quality of nursing care in their units.

It is our belief this new arrangement will benefit both the patients and staff of Bel Air General Hospital by increasing the authority of those who deal directly with patients.

Your cooperation is most appreciated.

Brian Hecht
Administrator

Laura read it again, then scanned the accompanying letter for the second time. It wasn't possible! Brian had never said a word to her about this. He wouldn't issue such an order without consulting her. He had always known that the nursing staff was her *peculiar* interest. He couldn't possibly be responsible for this.

Without looking at either Shaughnessy or Rosella, she said, "Excuse me," stood up, and went to the phone in the morning room. She got through to Brian at once. "Dana Shaughnessy is here with me—or, rather, she's in Oliver's study."

"I'm not surprised." Brian sounded perfectly calm.

"I'm holding in my hand a letter and administrative order addressed to her with your name at the bottom. I assume it is either some kind of prank or a forgery."

"I'm afraid not, Laura."

"You sent this?"

"Yes. Because I figured she'd run directly to you, I took the liberty of posting the order throughout the hospital before having it delivered to her."

"But, Brian—"

"I've also had copies sent by messenger to Quigley and Brookes."

Laura was actually shaking with anger, but her voice did not convey it. "You have been most efficient."

He heard the sarcasm, noting how unusual it was for her to engage in it. "Thank you," he replied in the same tone.

Long pause. "Brian, why?"

"I thought it wise—in the best interests of the hospital and yourself."

"I won't have it, Brian."

"Very well. Then you will have my resignation."

The threat struck her almost like a physical blow. Anger turned immediately to fear. "Brian, why are you doing this to me? What has happened?"

"I am not doing anything *to* you, but rather *for* you. And nothing has happened to *me*. I'm the same good ol' Brian I've always been."

"Oh, Brian, I feel like weeping—something I haven't done since Willard died!"

"There's nothing to cry over, Laura. The order was posted for good and sufficient reasons."

"What were they?"

"I can't tell you that just now, not over the phone. Just trust me."

Long sigh. "Will you please come up here and talk to me?"

"I can't right now. I'm late for an important lunch. It'll have to wait till this afternoon. I'll come as soon as I can."

"Very well." Struggling to regain her composure with all her will, Laura returned to the study, to find that Dana Shaughnessy's tears had evaporated, replaced by fury.

"That goddamned she-bitch of a whore did it! I *know* it!"

Rosella Parkins came to her feet. "Miss Shaugh-

224

nessy, you will *not* use such language in this house!"

Even in her outrage, Shaughnessy could not help being intimidated by the formidable Rosella. She began dabbing again at her eyes.

Laura sought to placate her. "I know you are upset, Dana, but there is no virtue in vituperation."

"But I *know* she did it! She went to Mr. Hecht, told him—"

"Of whom are you speaking, Dana?"

"Hillary George. I know you like her, Mrs. Carlyle, but she's nothing but a whore. Do you know that—"

"Stop it at once!" Laura's voice now showed her inner steel. "I will not listen to such talk." She turned to Rosella. "Please escort Miss Shaughnessy to the elevator. She may return when she has calmed herself and is prepared to speak civilly."

Shaughnessy gaped at her, then at once began to weep again. "Please; don't do this to me," she wailed.

"I've done nothing to you. It was entirely Brian's—Mr. Hecht's—doing."

"Don't let him fire me—*please!*"

She motioned to Rosella. "We'll talk about it later, Dana. Have some lunch. You'll feel better."

Hamilton Dodd was determined to control his temper and his tongue, for he was sure his anger, no matter how justified, would be self-defeating with the mother of Susan Raimond. Thus, when he had her alone in the lounge behind the nursing station he said in a voice that came as close as he could to sweet reasonableness, "Miss Farrell, have you had a chance to reconsider your decision concerning your daughter?"

"There is nothing to reconsider, Doctor."

He saw the woman as stubborn, willful—and, worse, a murderess. But he had talked to himself, hoping to make himself believe she really loved her daughter and was merely misguided. This he now tried to keep in mind. "It occurs to me, Miss Farrell, that perhaps I have failed to explain the situation to you adequately."

"I think you have done quite well, Dr. Dodd. Unless I permit my daughter to have a cesarean section, the baby will die. As much as I regret that, I must put Susan's welfare first. It is not my fault she has a *placenta previa.* I refuse to wallow in guilt or permit you or anyone else to attempt to make me do so."

Yes, a strong-minded woman. Too bad she was also stupid and cruel. "As I feared, you do not fully understand the situation."

"Oh?"

"It is not just the baby's life that is at risk, but your daughter's as well."

She smiled in a twisted, sardonic way. "Come now, Doctor, that is beneath you."

"If you do not trust my judgment, Miss Farrell, by all means seek a second opinion. Your daughter has persistent bleeding from the uterus and has had for some time. With the placenta above the os, there is no way to prevent it."

"I know that, Doctor, but she is receiving whole blood."

"Yes, but we are virtually pouring blood into her arm and having it run out between her legs. If your daughter goes to term, still at least a couple of weeks away, there is a considerable risk to her life. I cannot be responsible for that."

She shook her head as she favored him with a display of perfect teeth. "This hospital has tried everything, or so I thought, to force my daughter to have unnecessary surgery. Now a threat to her life is introduced. Personally, Doctor, I find this contemptible."

He wanted very badly to knock those perfect teeth down her throat, but managed not to show

226

it. "Miss Farrell, I have another patient across the hall from Susan. Her problem was different—an *abruptio placentae*—but she also had persistent bleeding. She was highly reluctant to have a cesarean. But she finally became convinced of the need for surgery when her blood-fibrin levels became alarmingly low."

"What is blood fibrin?"

"In simplest language, fibrin is the means by which clotting occurs. Persistent bleeding strips the blood of fibrin. Then when surgery occurs, the patient's blood will not clot. Bleeding continues, and the patient may well bleed to death."

"But Susan is receiving blood."

"True, but fibrin does not remain in blood which has been stored. Transfusions do not maintain the fibrin level." He watched her carefully. At least she was no longer scoffing at him. He had gained her attention.

"Is Susan's fibrin level low?"

He was between the proverbial rock and a hard place. He wished he could lie but knew he could not. "It is not as good as it should be, Miss Farrell."

"Is it dangerously low?"

"No, but with continued bleeding I cannot promise you that it will not become so."

"I see." She turned away from him, striding on high heels to the coffeepot, but not taking any. In a moment she said, "If you are endeavoring to frighten me, Dr. Dodd, you have succeeded."

"That was not my aim. I want only to apprise you of all the facts."

"And so you have." She turned back to face him. "Those facts now convince me more than ever that I am correct in not permitting the operation. If Susan's blood fibrin is low, the surgery would pose an intolerable risk for her. Letting the baby go to term is by far the safer course."

"Miss Farrell, I—"

"Doctor, am I not correct in stating that the location of the placenta is the cause of her bleeding?"

"Yes, but—"

"As soon as the placenta is removed the bleeding will stop, right?"

"Yes."

"In a normal birth there will be no need for incisions. She will deliver the child and all will be well." Now she smiled. "You see, Doctor, I do know something about all this."

Dodd could only shake his head in frustration. Before he could say anything, Nurse Tawari entered and whispered in his ear. "Very well, I'll be right there." He turned to Rita Farrell. "I have an emergency. I must go."

"You seem to have a great many emergencies, Doctor," Rita said. Then she turned and poured herself a cup of coffee with a steady hand.

228

# Chapter 12

Charles Bridges had hoped to find some gentle way
to tell his wife the tragic news, but the opportunity never came. Adriana now seemed so weak and
ill he could not bring himself to say anything even
during those brief periods when she was awake.
During one such period she had opened her eyes,
smiled wanly, and whispered, "We have a son,
Charles." That left him so choked up he couldn't
have said anything even if he had known what to
say.

As the morning wore on, activity seemed to pick
up. Nurse Tawari made frequent trips into the
room, checking Adriana's monitors, changing the
IV and bag of blood. On each successive trip she
looked more worried. Finally, Hamilton Dodd
hustled in, read the monitors, and took Adriana's
pulse, shaking his head all the while.

"What's wrong, Hamilton?" Bridges asked.

Dodd finished counting the pulse, pulled the

stethoscope from his ears, and faced his friend. "I have to take her back into surgery this instant."

Bridges paled. "What's wrong?"

"Her internal hemorrhaging is continuing. Her blood pressure is dangerously low, eighty over fifty. Her pulse is racing at one forty. We either have to stop the bleeding or we're going to lose her."

Charles Bridges's eyes widened. "You mean—" He shook his head in disbelief. "She might die?"

"I'm afraid so, unless a hysterectomy is performed at once. It is the only way left to us." He saw Bridges still registering shock. "I'd hoped the pitocin would work, shrink the uterus." He went to Bridges and put his hand on his shoulder. "I'm sorry. I've been afraid of this all along. I'd hoped the pitocin would work, but it hasn't."

"There will be no more children?"

"I'm sorry." Then he saw Bridges staring past him to the bed. Dodd turned and saw that Adriana's eyes were open. "You heard?"

"Yes." Her voice was barely audible. "At least we have one child . . ."

Brian's lunch was corned beef on rye in the office of Maurice Edgerton, attorney for Bel Air General. Their discussion produced mixed results for Brian. Edgerton felt there would be no particular difficulty with the Bridges matter. In a life-threatening situation the husband's right to overrule the wishes of his wife would surely be upheld in court. And, given the stability of the marriage and the prominence of the couple, he strongly doubted any legal action would be brought against Bel Air General.

The Raimond case was another matter. Under California law, the age of consent was eighteen unless the minor had been living as an independent teenager. Therefore, the mother, not Susan Raimond, had to give consent for the surgery. Yes,

230

it would be possible for the hospital to go to court on behalf of the unborn child. It would be a stupendous, precedent-shattering case, and the hospital might lose if it could be proved that the surgery posed a risk to the life of the mother. Did it? Brian wasn't sure. He said he'd find out and get back to Edgerton. Meanwhile, the best course of action was to continue to try to persuade Rita Farrell to give her consent.

When he returned to the hospital, Brian went directly to the Tower. Might as well confront Laura and have it over with. He had already decided to tell her at least some of his real reasons for getting rid of the three supervisors, but this plan came to naught when he discovered she was not alone.

Like her husband, Bobbi Hecht had awakened feeling low. Her bedmanship—or, rather, floormanship—with Judd Forbes had left a bad taste in her mouth. What had possessed her? She cared nothing for him, didn't even find him particularly attractive. She had simply acted out, with a virtual stranger, that which she wanted to do with her husband. In the light of day, what she had done was intolerable to her. Judd Forbes! Her husband's assistant! She must have been crazy. There could be no repeat performance. She was going to nip this thing in the bud at once. To this end, she had gone to see her grandmother, planning to offer some plausible reason why she was no longer interested in the outreach project. She had not yet worked around to it when Brian walked in.

As soon as he entered Oliver's study and saw his wife, Brian's anger flared. "Is this going to become a regular event, Laura?"

"Event? What are you talking about?"

"Are our discussions of hospital affairs now going to include members of the board of directors?"

Laura's back straightened at once and she

231

glared at him. "I believe that's uncalled for, Brian."

Bobbi felt as though he had slapped her. At once she got up, her anger showing. "I was just leaving."

"You'll do no such thing, Roberta. Please take your seat." Laura turned to her grandson-in-law. "My granddaughter is my guest. You will treat my guests with courtesy."

He bowed toward his wife, a gesture of pure irony. "Okay. How've you been, Bobbi? Everything okay?"

"Stop it this instant, Brian! I will *not* have such behavior in my house—especially from someone I love as much as you."

Brian suspected he was acting childish and petulant and he didn't like it very much. "Very well." He sat in a leather chair diagonally across from the two women. "Have you countermanded my order, Laura?"

"You know I have not."

"But you'd like to."

"Perhaps. What I'd really like is an explanation—in fact, several explanations." Suddenly Laura realized Bobbi didn't know what they were talking about. She turned to her and said, "Brian posted an order this morning reorganizing the nursing staff. He eliminated the position of Supervisor of Nursing." Now she turned back to him. "I believe I have a right to know why that action was taken."

Brian's anger still seethed. He disliked having this discussion in front of his wife. Her presence was to him an act of trespass on his turf, an outrageous invasion of his privacy. He certainly was not going to discuss Hillary George, Max Hill, or any of his real reasons in front of a third party, especially Bobbi. Words formed in his brain. He had a fleeting sense he ought to restrain them, but in his rage he was powerless to do so. "I had to

232

get that hundred grand back somehow. Eliminating the supervisors seemed a good way to do it."

"Damn you, Brian!" Bobbi cried.

"Stop it, both of you! I won't have it." Laura's voice was surprisingly sharp. Then she said, "I hardly think that is the real reason, Brian."

"It did cross my mind." Now he looked intensely at Laura. "I think I handled a difficult situation quite well. Frankly, I don't care much for being called on the carpet about it. I felt I took an action you would have come to yourself under the circumstances. In fact, I lifted a page out of your own book."

"My book?"

"Do you remember some months ago when you couldn't convince Ernest Wilkerson to resign? You simply made an endplay, denuding him of authority and creating the post of Chief of Surgery for Leon Kazinsky. I thought that was very sharp of you. I simply did something similar."

She shook her head. "I don't understand."

"The supervisors had to go, all three of them. I know that if I fired them as they deserved, there would be all sorts of trouble, including lawsuits, most likely. So I made an endplay. I eliminated their positions, calling it a reorganization."

Laura looked at Bobbi, but got no help there. "I still don't understand. Why did the supervisors have to go?"

Brian hesitated, sighed. "That I cannot tell you."

"Bobbi said, "You mean you won't say because I'm here."

Shrug. "As you wish."

"Anything you want to say to me, you may say in front of Roberta," Laura informed him.

"I just did. I cannot tell you why I fired the supervisors. Nor do I feel I have a need to. It was my decision, made for good and sufficient reasons."

"Bull!" Bobbi shot back. "You were just exercising your authority, proving what a big man you are."

Brian looked at her levelly. "That's entirely correct, Madame Director. With the president's granddaughter very much on the scene, ready to run to her with every little trial and tribulation, not to mention whim, I thought it was a splendid idea to establish once and for all who's the boss and who is running the hospital." Now he grinned. "If that was a mistake, then *mea culpa*."

Laura was so shocked and saddened she was nearly speechless except for, "Oh, dear, oh, dear."

When Brian looked at her, his anger began to fade, replaced not by regrets but by compassion for this old woman whom he loved. "I'm sorry, Laura. I probably should have discussed my actions with you in advance, but I felt the need to—"

"Exert your masculinity."

Brian glanced wryly at Bobbi. "That's one way to put it."

"Please be still, Roberta. Let a person think."

"If you can figure out how to get her to do that, then you're a better person than I am."

"Fuck you, Brian!"

"Stop it!"

Brian laughed. "One good thing about this, Bobbi—I doubt if you'll be horning into any more discussions of hospital affairs."

"I will not have it!" To make her point, Laura Carlyle rose to stand over the two of them. "This is . . . *unseemly!* Two grown people who love each other should not bicker like this. Please spare me any more of this in the future." She did have the effect of silencing them, so she slowly sat down again. "Brian, however justified you may think your action is, it still causes great difficulties for me. Dana Shaughnessy has been with this hospital for many years, Kathryn Quigley and Barbara

234

Brookes almost as long. I have always promised loyalty to our employees. You know how long it took me to replace dear Abby Main as Director of Nursing after her illness. In one impetuous act, you have undone something I spent many years to achieve."

"I was conscious of that, Laura. But loyalty is not a one-way street. Loyalty given must be loyalty returned."

"What do you mean? What has happened?"

Brian knew he had to say something. "What has happened is that an intolerable situation has developed. The three supervisors would not accept Hillary as director. They were constantly undermining her authority and slandering her character, losing no opportunity to do so. We either put Hillary George in charge of the nursing staff, or we don't. I simply carried out your wishes when you originally appointed her."

Laura looked away from him. "I just wish I knew what has been going on."

"No, you don't Laura. I'm quite sure you wouldn't want to know. All you need to do is trust my judgment in this matter." He watched the expression in her eyes as she looked at him. "But you can't quite do that, right?"

"The nursing care in this hospital has long been a special interest of mine, ever since I myself was a nurse." Laura sighed.

"You still are a nurse, Grandmother."

He sighed. "I might as well say it. Laura, I am either administrator of this entire hospital or I am administrator of none of it."

Laura looked at him with great sadness, shaking her head. She felt like weeping. "Oh, Brian, how did it come to this?"

The hysterectomy was in many ways routine for Hamilton Dodd. With his patient under full anesthetic, he reentered through the same incisions he had made for the cesarean section, tying off the Fallopian tubes, excising the uterus, taking great pains to tie off all the blood vessels leading to it. With the bleeding stopped and the administration of plasma containing fibrin, Adriana Barre would now recover.

But in other ways, of course, the surgery was anything but routine. Even while his hands were technically proficient, Ham Dodd's mind dwelled on the fate of this woman. Her long battle to have a child was now ended. The one child she'd borne alive was dying, if not already dead. She didn't yet know that. She would have to be told soon.

It was uncharacteristic of him that his frustration took the form of irritability. One by one, he bit off the head of everyone in the OR. But when he had sewn up his patient and finished, he stopped at the door and apologized to all in the room. He needn't have, for they understood. They felt just as badly as he did, as the entire hospital staff did. Word of the tragic events in the life of Adriana Barre had spread through the hospital grapevine almost as soon as they had occurred.

On his way down from the Tower, Brian stopped at Sheryl James's office on impulse. She was alone. "You said if I ever wanted to talk, you'd listen," he said. "I want to talk. Got time?"

She smiled. "Sure. Come in." She motioned to the chairs where they usually sat. He remained for perhaps a full minute without speaking. Sheryl simply waited, sensing how very upset and confused he was.

Finally Brian said," I realized this morning why I love Jenny—miss her so. She was the one person I could always talk to. She was my sounding board, someone to discuss my problems with."

"And without her you have no one."

"That's about it. Want to volunteer?"

"I can't be Jenny, Brian."

236

"I know. How are you at confidences?"

She smiled. "You must know the answer to that. It's my stock in trade."

He nodded. After a long pause he began. "I just left a rather nasty scene. I'm not sure how much of it was my fault. I went to the Tower to explain to Laura why I posted the order reorganizing the nursing staff."

" I saw it."

"My wife was there." Pause. "The simple fact is that I resented her presence greatly. Things I would have said privately to Laura I could not say in front of her. But Bobbi is Laura's granddaughter and a director of this hospital. What could I do?"

Sheryl smiled. "Get angry?"

"You got it. I feel emasculated, having her work in the hospital. The plain fact is I should've discussed the order with Laura in advance. The nurses have always been her special bailiwick. But I didn't because—"

"You wanted to exert your authority."

He glanced at her. "You really are sharp, aren't you?"

"It isn't too hard to figure."

"Familiar stuff, eh?"

"Which is not to say it isn't important. How do *you* feel about it—about yourself, I mean?"

"Not too great, obviously, or I wouldn't be here, Doctor."

She laughed. "No need to be so formal, Brian. There's no fee being charged."

"Professional courtesy?"

"Or being scared of the boss. Seriously, has it ever occurred to you that you may have two separate problems and are confusing them?"

"Maybe."

"You've had a problem with Bobbi for quite some time. Now you've let Bobbi create a problem with Laura where there wasn't one before." She

237

saw him looking intently at her. "How'm I doing so far?"

"Not bad. Go on."

"Or maybe it's a mistake to personalize the problems. Was there another reason which made you decide to reorganize the nursing staff?"

"Yep." He hesitated. "I really shouldn't tell you, Sheryl, but . . ."—he shrugged—". . . I did come to talk. Confidential?"

"Absolutely."

"The three supervisors were trying to blackmail Hillary, get some dirt on her, force her to resign so one of them could replace her."

"Sheryl was appalled. "You're kidding!"

"Nope. I decided to come down on Hillary's side and get rid of the troublemakers. Firing them would have led to questions, so I did everyone a favor by eliminating the positions."

"Has Hillary actually *done* anything? Strike that. It really doesn't matter, does it?"

"No. I don't know and don't want to know. All that matters is that she is a fine woman, she's Director of Nursing, and she needs my support."

"And you don't want to go into any gory details, even with Laura."

"That's about it—except there are no gory details as far as I know. Just three old biddies snooping into someone's private life, hoping for dirt."

She nodded. "Would you have told Laura what you just told me if Bobbi hadn't been there?"

"Probably."

"But you got your back up instead."

"I claimed the right to make such decisions." He sighed. "I even threatened to resign if my authority wasn't complete."

Sheryl nodded. "Too bad you don't get along with your wife."

"It's an intolerable situation for me. With her in the hospital, everybody's going to run to her with their—"

238

"No, they're not."

"—complaints. She'll backstop everything I do. This place will become a two-headed monster."

"Has this happened?" Sheryl asked.

"Not yet."

"Then aren't you blaming her for something that hasn't happened and may very well *not* happen?"

"Possibly."

"Are you always this prescient? Or should I say, do you always borrow trouble before it gets here?"

His smile was rueful. "It doesn't hurt to be prepared."

"True. But it helps to be prepared for several possibilities rather than focusing on just one."

Brian shrugged and made no comment.

"Funny thing about you and your wife. All she wants is to be near you, part of your life, and you want to drive her away." She saw him start to speak and silenced him by raising her hand. "She had nothing to do with Jenny's rape, Brian."

"So you've told me."

"I've talked to her. I know for a fact she feels almost as badly about what happened to Jenny as you do."

He looked away. "Let's talk about something else, all right?"

She was puzzled by his attitude. Why was it so essential that he blame Bobbi? But she said, "All right."

"Are you having any luck with Susan Raimond?" Brian asked.

"Lots with Susan, not much with Rita Farrell. She's got her back up, something you might understand. Nobody's going to get through to her."

He firmed his lips. "I talked to the hospital's attorney. The only alternative is to have the unborn baby declared a ward of the court. The judge could order the cesarean to save its life."

"Complicated. And messy."

"Very. The press would love it. Any chance the mere threat of a lot of bad publicity would change the mother's mind?"

"I doubt it," Sheryl said. "She'd probably welcome any publicity at all. By the way, have you heard the latest?"

"I'm afraid to ask."

"You should be. Leon Kazinsky told me at lunch that Dr. Dodd had a most *unfortunate* talk with Rita Farrell. He tried to frighten her by saying the continued bleeding puts Susan in danger. All he did was convince the mother that lowered blood-fibrin levels would put Susan in danger if she had surgery."

"Lord! In court she'd argue that she's acting in her daughter's best interests."

Sheryl leaned closer to him. "Brian, I'm convinced that with a little time we can talk Susan into having the baby," she said earnestly.

"How? In California the age of consent is eighteen unless the child has been an independent minor."

"I know. It seems hopeless, but there's a solution to this problem, I'm sure of it. I just need a little time."

"You got it. As they say, you're the only sail in the wind at the moment." He stood up to leave. "Thanks for listening to me."

"Anytime." She stood, too, accompanying him to the door of her small office. "I was so sorry to hear about Adriana Barre."

"That her baby is going to die? Yes."

"Not to mention the hysterectomy she just had."

He gaped at her. "I didn't know about that."

"Then you're the only one in the hospital who doesn't."

Wally Dykes was uneasy, In fact, he was just plain nervous. Nothing was going the way he'd planned. He'd figured on dealing directly with Stillwell, a

240

man easy to handle. The nastier he was with him, the quicker he folded. But the black priest was something else. Dykes felt he couldn't control him, if only because he had nothing on him. Over and over Dykes told himself that everything was okay. He couldn't really expect Stillwell to hand over the money personally. Some sort of arrangement like this, making it look like a charitable contribution, was probably inevitable. But that didn't make Dykes like it any better.

What he liked even less was that his wife was now deeply involved in the whole deal. He had hoped—still hoped—to get the money and bug out on wife, kid, mother-in-law, the whole shebang. He would disappear. Planning just how to do it had been his major preoccupation. But then his blasted mother-in-law had ruined that when she came over, blabbing about how she didn't want any blackmail. Maureen had heard, supported him, even joined in. Had she ever! It was all she talked about now. And suddenly she loved him. She was all over him in bed, and it had been a long time since that had happened. Shit!

The worst thing was that she wanted to *participate*. Had to know every detail about the meetings with Stillwell and the black priest. She'd even listened on the extension when the priest talked about the "gift" for the Cardinal.

"Give the negative to him, Wally. Half a million is enough."

Hell, no! You never give up something like that. It would be good forever. You could bleed a man dry with something like that.

"Wally, it's a onetime thing, isn't it? That Cardinal will never hang around. He'll probably resign, disappear someplace. You'll never get any more money out of him."

Yeah, but the Church would still be there.

"Let him have them, Wally. We'll take what

we got, enjoy it. We'll invest it someplace. We'll be set for life."

*You mean trapped for life.* He wasn't going to do it, no way! A sealed manila envelope—there was no way for anyone to know what was in it. When Maureen insisted on watching him seal the photo and negative inside the envelope, he went along. He was less happy when she also insisted on riding with him to the church. Okay, so he'd dump her later. In the meantime, she'd have to wait in the car.

"Father Jackson" met him on the steps of St. Bonaventure's with a big grin and a hearty handshake. "Right on time, Mr. Dykes. Punctuality is a rare and blessed quality these days." They went around the side to the rectory. "I don't know about you, Mr. Dykes, but I consider this a red-letter day. I couldn't be happier. I'm sure you feel the same way."

"Oh, yeah, sure."

"It gives me goose bumps just thinking about all the help those poor suffering men and women will receive as a direct result of what we do this day."

Wally saw the broad smile on the black face. Unreal was what it was. Nobody, but *nobody*, could be that goody-goody, especially when giving away half a million bucks. "Me, too, Reverend— I mean, Father . . ."

"Jackson, Father Jackson." He went behind his desk, saying, as he reached underneath, "We might as well get to it, hadn't we?"

Dykes felt he couldn't breathe as the priest placed a brown vinyl suitcase, about the size of an overnighter, on the desktop and fumbled in the pocket of his cassock for keys.

"Father Jackson" laughed, embarrassed. "Why is it that as soon as you know a suitcase contains something valuable you feel the need to lock it? If it just held clothes or something, you'd never think of it." Another chuckle. "Don't you think that strange, Mr. Dykes?"

Wally couldn't reply. He only watched intently as a pair of locks was turned, another pair of fasteners unlatched, and the lid opened to reveal neat stacks of very green money.

"You may count it if you wish, but I assure you it is all there."

Dykes glanced upward, saw the big grin on the priest's face. Then he looked at the money again, stepped forward to touch it. God, it was beautiful! His fingers positively tingled as they felt the smooth, crisp bills.

"I know you'll put this to the best possible use, my friend."

Now he could smile. "Yeah, better believe it!" But when he looked at the money again he realized something was bothering him. "I wasn't expectin' new bills."

"It would have been very difficult to raise this much money in old bills, and would no doubt have taken much longer to accumulate. Why does it matter?"

Dykes glanced at him. "It's easy to trace the serial numbers on new bills."

Max Hill laughed. "Now who on earth would want to do that? And what would it matter if they did? This is a perfectly honorable transaction."

Dykes blinked at the smiling face, felt reassured. "I guess you're right."

"I know I am, but I don't blame you for being nervous. I know I was, just knowing I had such a large sum in my possession." He closed the case but did not lock it. "I am truly happy to pass it on to someone else." He shoved the case toward Dykes, then clapped a hand to his forehead. "Good heavens! How thoughtless of me! The banks are closed. What are you going to do with this overnight?"

Dykes hesitated. "I see what ya mean. Oh, it'll be taken care of. Don't you worry."

"You've arranged for a night deposit, I suppose."

Dykes lifted the suitcase from the desk. For the first time he felt the thrill of victory. Five hundred thousand bucks! But he managed to restrain himself to a broad grin. "Heavy little sucker, ain't it?"

"Yes, money has surprising weight and is a great reponsibility, I might add, for any man."

"Don't you worry none, padre. This'll be spent very wisely."

"I'm sure." Max came around the desk, clapped Dykes on the shoulder. "I guess that about wraps up our business here. Let me accompany you to the door." They made a couple of strides across the rectory. As Max reached for the doorknob, he said, "Oh, I almost forgot. You have a little gift?"

"Oh, yeah, the gift. Almost forgot myself."

Max watched Dykes reach inside his suit and extract a five-by-seven envelope. He accepted it. "I know I shouldn't, but I just have to see what you've given him." He strode back to the desk and reached for a letter opener.

Dykes raised his brows. "Are you sure you wanna do that?"

Max slit it deftly. "My sin of curiosity is well known. He'll understand." The contents were pulled out and looked at. Max smiled beatifically. "A photograph of yourself. I'm sure the Cardinal will treasure it."

"Won't he, though?" Dykes just couldn't resist grinning in return.

"Well, let's be on our way."

At the door of the church Max elaborately shook Dykes's hand, wishing him Godspeed and good fortune, then watched him descend the steps. As he reached his car, Max waved at him with the envelope. Then he turned and reentered the church.

244

Detective Lieutenant Frank Elgin was out of his car and moving toward Dykes even before he saw the signal. It caused him to mutter, "The dumb greedy bastard!" The envelope in Max's hand meant that the incriminating photo and negative had not been turned over.

Elgin reached Dykes just as he was opening the trunk of the car to put the suitcase inside. The detective roughly pulled him away and shoved him hard against the side of the car. "Spread 'em. You know the drill, Dykes."

Dykes stared at him. "What's goin' on?"

"Dammit! I said spread 'em!" He shoved Dykes's head down hard against the roof of the car, then quickly patted him down for a weapon. "At least you got enough sense not to carry a piece."

"I ain't done nothin'," Dykes whined, frightened out of his wits.

"That's what they all say." Elgin produced his gold badge, shoved it in front of Dykes's nose. "You're under arrest. Suspicion of counterfeiting. Read 'em his rights, Sergeant."

Hank "Beanie" Bean was a sergeant, all right—with the fire fighters. Elgin had recruited him from his parish, telling him almost nothing about what was really going on, because he needed assistance and didn't want to involve another cop. That would have meant either some kind of arrest report or a lot of lies, which he didn't want to become involved in.

Bean produced the card Elgin had given him and began to read. "You have the right to remain silent. . . ."

"Hey, I ain't no counterfeiter!" Dykes squawked.

"Leave my husband alone!" A very frightened and angry Maureen Dykes had gotten out of the car and now came over to Wally, Elgin, and Bean.

"Stay outta this, lady. Okay, Dykes, you gonna open that suitcase, or am I?"

"There's nothin' in it."

"Fine. Then open it." When Dykes hesitated, Elgin shrugged and said, "Okay, Sergeant, *you* open it."

Dykes wavered a moment but could think of no way out. "All right, all right. There's money in it, but it's legit—a charitable contribution. I ain't no counterfeiter."

"And I'm Charley's aunt. I've been following that case all day. I'll hand it to you—it was half-way smart of you to use a church as a dropoff."

"Take a look at this, Lieutenant."

Elgin went to stand beside Bean and pulled out a couple of bills from beneath their wrappers. He held them up and laughed. "These couldn't be any phonier if you put a three on them!"

Dykes snatched the bills from the detective and for the first time looked at them closely. "Oh, God!" he groaned.

"Not even good stuff, Dykes," Elgin said sadly. "I've seen better money in a Monopoly set."

Panic rose in Dykes. "I don't know nothin' about this, Officer, honest. I'm no counterfeiter."

"I believe it. Your job is to peddle the stuff. But it's all the same to me. Cuff him, Sergeant."

"Wait! I'm tellin' the truth. I was just told to pick up a suitcase. I had no idea what was in it." He saw the cop was at least listening to him. "I got the case from a priest. Who'd think a priest would—"

"What priest?"

"There. Inside the church. Father . . ." He couldn't think of the guy's name all of a sudden.

"Father who?"

Maureen came to his aid. "Father Jackson. He's a black priest."

"Yeah, Father Jackson. Go in and ask him," Dykes babbled. "He'll back me up."

Elgin seemed to hesitate, looking at his "sergeant." "Okay, let's go talk to this Father Jackson." He started up the stairs.

"I wanna come, too," Maureen said.

"Okay. We'll all go. Sergeant, bring that satchel. We'll see what this Father Jackson knows about this."

A minute later, Elgin rapped on the rectory door. It was opened by a white-haired priest with a kindly pink face, truly benevolent-looking.

"Are you Father Jackson?" Elgin asked.

The man looked surprised. "No, I'm Father Norris."

Dykes gaped at him in disbelief. "The black priest—where is he? I was just talkin' to him a minute ago!"

"A black priest?" Father Norris repeated.

"Yeah—Father Jackson."

The elderly priest, much beloved by the parishioners of St. Bonaventure's, shook his head slowly. "I'm sorry. We have no other priest at St. Bonny's. You must have the wrong parish. There's a black priest at St.—"

"Naw, it was *right here!*" Dykes gestured frantically. "I was standin' in this very office when he gave me the suitcase!"

Father Norris looked even more perplexed. "Suitcase?"

"Yeah, this one right here." He pointed.

The priest looked at it. "You must be mistaken. I never saw that before in my life."

"But . . . but . . ." Dykes felt the strong hand of Lieutenant Elgin on his arm, pulling him away. "There's some . . . mistake!"

"There sure is, and you made it. C'mon." He turned to the clergyman. "Sorry to bother you, Father. I'm Lieutenant Elgin, LAPD."

"What's going on, Lieutenant?"

"Nothing that concerns you or St. Bonny's, Father. And nothing we can't handle." Quickly he

247

led Dykes outside and shoved him in the backseat of the police car, climbing in after him.

"Where are you taking him?" Maureen cried.

Elgin saw the fear in the wife's eyes. "The station. That's where we book 'em, you know." He suspected she'd probably spill the whole story if given half a chance. "You can come along if you want."

"She's done nothin'," Wally said quickly.

"Then the ride won't hurt her. Get in front with the sergeant, ma'am." Elgin watched her scramble in.

"You're makin' a big mistake, Lieutenant," Dykes blustered.

"Am I? You're carrying around a suitcase full of funny money, which you say you got from some nonexistent priest. I imagine the DA won't think it's much of a mistake—the federal DA, that is. Counterfeiting is the big leagues, Dykes."

Dykes blanched. "How do you know my name?"

"I've had my eye on you for quite some time. I thought you were penny ante stuff, but I see you got greedy for the big time. Well-l, that's what you're gonna get—big time." He looked to the front. "Let's go, Sergeant."

"No, wait!" Dykes tried desperately to think. "Look, I'm tellin' the truth. I got the money from a black priest. I didn't know it was counterfeit, honest."

"How dumb do you think I am, Dykes? There's a lot of money in that suitcase, maybe half a mil, I'd guess if it was real. Where would a priest get that kind of money? And why, pray tell, if there was such a priest, would he give it to *you*?"

Dykes hesitated, then muttered, "It was a contribution—for AIDS research."

"*You're* into AIDS research, Wally?" Elgin began to laugh. "You should be a comedian. You'd knock 'em dead!" His laughter increased.

"It's the truth, dammit!"

248

"Sure, sure. Let's go, Sergeant."

Maureen heard the motor start. "No, please, wait." She twisted around and leaned over the backseat. "Tell him, Wally."

"No."

"Ya gotta. It's all over."

This was what Elgin had been waiting for. "What's all over? Tell me what?"

"Dammit, Maureen! Keep your fuckin' mouth shut!" Wally bellowed.

Elgin looked only at Maureen. "Mrs. Dykes, if you have some information about all this, I suggest you tell me now. It may save you and your husband a great deal of trouble."

She hesitated, looking back and forth between her enraged husband and the craggy face of the detective. "I have to, Wally," she whispered at last. "Lieutenant, my husband got a photograph of a Catholic Cardinal—"

"Dammit! Maury, *shut up!*"

"—in bed with a black woman. He was just gettin' some money to keep quiet about it."

"In other words, blackmail," Elgin said calmly.

"It wasn't blackmail, it was—"

"Blackmail is blackmail, no matter what you call it. I believe the statute number is—"

"Wally was just accepting a contribution—"

Elgin laughed. "Oh, yeah, for AIDS research."

"It's the *truth*, dammit all to hell!" shouted Wally. "That money was supposed to be real secret. Not even the Pope knows about it!"

The detective grinned. "Sure, Dykes. A nice tale." He laughed. "Okay, suppose I believe this story, like I believe in the tooth fairy. Got any proof of why some priest would be nuts enough to give all that dough to *you?*"

Maureen was almost bawling. "We did have, but Wally gave it to the black priest."

Loud laughter. "The nonexistent black priest

249

again. Have you ever heard the beat of this, Sergeant?"

"It's the truth!" Maureen wailed. "Wally gave the priest the photo and the negative."

"What photo and negative?"

"Of the Cardinal in the sack with the black chick!"

Elgin doubled up with laughter. "Too bad we aren't recording this, Sergeant. The boys at the stationhouse aren't ever going to believe it."

Now frantic, Maureen pounded on his shoulder. "It's the truth! You have to believe me." She turned to her husband. "Tell him it's the truth, Wally, or they'll send you up for counterfeiting. They can't charge you with blackmail if the money you got isn't real. Tell him. It's the only way." Suddenly she gaped at him. She saw it in his eyes, in the movement of his mouth as he cursed her. "You didn't give it to him, Wally? You switched it? Thank God!" She lunged over the seat, stuck a hand inside his suit jacket and extracted a manila envelope.

*"Goddammit! Give that back!"*

"Here, Lieutenant. Open it. See for yourself," Maureen said triumphantly.

Elgin accepted the envelope, tore it open. It was very difficult for him. He didn't want to look at the photo, but he knew he had to. He glanced at it, suppressing his inner revulsion, then said casually, "This is a photograph of a man in bed with a woman. It happens all the time in Los Angeles."

"That's Quentin Cardinal Stillwell!"

Elgin glanced at it again. "Is it? It sorta resembles my Uncle Bill, if you want my opinion."

"It *is*, I can tell you. It is—"

"Okay, Mrs. Dykes, I heard you." He made sure the negative was there, then closed the envelope and inserted it in his pocket. "Okay, I'll tell you what. The photo is some evidence for your story, Dykes. I'm gonna keep it—and the money. I'm gonna see if I can locate this black priest, find out what he says, where he got the money."

"Talk to Stillwell," Dykes said wearily.

"Oh, sure, Wally. I can just see me going up to a Cardinal and asking him if he was ever in bed with a black woman. What I'm *really* going to do is check out your story, and I mean really check. Meanwhile, you'd better keep your mouth shut. And your life had better be as pure as the driven snow—not much of which we get in Los Angeles. In fact, every cop in Southern California better be able to read your hubcaps at every stop sign. Get my meaning?"

Maureen stared at him. "You mean we can go?"

"For now. And believe me, *just* for now."

"C'mon, Wally!"

Elgin saw Dykes hesitate, his anger almost bursting from him. Then he slowly opened the door and got out. The couple headed for their car. "Let's go, Beanie," Elgin snapped.

When the cruiser was a block away, Elgin got out his lighter and set fire to the envelope and its contents. He held it until all but a corner was consumed. Then he dropped it out the window.

"Was that really Cardinal Stillwell?" Bean asked, intrigued.

Elgin leaned back in his seat. "Naw. Didn't look like him at all."

Half an hour later, Elgin returned the counterfeit money to the police property room, slipping the clerk a twenty as he said, "You shoulda seen the eyes on those kids at school when they saw all that funny money."

# Chapter 13

Sheryl James had invited Leon Kazinsky to her place for dinner. She wanted to make sure she was over her annoyance at him, and found that she was. She laughed and flirted with him. All seemed to be well with their relationship—whatever that was. She remained uncertain just what there was between them and where it could possibly lead, but at least she was still able to enjoy it, and that was the most important thing right now.

The phone rang just about the time Sheryl and Kazinsky were getting down to some serious love-making prior to going to bed. It was the switchboard operator at the hospital. Susan Raimond was asking for Sheryl, said it was important. Could she come over right away? Sheryl was impressed. Clinical psychologists didn't usually get emergency calls, at least not those with the type of practice she had. She said she'd come at once. When she told Leon, he just said, "Really?"

It made her a little defensive. "Don't *you* get called in sometimes?"

He was immediately aware of his tactlessness. "And there's no reason why you shouldn't, right?"

She eyed him a moment. "Right."

"Susan Raimond, huh? Maybe somebody's changed her mind."

"Let's hope so, but I wouldn't count on it."

"What else could she want?"

"I'll let you know later. You *will* be here later?"

"I think so. It was getting interesting." He saw the warm smile she gave him. "I'll stay."

"Then do the dishes," she suggested on her way out the door.

Susan Raimond was alone and upset. It was obvious she had been crying.

"What's the matter, Susan?" Sheryl asked.

The girl found it difficult to speak. The words she wanted to say choked her and fresh tears filled her eyes. "I—I just . . . learned about . . . Adriana Barre."

"Learned what?"

"Her baby's going to die. And they did . . . a hysterectomy. Isn't that . . . what . . . it's called?"

"Yes."

"She can't have another child?"

"I'm afraid not."

"Oh, it's so awful!"

Susan broke down, sobbing uncontrollably. Sheryl was rather surprised that the girl was taking another's tragedy so personally. But then, Susan Raimond was so young and so sheltered that she'd probably had little experience with grief. Then Sheryl remembered Susan had lost her father. She knew grief, all right. Maybe that had something to do with it. Sheryl wanted to comfort her, but was uncertain whether she should. Something was happening here. She decided to wait and find out what it was.

253

"Would . . . Adriana . . . take my . . . baby?" Susan finally managed to say.

Sheryl was astonished, but managed to keep her voice level, replying honestly, "I don't know."

"I—I want her . . . to have . . . my baby."

Sheryl was deeply moved. She didn't know what to say.

"Would you . . . ask her . . . for me?"

"I suppose I could, when the time is right," Sheryl said.

"Ask her . . . *now*—please."

"I can't just now, Susan. I don't know if she's recovered from her surgery. I'll have to speak to Dr. Dodd, and to others. What's the hurry?"

"I want to have the cesarean," Susan said.

Sheryl's brows arched. "Right now?"

"Yes."

Would wonders never cease! "Does your mother know this?"

"No. She's gone home for the night. That's why . . . I want to have . . . the surgery now."

"So she won't be able to stop it and it'll all be over by the time she finds out?"

Susan nodded vigorously.

Sheryl sighed. "I'm sorry, Susan. That's impossible. You're under age. Your mother must give her consent."

"But I *want* my baby now. I want to . . . *give* him—or her—to . . . Adriana."

Sheryl went to her, bent over the bed, and kissed her wet cheek. "You really are a dear, good person, but the hospital cannot go against your mother's express wishes. She could bring legal action, particularly if anything happened to you."

"I'll be all right."

"I'm sure you will, but what you want is still impossible. Neither Dr. Dodd nor any other doctor would perform the surgery under these circumstances."

"Oh, Lord!" Susan burst into tears again.

254

Sheryl put her arms around the girl while she cried, then asked, "Have you spoken to your mother about what you want to do?"

"No. She won't . . . listen."

"She might. If you told her how badly you want to have the baby, she might change her—"

"Never! You don't know my mother." A surge of anger replaced her tears. "I've never been . . . able to cope with her. My dad was the . . . only one who could."

"You miss your father?" Sheryl asked gently.

"I think about him all the time. I miss him . . . terribly. This wouldn't have . . . happened if Dad was alive."

Sheryl thought about defending the girl's mother, then reconsidered. At the moment she just didn't feel like putting in a good word for Rita Farrell. "You have been able to stand up against your mother sometimes, haven't you?"

"No," Susan said wearily. "She always wins."

"That can't be true, Susan. I hardly think your mother wanted you to become pregnant."

"That's true."

"Have you told her who the father is?"

"His name's Tex. That's all I know."

"You don't *know* the father?"

"Not really. I met him on the beach. I've never seen him since."

"You mean, you just met him and you—"

"Only the one time."

"Oh, Susan, that was very foolish." At once she regretted her words. "You must have wanted to hurt your mother very much."

"I suppose. Mostly I wanted to get away from her."

"And it didn't work."

"It did for a while. I went up to a little town in the mountains where she couldn't find me. I loved it. I felt like a real person. I was so hap-

255

py. . ."—deep sigh—" . . . until she tracked me down and brought me here."

"You lived by yourself?"

"Yes, for months. It was wonderful."

"Then why didn't you refuse to come back with your mother?"

Sigh. "I was bleeding—scared, I guess. It seemed the best thing to do."

"I suppose it was." Sheryl sympathized with this extremely immature young woman trying to break away from her strong-willed mother and not being able to. She also knew that this child—for Susan really was still a child—needed help. "Tell you what, Susan." She smiled. "When all this is over, why don't you come to see me? We'll have a talk. Maybe I can help you . . ."—she paused to choose the right words—". . . help you make better choices in the future."

"I'd like that." The expression in the huge brown eyes left no doubt of the girl's sincerity.

"Then that's what we'll do. I'd better let you rest now."

"Will you speak to Adriana?" Susan pleaded.

Sheryl hesitated, then said, "I will, if I get a chance and when it seems right. I'm sure she'll be pleased by your offer."

"I mean it, Sheryl. I want her to have my baby."

Max had listened for quite a long time. When Elgin had finished filling him in, he said, "Thanks a lot, Frank. I owe you." Then he hung up the phone and turned to Quentin Stillwell. "The photo and negative are destroyed. It's over."

The Cardinal slumped in his chair. Max thought the man had visibly aged in the last few days. Softly he said, "It will never be over."

"You're wrong. Dykes and his wife are scared to death. And even if they weren't, they no longer have any proof. And the three nursing supervisors

256

have been canned." He smiled. "It's worked out better than we ever dared hope for." But Stillwell was repeatedly shaking his head. He looked extremely sad. "Oh, I see what you mean. What are you going to do now?"

Stillwell's voice was low. "What I've always planned—confess to the Holy Father, resign, and hope he'll permit me to enter a monastery. After that . . ."—he shrugged—". . . my future is in the hands of God."

For perhaps the first time, Max felt a little sorry for him—but not too much. "I think maybe that's a good idea."

"Yes. It is the only path for me." He looked up at Max, who was standing beside his desk. "Tell me again the name of the man who helped you."

"Detective Lieutenant Frank Elgin, LAPD."

"Does he know about me?"

"Yes. I had to tell him. But he doesn't know about Hillary. My chief aim was to protect her."

"I understand. You did the right thing."

"But Elgin is the *only* one who knows about you and I guarantee he'll never speak of it."

Stillwell looked at Max a long moment, although it was debatable whether he actually saw him. He seemed to be looking through him, witnessing events at a far greater distance. "What does he . . . think of me?"

"Frank is a devout Catholic. I believe he is . . . disappointed. I guess you might say he shares your opinion of yourself," Max said dryly.

"As he well should. He sounds like a good man."

"For what it's worth, he expects you to resign."

"Yes. When you see him, thank him for me. Tell him . . ." Stillwell hesitated. "Tell him I'll pray for him, if my prayers have any value."

"I'm sure they do, Your Eminence." Now Max paused, forming words in his mind. "Cardinal Stillwell, I'm no expert in religion, but it seems to

257

me yours were sins of the flesh. I have an idea there are far worse ones."

"You're right, you are *not* an expert. Broken vows, years of deceit are hardly mere sins of the flesh."

Max shrugged. "Have it your way. I have two requests to make of you. One is that in your confession to the Pope or to anyone else, you refrain from identifying Hillary. I see no value in it. Her sin, if that's what it was, is entirely her affair."

"I agree. I hadn't planned to implicate her."

"Second, I want you never to see her again."

"I'd planned not to, of course. It is an essential part of my atonement. But I had . . . hoped to say . . . good-bye to her."

"No."

"I want to . . . tell her how things . . . worked out, what . . . you did."

"I'll tell her something—just how much, I don't know at the moment. Cardinal Stillwell, I want your word that you will never see her again."

Sigh, deep and long. "Very well. You have my word."

When Max left the diocesan offices, he went straight to Bel Air General. In Pediatrics he entered Tommy's room. Hillary had fallen asleep in the chair beside his bed, her head flung back against the cushions. Good. She must be exhausted. He looked for something to cover her, then found a light blanket in a closet and draped it over her.

Then he heard a muffled sound.

He glanced over at Tommy. His eyes were open, such beautiful brown eyes, and he was trying to talk through the oxygen mask that covered his mouth. So long famous for his grin, Maximilian Hill now rendered the biggest one of his life. "You awake, old buddy?" He saw the boy's head nod. " 'Bout time. You're turning into a bed freak, you know that?" He hesitated, looked around, said

"What the hell" to himself, and removed the mask. "What have you got to say for yourself?"

"I'm thirsty," Tommy whispered.

"I'll bet you are." Again he looked around. Should he? Hell, water never hurt anybody. He brought the glass and bent the straw to the boy's lips and held it for him a moment. "Just wet your whistle." Then he glanced at the monitor. Tommy's temperature was just above one hundred. The boy's fever had broken. He was going to be all right.

"Where's Mom?"

Max motioned toward the chair. "Having a snooze. She's been here with you every minute for days. Let's not wake her."

"Okay. I'm kinda tired, too."

"Then saw off another log. We'll talk later."

He gave him another sip of water and replaced the mask, waiting till Tommy's eyes closed. Satisfied the boy was asleep, Max left the room. At the nursing station, he told the nurse on duty what had happened. The reaction to his news was what he had expected.

"Thank God!"

Sheryl returned to her apartment, unable to get Susan Raimond off her mind. To Kazinsky she said, "It beats anything I've ever heard of. She wants to have the baby so she can give it to Adriana Barre."

Kazinsky watched her closely, as a doctor observed a patient, looking for visible evidence for a diagnosis. "Are you upset?"

"I don't know if *upset* is the word. But it does grab you a little. Think of it, Leon! That poor, dumb, scared, grossly inhibited kid wants to do what's right, but can't because of her—" She grimaced, an expression of her thoughts about Rita Farrell.

259

Kazinsky laughed. "You can swear if you want. I've heard it all before."

"Swearing isn't all I'd like to do to her. Leon, what possesses a mother to ruin her daughter's life?"

"At not quite eighteen, no one's life is ruined."

Sheryl sighed. "I hope you're right. Maybe Susan will find the strength to break away from her. I asked her to come see me when this is over. Maybe she will."

"And I'm sure you'll help her if anyone can."

Sheryl went into the kitchen, poured herself some wine, asked if he wanted some. He didn't. "I see you did the dishes."

"I was well trained in obedience."

"No, you just like being henpecked, I can tell." Then her mind returned to Susan Raimond. "Susan wants me to ask Adriana if she'll take her baby."

"What's the point of that? There's not going to *be* a baby unless the girl's mother has a sudden change of heart."

"I know, but maybe if Rita Farrell knew there was a fine home for the child, she'd change her mind."

"Uh-uh, Sheryl. Adriana Barre doesn't yet know her baby isn't going to live, and in her present condition nobody's in any hurry to tell her. So you stay out of it, hear?"

Sheryl looked at him. "I hear. I'm sure you're right. Who's going to tell her?"

"Nobody's very sure at the moment. You may be needed."

"Thanks. I get all the cushy jobs." She went over to him and lay down next to him, her head on his chest. "I feel so rotten about all this."

"I thought shrinks didn't take patient's problems personally."

"Apparently this one does." She raised her head,

260

kissed him lightly. "Where were we before the phone rang?"

His kiss was considerably more ardent, and he felt her response. But he asked, "Do you still feel like it?"

"Dunno. Let's find out."

At first she figured it wasn't going to work. There was something about being naked and caressed by a man that made her mind dwell on Susan Raimond, that poor, foolish child, grappling on the beach with a man she didn't know, getting pregnant, letting her mother run her life. Such sadness, such folly, such waste. Sheryl felt more like crying than making love. But as Leon Kazinsky fondled and stroked her body, kissing her lips, she began to feel the beginnings of erotic pleasure. Soon she was returning his kisses and caresses as he aroused her passion.

But it was not to be. At the worst possible moment—or one of them—just as he was about to enter her, she suddenly said, "Forgive me, Leon, but I just thought of something!"

"What?" It was not a query about what she'd thought of, but a reflection of his own consternation over his shattered concentration.

"I have to make a phone call."

"A *phone call?* You're kidding!"

"I'm sorry." She squirmed away from him and rolled off the bed. "I just had an idea about Susan Raimond." She saw the look on his face. "I know. This is terrible." She swallowed hard. "Stay there. I'll be . . . right back." She picked up the phone at her bedside, started to press buttons, then stopped. "Do you have Brian Hecht's home phone number?"

He stared up at her nakedness, so ripe for passion, and shook his head in disbelief that this was happening. "I think maybe, in my pants." He, too, squirmed off the bed, found his pants, and located his wallet, which contained a typewritten list of names and phone numbers. He handed it to her, watched her dial. As he glanced at his wilting erection, he growled, "I guess I don't need to tell you this call had better be important!"

Brian's interruption was not quite as inopportune as Kazinsky's, but he was naked, in bed with Lorraine Paul, and more than a little preoccupied. He let the phone ring several times, hoping whoever it was would give up, then sighed, reached across Lorraine, and clasped the receiver to his ear.

"Brian, I hope I'm not disturbing you," said a woman's breathless voice.

"Who's this?"

"Sheryl James. I wouldn't call if it wasn't important."

"Go ahead." Brian grimaced in frustration at Lorraine, who was holding her hand over her mouth to suppress a giggle.

"Susan Raimond called me over to the hospital tonight. She said it was important."

"Yes?"

"She wants to have her baby and give it to Adriana Barre."

He felt Lorraine move, felt her hands clasping him. He shook his head for her to stop. "Does the mother agree?" With his free hand he tried to push her away but failed, or maybe he didn't try too hard.

"No."

"Then why are you calling to tell me this, Sheryl?"

"In talking with Susan, I learned something that may be important. Didn't I hear you say the age of consent in California is eighteen *unless* the person has lived as an independent minor? Or something like that?"

Lorraine had pushed him down on his back and was now straddling him.

Oh, Lord. . . . "Yes. That's what . . . I said."

262

"Listen to this, Brian! After Susan got pregnant—by some guy on the beach she didn't even know, I might add—she ran away from home and lived in some little town in the mountains for months! Doesn't that make her an independent minor?"

In utter fascination Brian watched Lorraine raise her hips, guide him inside, then felt her nestle down on him. He gasped, couldn't help it. He shook his head at her to stop—how, he didn't know—but her wide, teasing smile told him it was no use. "It might, Sheryl. I don't know." He thought his voice sounded quite good, considering.

"She said she'd never been so happy in her life until her mother finally found her. I gather that happened only a couple of days before she entered the hospital. Doesn't that make her an independent teenager?"

Lorraine's movements were driving him crazy—so slow, so persistent. He tried to swallow, couldn't. "It certainly would . . . seem so."

"I think so, too, Brian. If she really wants to have the baby by cesarean, then it seems to me she would be legally able to give her consent. What do you think?"

What Brian thought was that he was about to die. He couldn't hold off. "Sheryl, could you . . . hold on . . . a minute?" He didn't wait for an answer, just let his arms fall away, one hand over the mouthpiece, as he surrendered mindlessly to an aching, throbbing orgasm, although he did manage to suppress his groans of pleasure. When it finally ended and he tried to bring the phone back to his ear, he couldn't. Lorraine had collapsed on him, grinding her hips in the throes of her own orgasm. It seemed forever until he could return to the phone. "I'm sorry to keep you waiting, Sheryl." His voice was almost back to normal. "Someone just . . . came." Lorraine really did gig-

263

gle now. He made a face at her as he quickly covered the mouthpiece.

"That's okay. Brian, I think Dr. Dodd ought to go ahead and do it now, while she wants to, before the mother has a chance to . . . to do a number on her, talk her out of it."

"I don't know, Sheryl."

"Look, you certainly have a legal basis. If you consult the mother, she'll probably go to court to block it. If you authorize it now, it'll be done. She can scream and holler later. Only she won't—"

"Because she'll look like the Wicked Witch of the West?"

"Something like that. I say do it *now*, Brian. We have the law on our side. And we sure have morality, too."

Hesitation. "Let me think about it, talk to Leon Kazinsky."

"He's right here," Sheryl said promptly. "You want to speak to him?"

Brian again hesitated, looking over at Lorraine Paul. "Let me call you back in a minute, okay? Do I have your number?"

She gave it to him.

"Okay. Only be a couple minutes. I have to . . . think."

Lorraine took the phone from him, hung it up. Then they both collapsed, laughing, into each other's arms. "Didn't you ever do it on the phone before?"

"That's a first."

"How was it?"

"C'mere."

"I already *am* here."

"I think he was doing it with somebody," Sheryl told Kazinsky after she hung up the phone.

"He's a luckier man than I am." Kazinsky was pulling on his pants, feeling somehow uncomfort-

264

able at the idea of speaking to Brian Hecht stark naked.

"I'm sorry, Leon. I'll make it up to you." She smiled. "As only you know I can. What d'you think?"

"About Susan Raimond? I think it's a damned interesting possibility."

Sheryl beamed. "Then you'll back me up?"

"I'll do anything as long as you're dressed like that."

She had forgotten her nakedness. Now she looked down at herself and laughed.

"This may be the first time in history that a major medical decision was based on sexual frustration."

"Oh, I'm sure it's not." She went over to him and rubbed her breasts against his chest.

"Do we have time?" Kazinsky asked.

Sheryl made a face. "He said he'd call in a minute."

"I'll bet he doesn't."

Kazinsky would have won. It was closer to forty minutes later Brian Hecht returned the call. "I'm sorry to be so long, but I wanted to talk to Maurice Edgerton." It was only partly a lie. "After a lot of hemming and hawing, legal mumbo-jumbo, and some priceless equivocations, he said to go ahead if both you and Dodd agree, Leon."

"I agree. It's the only option we have. I'll phone Dr. Dodd."

Brian paused. "I hope we're doing the right thing."

"Stop worrying, Brian. This is about to become a medical decision, which means it's out of your hands." When he heard Brian sigh, Kazinsky said, "It can't be any worse than the Claiborne transplant."

Charles Bridges had sat beside his wife's bed all afternoon and evening, then into the night. She

265

had come out of the anesthetic and said a few words, but mostly she slept.

Bridges knew he had every reason to be encouraged. The reports from the doctors and nurses attending her were all optimistic, and the monitors at her bedside confirmed the good news. Apparently the hysterectomy had been a success. Adriana's internal bleeding had stopped. Her blood pressure, pulse, and respiration were moving toward normal. His wife, his one true love, was going to recover. Because of the two surgeries and the severity of her condition before the second one, there would be a long, slow recuperation period. But she was going to be all right.

He tried to hold on to that as he sat beside Adriana's bed. Wasn't that what was truly important? To him, yes. But to her? Would she be able to accept the loss of the baby? During one of her brief periods of wakefulness she had said, a sweet smile on her face, "How's our baby?" Her words had seemed to wrench his heart right out of his chest, for he had just been informed that the child had died.

"Is that you, Charles?" she whispered now.

"Yes." At once he stood up, took her hand. "How are you feeling, my darling?"

"Drowsy. Thirsty."

He gave her a little water. "How are you, other than thirsty?"

"Just tired, very tired." She squeezed his hand. "You're married to a . . . sleepyhead."

"Then sleep. It's the best thing for you."

Long sigh. "I hope so."

"The doctors say you're much better, Adriana. The bleeding has stopped. It's just a matter of time now."

"That's nice." She was silent so long he thought she'd gone back to sleep. "You needn't stay, Charles. You can . . . go home."

266

"I will soon. I like being with you." The pressure of her hand in his filled him with emotion.

"How's our baby?" she asked again.

*Oh, God!* He knew he should tell her their son was dead, but he couldn't. He wanted to lie to her, but he couldn't do that either. "I think perhaps I ought to check." That really wasn't a lie, was it?

"Oh, do, please." He tried to free his hand, but she held him tightly. "We have a son, Charles."

Tears filled his eyes. "You'd better rest, darling."

"Yes, I will."

Now he freed his hand.

"I'm so happy, Charles, so . . . blessed."

Then mercifully she fell asleep and did not hear the sob that was wrenched from him.

# Chapter 14

Hillary couldn't stop crying. Tears of joy flowed like a flood and she was powerless to stop them. When she opened her eyes to find her son smiling at her, it seemed like a glorious dream. So sure had she been that Tommy was going to die that she was certain at first that she was still asleep. Only the presence of Max Hill convinced her of reality. Then all the days of desperate worry overcame her and tears were her release.

She wept as she hugged her son, so hard and so long he finally wriggled uncomfortably and said, "Aw, Mom!" She wept in Max's arms, trying so hard to smile, managing a watery one before a new deluge came. She wept as she was hugged by doctors and nurses who came in to express their happiness for her and Tommy. It was indeed a wet scene.

Among those who hugged her was Tina Chung, head nurse in Pediatrics. Against Hillary's ear she

268

said, "I'm so pleased by everything that's happened!"

"Yes. Tommy's going to recover."

"I didn't mean just that." The dark-haired woman stood back, smiled. "It's wonderful news. But I was talking about the reorganization. I'm so delighted! You have my total support."

Hillary stared at her, confused. "What are you talking about?"

"You don't know? I guess you wouldn't." Tina started to tell her, then thought better of it. Instead, she handed her a folded sheet of paper. "Here. Read this when you have time."

Hillary took it but had no time to look at it, as another person came to greet her. The paper ended up in her purse, unread.

Finally Max insisted on taking her home. "I'm putting you to bed," he told her. "When you wake up tomorrow this medical miracle will still be here." She protested, but gave in when Carmen Rodriguez arrived to sit with Tommy.

In her own apartment her tears finally dried, or maybe she simply ran out of them. "Oh, Max, you've been so strong, so good." She sighed.

He grinned. "Now that is nice to hear. Strong and good. I like it."

"It's true, absolutely true. I couldn't have made it without you."

"Nonsense. It was all your doing. As I recall, I've been to the hospital to see Tommy precisely twice."

"But I knew you were with us, supporting us. That meant so much."

He looked carefully at her, as though appraising her. "Yes. I *was* with you. I want to be—always."

"Oh, Max . . ."

Big grin. "Now into the sack with you—alone, however much that grieves me."

269

Smiling, Hillary said, "I suppose. I *am* exhausted."

He kissed her lightly. "Can I trust you to go straight to bed?"

"Yes. I'll just shower first."

"Do you want a drink? It might help you to sleep," Max suggested.

"I don't think I need help." She accompanied him to the door and kissed him. "Thank you, Max—for everything. You are a love. You're always here when I need you."

He smiled. "Keep that in mind for the future."

Hillary had showered and was in her nightgown sitting on the edge of the bed when she remembered to thank Someone else. She fell to her knees. It was no elaborate prayer, just a few simple words from an overflowing heart. "Thank you for saving my son's life. I will do my best to be worthy of this wonderful gift."

Then she climbed into bed. It felt so delicious, utterly so, and in a moment she had turned on her side, her usual position for falling asleep. Half-asleep already, she remembered the paper in her purse. What was that all about? It could keep till morning. But her curiosity got the better of her. She tossed back the cover and went to her purse, hanging on a chair.

The administrative order by Brian Hecht first puzzled her. A second reading produced disbelief. A reorganization of the nursing staff? No one had discussed it with her. Elimination of Supervisors of Nursing? Greater authority for floor and head nurses? That would never work. . . . Then the full import of the order struck her. Dana Shaughnessy, Kathryn Quigley, Barbara Brookes—gone. Just those three. Then she knew that this was no mere reorganization. This was the elimination of her bitterest enemies. Shock and amazement dissipated her fatigue.

270

Brian Hecht. His order. But there was no possible way he could have been aware of what those three were doing. Unless . . . She ran to the bedside phone, intending to dial Brian, then thought better of it. Who could have told him? Arthur? He would never. Max? But he didn't know about the blackmail—or did he? His enigmatic words at their lunch came back to her—"Everything is going to be all right." What did he *really* know? What had happened?

Her second impulse was to phone Max, but again she thought better of it. Instead, she dialed Arthur's hotel, to be told that Cardinal Stillwell had checked out. Thoroughly alarmed now, she dialed the diocesan offices until she finally got a sleepy response. "I know it's late, but is Cardinal Stillwell there?"

"Just a moment." Hillary waited for what seemed an eternity. "Cardinal Stillwell is not here. He's left for Rome, the Vatican."

*Oh, God! No!* "Are you sure?"

"Yes, but let me check." Another eternity. "His flight is from Los Angeles to London, then Rome. He should be boarding shortly."

"Thank you." Slowly Hillary hung up, filled with anguish. It was all going to happen. He was going to give up everything, and it was all her fault. She had to stop him. There had to be some way. She dashed for her closet, threw on clothes.

Ham Dodd listened to the succinct explanation by Leon Kazinsky. Independent minor. A loophole. Susan Raimond wanted the surgery. *Do it now.*

"I don't know, Leon," he hedged when Kazinsky had finished.

"I have talked to Brian Hecht, who spoke to the hospital's lawyers. There is some legal risk, but if you and I agree the surgery is necessary, and the girl agrees, as well, the decision is ours to make."

Still Dodd hesitated. "How did this come about?

271

The last thing I knew we were talking infanticide."

"Sheryl James has been working with the Raimond girl. She got her to— Hold on a minute." Kazinsky did not want to relinquish the phone to Sheryl. It would be difficult to explain what the two of them were doing together at this hour. But she gave him no choice. She grabbed the receiver out of his hand.

"Dr. Dodd, this is Sheryl James. Susan called me to the hospital tonight. She was upset about Adriana Barre. She wants to have the child and give it to Adriana."

"That's impossible!"

"Is it? In talking to her, I learned she'd lived completely alone for several months during her pregnancy. That makes her an independent minor."

"So it would seem. Has Susan Raimond given her formal consent?"

"She hasn't signed the form, but I'm sure she'll be willing to."

Dodd thought a moment. "Put Leon back on." When he heard Kazinsky's voice he said, "Do you want to do this thing?"

"It's the only way to save the baby."

"I agree. Let's do it. I'll be right over to scrub. Meanwhile, get that girl's signature on the dotted line."

"I think Sheryl James should do that. She's the only one Susan really trusts."

In the background, Dodd heard a female voice scream, "Hot diggety-damn!"

An hour later Sheryl entered the scrub room. To Dodd she said, "Susan has signed. She is on her way to the OR."

"Very good, Dr. James."

"Are you giving her a spinal block?"

"Yes."

272

"She has asked if I might remain with her."

Dodd glanced at Kazinsky, who was to assist. "That might be a good idea. You'll have to scrub."

Sheryl had scrubbed before, but not for some time. As she bent over the sink with brush and soap, she heard Dodd grumble, "What I dislike about this is the hour."

Kazinsky laughed. "Who ever said surgeons are supposed to need sleep?"

"I don't mean that. It looks like secret, dead-of-night cutting, particularly since we haven't consulted the mother."

"That's not what worries me. What if something's wrong with the child?"

"Don't even think about it!"

They lathered and rinsed in silence for a time. Sheryl finally said, "Dr. Dodd, when I said Susan wanted Adriana Barre to have her baby, you said it was impossible. Why is that?"

He glanced sideways at her. "You must know it is. Babies are not substituted anymore except in bad novels. No hospital would permit it."

"I wasn't talking about that. Couldn't Adriana and her husband adopt Susan's baby?"

"Oh, I see what you mean." He shrugged. "I suppose it's possible. But that's down the road a piece. We don't even know if they want to adopt."

"I suppose you're right."

In the OR Sheryl stood beside Susan, holding her hand, smiling reassuringly at her. The operation went beautifully and the baby let out a lusty cry as Dodd handed him to the pediatrician, Dr. Randall.

"You have a boy, Susan, a fine healthy boy," Sheryl told her.

"Are you sure?"

Sheryl glanced over at the baby, then at Randall for confirmation. She saw his nod. "Yes, Susan. He's fine. Lots of dark hair."

"Oh, that's so wonderful!"

Sheryl did not wait for the closing. She left the OR, stripped off her gloves, mask, and scrub suit, and headed for a phone.

Hillary was never so glad a plane was late in her life. Even then she almost didn't make it, running through the airport, finally shouting "Arthur! Arthur! Wait!" to stop him just as he was preparing to board. She ran directly into his arms, grateful that he was not dressed in clerical garb.

"Don't do this, Arthur! I won't let you," she whispered.

"I must, Hillie. It is the only way."

She saw the agony in his eyes, and it intensified her own. "Don't go! There has to be another solution."

Then he remembered. "Why did you come? I promised Max I wouldn't . . . see you again."

Protests formed in her mouth. Then she stopped, shook her head sharply, blinked. "Max? What's he got to do with this?"

"Everything. We owe everything to Max."

Hillary stared at him. "I don't understand."

"Haven't you seen him? Hasn't he told you?"

"I've seen him, but he said nothing."

A slow smile touched Cardinal Stillwell's lips. "No, I guess he wouldn't say anything. Quite a man you have there, Hillie."

"Say anything about what?" She saw flight attendants waiting at the doorway. Nearly everyone else was aboard. "We haven't much time. Tell me, please!"

"All right. You should know. Here it is quickly. I went to see Max, to confess to him. He apparently already knew about us, but not . . ."—he looked around to see if anyone was overhearing them—". . . about the blackmail. He took care of everything."

It was difficult for Hillary to grasp at first, so agitated was she, but as Stillwell continued to

274

speak, she began to listen, if not entirely to comprehend: Max a priest; Max conning Dykes; a cop named Elgin joining in, supplying counterfeit money; the fake arrest; obtaining the photo and negative; destroying them.

Stillwell finished by saying, "It's all over, Hillie. We're safe now."

"Did Max talk to Brian Hecht about the supervisors?" she asked.

"Yes, I think so."

She had a million more questions, but there was no time for any but one. "If we're safe, then why are you leaving?"

"I have to, Hillie. I must."

"But if no one knows—"

"I know and God knows, and soon the Holy Father will know. This is my only chance for salvation. I must take it. Don't ask me not to."

"The monastery?" she whispered.

"I hope so, God willing."

His smile was positively beatific, but that did not prevent Hillary's eyes from filling with tears. "Don't, Arthur, please."

"I must, Hillie,"

"But I feel so guilty. It's all my fault."

"That's not true. The fault was mine."

"But there's so much for you to do in the world. . . ."

He put his fingertips to her lips to silence her. "I've made my decision, my darling. What you and I had was beautiful, but it was wrong. It had to end, you know. This is the only way, believe me."

Hillary wanted to cling to him, to weep, to beg him not to go, but she struggled against it. "I'll . . . always . . . love you, Arthur."

He nodded, smiling tenderly. "And I will love you, but in a better way, the way it should have been all along, Hillie."

She couldn't speak, could hardly breathe.

"I have to go. I'll miss my plane." He turned, took a couple of steps, then stopped and looked back at her. "Love Max. Be good to him. He loves you, too."

Through tear-dimmed eyes she watched him walk away from her. She stood motionless for a long time, unaware of her surroundings or the curious glances of passersby. Finally she turned away and slowly walked back through the terminal toward her car, her mind constantly repeating: *The only way, the best way, the right way. . . .*

She didn't drive home. Instead, she headed for Malibu and Max's beach house. Rapping on the door and ringing the bell, she faced him at last.

"Why didn't you tell me what you did?" she demanded as he opened the door.

"How'd you find out?"

"I went to the airport. I saw Arthur. He told me."

Max swore under his breath. "The bastard promised not to see you again!"

"He's *not* a bastard. And he didn't see me—I saw him. Why did you do it, Max?"

"Why do you think? Because I love you, you sap! I couldn't let anything happen to you." He seized her upper arms, giving her a little shake.

She looked at him a long moment, as though she'd never seen him before. Then a brilliant smile slowly lit up her tired face. "I guess it's serious, then."

"What's serious?"

"How much you love me."

"Oh, it's serious, all right." Soberly he added, "I thought you were going to bed."

"I am. Right now. Might as well get used to sleeping with you—it looks as if I'll be doing it for the rest of my life."

Gently, Max enfolded her in his arms.

* * *

In the dawn's early light, Hamilton Dodd left the operating room. He showered and changed back into street clothes, then went to look in on Adriana Barre. He didn't awaken her, just checked the monitors, nodding approval of what he saw.

Ham Dodd did not think of himself as an emotional man, or even as an introspective person. But he did have a good feeling about this night's work. The life of a baby boy had been saved. Susan Raimond's child was going to have every chance for a long, happy, healthy life. And so was Adriana Barre. Time and her husband's love would ease the pain she had suffered, both physical and emotional.

He heard footsteps behind him, turned, and saw Charles Bridges standing there. "She's going to be all right, Charles," he whispered. "You should be home in bed."

"I was, but I came in hoping to see you." He motioned and Dodd followed him out into the corridor. "I get bad vibes from that nursing lounge. Can we talk here?"

"Sure. Have you told Adriana about the baby?"

"Not yet. No real chance. And I guess you know it's not going to be easy."

"I know. Well, I guess there's no real hurry. Bad news can always wait awhile. It never really goes away."

"Did you deliver the Raimond baby?" Bridges asked.

"Yes, but how did you know about that?"

"It's a boy, isn't it?"

"Yes, but—"

"Healthy, normal in every way?"

Increasingly puzzled, Dodd said, "As far as we know, yes."

"I understand the mother wants Adriana to take her child since she can't keep him."

"How do you know— Oh yeah!" Light dawned, and Dodd scowled. "That damned Sheryl James.

Did she phone you?" He saw Bridges hesitate. "It's obvious she did."

"Yes, she did, and I'm very glad of it. I want that baby, Ham. For Adriana and for myself."

Dodd was amazed. "I know how upset you are over the loss of your son, Charles. But, Lord, man, think a minute!"

"I *have* thought. I've thought about nothing else for the past hour."

"We don't just pass out kids in this or any other hospital, Charles," Dodd blustered. "Lose one? Here—take another."

"Don't mock me, Hamilton." Now Bridges was scowling.

"God, that's the last thing I'd do. But—"

Bridges interrupted. "I want to adopt the Raimond baby. Isn't that possible?"

"I suppose so, yes," Dodd admitted. "But you must know there are certain procedures that must be followed."

"I'm sure there are."

"They take time, Charles—days at least, sometimes weeks, maybe longer. You and Adriana have to be checked out. The legal papers have to be prepared. A judge has to—"

"I know all that, Hamilton. But is there any reason Adriana can't know that this baby is going to be our son?"

"Don't be absurd. It just isn't done that way." Dodd was getting more distressed by the moment.

"Isn't it? Has no baby ever been born to one mother in a hospital and gone home with another woman?"

"Oh, God." He stroked his pate. "Yes, it probably has, but it's in the so-called gray area of adoptions. It's ethically frowned upon. You must know how many couples are on the waiting lists to adopt healthy white babies."

"I don't care about them," Bridges said impa-

278

tiently. "I care about Adriana. Who has more love to give a child? Who will provide a better home?"

"No one, of course." Dodd sighed. "Look, Charles, if you're determined to go ahead with the adoption, there's nothing I can say or do."

"Why would you want to?"

Right then Hamilton Dodd could cheerfully have throttled Sheryl James. "I don't, my friend. But I have to ask you a question, and I expect a straight answer. Okay?"

"I have no other kind," Bridges said simply.

"I'm beginning to wonder. Are you determined on this adoption because you really want the child, or because you don't intend to tell Adriana that her natural son has died?"

Charles Bridges turned away, walked a few steps down the hall, then back. "Both," he admitted at last. "I want the child and I *don't* want to tell Adriana about—"

"I thought as much. It won't work, Charles. I'll tell her myself, just as soon as she wakes up."

"I forbid it!"

"I'm sorry, Charles. I have to."

Bridges's distress was most apparent, but he gave in. "All right. I agree she has to know. But is there anything wrong in delaying telling her the truth for a couple of days?"

"Meanwhile, letting her think the Raimond baby is her child?" Dodd was shaking his head as he spoke. "It won't work, Charles. Suppose something goes wrong with the adoption? Suppose the Raimond girl changes her mind? Suppose Adriana won't accept another woman's son? I can't let you do it, Charles. It's too dangerous. And it's potentially too cruel."

When Hamilton Dodd told her later that morning, Adriana Barre seemed to take the news surprisingly well. But then, everyone had forgotten for the moment what a consummate actress she

279

was. Privately she was devastated, but her display of genuine grief lasted only briefly, for she saw and could not bear the agony on the face of her husband. It overwhelmed and submerged her own.

"I feared as much," was all she said.

"Adriana, I—I'm . . . so sorry," Bridges whispered.

"I know." She reached out, squeezed his hand in comfort, then turned to her right. "I know you did everything you could, Hamilton."

"Yes. It couldn't be helped."

She nodded silently.

Overcome by admiration and love for his wife, Charles Bridges said, "I didn't want you to know so soon. I've been so . . . afraid to . . . tell you."

She tried to smile at him. "Charles, you never were very good at keeping things from me."

Ham Dodd was so relieved he almost laughed out loud.

Now Bridges put his arms around his wife. "Adriana, I have something to ask you. There is a young woman across the hall who just had a baby early this morning, a little boy. I believe you know her—Susan Raimond."

"Susan Raimond?" Adriana echoed. The name obviously didn't ring a bell.

"Yes, with an *i*. The child actress. I believe she was in one of your films."

"Oh, yes, Susan Raimond. Now I remember. She was a lovely child. Such eyes . . ."

"It seems, dear, she's not married and can't keep the child. She wants you and me to adopt him."

Adriana stared at him. "Adopt . . . ?"

"Yes. He is healthy and normal in every way. Isn't that right, Hamilton?"

"It appears so, yes," Dodd muttered.

"A boy?"

Bridges nodded, holding her close. "Yes, a fine, healthy boy. Lots of dark hair, I hear."

280

"Have you seen him, Charles?"

"No, not yet."

She turned to Dodd. "Could we see him?"

He hesitated. "Well, I suppose so." Then he shrugged. "Why not?"

He left the room and gave an order at the nursing station for the Raimond baby to be brought from the nursery to room 227. Then he went across the hall to Susan Raimond's room. She was awake and not in too much discomfort. She was doing fine, in fact.

"Mother was just here," she told him immediately. "She's real angry at both of us."

Dodd grimaced. "I should imagine."

"She's planning to sue you." She saw his glum expression, and laughed.

"No, she isn't. I won't let her!" The brown eyes were sparkling. "I really mean it. I'm not a child anymore, Doctor. I've had a baby, so that makes me a woman, right? I'm not going to let Mother keep running my life. I can handle her, just you wait and see!"

Ham Dodd slowly nodded. He was beginning to feel a kind of grudging admiration for this troublesome brat.

"Is Adriana going to take my baby?" Susan asked eagerly.

"I wouldn't be surprised." Dodd smiled. "I wouldn't be at all surprised."

When Ham Dodd reentered the room across the hall, he was indeed not surprised to see Adriana Barre holding a baby in her arms. Her eyes were filled with tears, but she was smiling, and so was Charles Bridges. Neither so much as glanced at Dodd. Very quietly he stepped into the corridor and closed the door behind him.